Mistletoe and Magic

HELENE SULA

Harper
North

HarperNorth
Windmill Green
24 Mount Street
Manchester M2 3NX

A division of
HarperCollins*Publishers*
1 London Bridge Street
London SE1 9GF

www.harpercollins.co.uk

HarperCollins*Publishers*
Macken House,
39/40 Mayor Street Upper,
Dublin 1, D01 C9W8, Ireland

First published by HarperCollins*Publishers* Ltd 2025
1

A catalogue record for this book is available from the British Library.

PB ISBN: 978-0-00-877434-9

This novel is entirely a work of fiction. The names, characters and incidents portrayed in it are the work of the author's imagination. Any resemblance to actual persons, living or dead, events or localities is entirely coincidental.

Set in (Sabon LT Std) by (Amnet)

Printed and bound in the UK using 100% Renewable Electricity by CPI Group (UK) Ltd

MIX
Paper | Supporting
responsible forestry
FSC™ C007454

This book contains FSC™ certified paper and other controlled sources to ensure responsible forest management.

For more information visit: www.harpercollins.co.uk/green

For Mom—who brought me the magic of England and beyond when I was young, encouraged every journey, celebrated every departure, and somehow made me brave enough to live out my wildest dreams.

Chapter One

The Proposal/Promotion That Wasn't

It started, as so many bad ideas do, with a spreadsheet. A carefully colour-coded one, naturally. Eva Coleman didn't believe in chaos—she believed in structure. In neatly labelled tabs, in conditional formatting, in the quiet satisfaction of a cell turning green when a task was complete.

Column A was the timeline. Column B, the goals. Column C, the expectations her mother had lovingly but relentlessly installed in her brain since childhood.

By twenty-nine, she was meant to be:

- Engaged (yellow—Richard kept hinting it'd be 'soon')
- On track for promotion (yellow—trending red)
- Homeowner (grey—pending divine intervention)
- Planning a family (red—blinking)

On this particular December morning she was supposed to tick off two major boxes—proposal and promotion—she woke up early, wrapped in the comfort of her colour-matched pyjamas. She smiled at the ceiling, sighed and whispered to herself, "today's the day." Eva Coleman believed in signs. Not in a spiritual way or anything—she wasn't about to start reading tarot cards or consulting star charts. But she did believe that the universe occasionally nudged you in a particular direction. Like when her favourite coffee shop closed unexpectedly the morning of her big presentation, forcing her to try the new place across the street where she discovered a lavender latte that became her new obsession. Or when her third-grade teacher moved her next to Timothy Allen, who shared his animal crackers and later became her first kiss behind the science lab in ninth grade.

And today the universe was practically screaming at her in size 14 font, bold and underlined. Eva could barely sleep the night before, too excited. *Today was the day*. She peeled back the covers and hopped out of bed, then replaced her crisp white comforter and bright white sheets to their rightful place. Shimmying out of her matching blue Nordstrom pyjamas and Ugg slippers, she turned on the shower and commenced the morning get-ready routine. Today she'd wear the outfit from her mom's boutique—a crisp blazer and pencil skirt combo that her mother, Sandy, insisted made her look 'professional without being intimidating'. She stared at herself in the mirror as she applied mascara with careful precision, then brushed her pale cheeks with the perfect shade of Charlotte Tilbury 'Cheek to Chic' blush in deep rosy pink.

"*Today* I'm getting a promotion," she assured her reflection. "*Tonight* I'm getting a proposal." She carefully wiped away the blush so it wasn't too bright. Richard had once told her that her skin was a little too pale to wear such a bright colour. She hadn't made the mistake again.

Eva sometimes wondered when she had last dressed for herself.

The thought of disappointing him made her stomach clench—the same feeling she got whenever she imagined her mother's pursed lips and that particular sigh that meant Eva had fallen short.

But today would make it worth it. The fairy tale she'd earned was about to begin. She even pictured it: Richard down on one knee, the ring sparkling, and then the two of them riding away into the sunset on horseback, like the end of a movie she'd half-believed in since she was a girl. Her prince, her moment, her life at last neatly slotted into the spreadsheet's green column.

She had followed every rule—stayed late at work, smiled when she wanted to scream, wore the right clothes, dated the right man. If she just kept checking the boxes, eventually she'd earn the fairy tale: the ring, the house, the life. That was how it worked, wasn't it? Do everything right, and you'll be rewarded.

Today, the reward was supposed to arrive on schedule. Promotion at noon; proposal at seven. Her mother had already texted twice: Any news? Remember to smile. Eva texted back a thumbs-up and swallowed the small panic at the back of her throat.

At work, she'd managed to parallel park without a single adjustment—a Christmas miracle on par with the parting of the Red Sea, at least in downtown Nashville. The office peppermint bark hadn't run out yet. Her flawlessly applied Christmas-red nail polish ('Cranberry Spritz' by Essie) hadn't smudged despite her rushing to type up meeting notes for the head of A&R. And tonight—

tonight—was her two-year anniversary with Richard. She was wearing the lipstick he liked in anticipation. He was taking her to Kayne Prime. Another delightful way to celebrate getting a promotion at work. Everything felt beautifully, suspiciously aligned.

The Christmas spirit at Monarch Music was at full capacity. Garlands hung from every doorway. Someone was definitely burning a contraband pine-scented candle. 'Jingle Bell Rock' drifted faintly from the break room. Her desk was a cheerful contradiction—a miniature twinkling tree perched precariously between stacks of marketing briefs, a candy dish of peppermints next to scattered paperclips, and a bright yellow Post-it note where she'd written 'CANCÚN!! — 3 DAYS!' in her neat handwriting, underlined three times.

She was supposed to be finishing a draft of a sponsorship deck for the Brooks tour—a country singer known for rhinestone jumpsuits and glitter budgets. But instead, she was rereading a text from Richard.

Can't wait to see you tonight. 7pm. Don't be late. ♡

Eva smiled and tapped her phone against her chin. He was going to propose. She was sure of it. Things were aligning perfectly, she'd done everything she was supposed to and now (finally) she was going to reap the benefits and write her own fairy tale ending.

Blake from promotions popped his head over her cubicle wall, his white teeth reminding her of fangs. "Hey, Eva, you're doing the Secret Santa thing, right?"

She blinked, jarred from her daydream. "Yeah . . . why?"

"I forgot to get a gift. Any chance you could pick something up for me?"

"Blake. The party's in an hour," Eva crossed her arms but held a tight smile.

"I know, I know. You're amazing. Just something festive and classy. Nothing too weird. Budget's like . . . twenty?" Blake said, already walking away. You could barely tell from the front that he had honey blonde highlights, but from the back it was obvious. Eva sniffed.

"One day," Eva muttered to her computer screen, "I'm going to say no to someone and the sheer shock of it will cause a minor earthquake in Middle Tennessee."

Eva sighed, already reaching for her purse. Some distant part of her brain—the part that had once dreamed of writing stories instead of marketing copy—whispered that she could say no. But she'd never been good at refusing people, especially when they looked at her with that mixture of hope and expectation.

Besides, there was something comforting about being the person everyone counted on. It showed she was reliable, that she'd earned her place. Even if it meant feeling like she constantly had to prove she deserved to be here, that she was more than just Sandy Coleman's daughter. More than the girl who had a family connection that got her the job.

Twenty minutes later, Eva returned from a gift shop three blocks away, out of breath, with a locally made cinnamon candle in hand. She'd seen another one she liked better, with hints of pine and cedarwood, but it was thirty-five dollars. Blake had only given her twenty, and she wasn't about to subsidise his Secret Santa gift—not when she'd already stayed late three nights this week fixing his social media campaign errors. As she walked back through the entrance of the office, Eva scrolled through Instagram, pausing on a photo of her younger sister Lily's baby announcement. "Baby #2 coming in June!" the caption read, with Lily, her perfect husband, their toddler, and their golden retriever all wearing matching Christmas

5

jumpers. Eva's youngest sister, Maddie, had got married six months ago in a Pinterest-perfect barn wedding. Both sisters, though years younger than Eva, seemed light-years ahead in the life checklist their mother considered non-negotiable.

"You're the oldest, Eva," her mother would say. "You should be setting the example." But somehow, Eva—always the responsible one, always the rule-follower—had fallen behind in the race to traditional milestones. She was pushing thirty with no ring, no babies, no house with a picket fence. Just a decent job and a boyfriend who, after tonight, would hopefully make her mother stop introducing her as "my first, Eva, still no ring on her finger" at family gatherings.

Tara met her at the elevator when she returned, eyeing the small shopping bag as they walked back to her desk.

"Please tell me you didn't just run an errand for Blake."

Eva handed her the bag. "It was either this or watch him wrap a protein bar in tinsel again."

"You are too nice."

"I'm festive."

"You're like a human Hallmark movie," Tara said, "except instead of saving Christmas, you're saving grown men from their own incompetence."

Eva grinned and cast her eyes down to her Post-it note of the Cancún countdown.

Tara paused, then said, "So . . . what are you wearing tonight?"

Eva blushed, her fingers subconsciously touching the empty space on her ring finger. "The green silk dress. The one with the sleeves."

"Ooh. You think he's going to do it?"

Eva tried to play it cool, but her voice cracked slightly. "I mean . . . we've been together two years. He booked the steakhouse. And he prompted me to have my nails done in a totally casual, definitely suspicious way."

"Please. You've been walking on air all week." Tara lowered her voice. "Did you find the ring?"

"No!" Eva whispered back, then reconsidered. "I mean, not exactly. But I found the browser history. Tiffany's."

Tara squealed, drawing glances from across the office. "I knew it! Two years is exactly when it happens. Adam proposed to me at two years and three days."

"Speaking of Adam, weren't you two supposed to go to Hawaii last month?" Eva asked.

"We did. Those photos I showed you of the sunset from our balcony? That was Maui," Tara said, giving Eva a strange look. "Don't you remember? I was talking about it for weeks."

"Right, of course! The sunset was gorgeous," Eva said quickly, embarrassed she'd forgotten. "I guess I've just been so caught up in planning for Cancún."

She'd been so focused on proving herself at work—staying late, taking on extra projects, triple-checking every piece of copy—that she'd missed her friend's vacation stories.

"You deserve it. When's the last time you actually took a vacation?"

Eva tried to remember. "I took that long weekend to go with my parents to visit my grandma last Christmas."

"That's not a vacation, that's an obligation," Tara laughed. "I can't believe you still have all your annual leave. Most people would kill for your vacation days."

"I know, I know," Eva said. "But there was the album launch, and then festival season, and then . . ."

"And then you just never prioritised yourself," Tara finished for her. "Always trying to do the right thing for everyone else. When are you going to think about Eva?"

The words stung because they were true. While everyone else took their annual leave without guilt, Eva hoarded hers like evidence of dedication, proof that she wasn't just coasting on her mother's connections. "Well, Cancún's going to change that. Sun, sand, and hopefully a big shiny rock on your finger. Then you'll finally have caught up with your freakishly accomplished friend group."

Eva smiled weakly. It was true—everyone in her circle seemed to have figured life out. Tara was happily married with a promotion already under her belt. Courtney—her best friend since first grade when she'd shared her own Dunkaroos after Eva forgot her lunch money— had her own catering business that was taking off. Even her college roommate Rachel, who once forgot to wear shoes to an exam, now had a thriving dental practice, twins, and a house in Belle Meade.

And then there was Eva—always reliable, always doing everything right, yet somehow still waiting for her real story to begin.

Tara glanced at her watch. "Hey, aren't you supposed to meet with Jacqueline? The big announcement?"

Eva's stomach flipped. Right. *The promotion.*

She smoothed her skirt, tucked her auburn hair behind her ear, and grabbed her notepad. As she walked to the conference room, she tried not to think about how much she wanted this—not just because of the title or the money (though both would be nice), but because it would mean she was finally *enough*.

She'd earned it. She'd stayed late. Covered everyone's mistakes. Taken on the projects nobody wanted—like the glitter budget for a C-list country singer—without losing her mind.

She deserved this.

Twenty minutes later, Eva stepped out of the conference room with a hollow smile frozen on her face.

"You're such a valued part of the team," Jacqueline had said warmly, handing her a Starbucks gift card like a consolation prize. "But we're looking for someone with a little more . . . edge for the new role. We want you to stay exactly where you are, Eva—you're so good at it."

She looked at Tara and shook her head.

"You didn't get it?" Tara asked coming over.

"Nope. It went to Blake," Eva said moving her mouse to wake up her computer screen.

"HIGHLIGHTS?! Eva, are you joking? You have to stick up for yourself. You can't just let other people take the credit," Tara said sitting on top of Eva's desk.

"That's easier said than done," she said. "Blake's been here longer than me anyway."

"No, you handled that catastrophe with the beer and fried chicken song, you came up with the idea of the Instagram trend to show off your boots for the Mississippi Mischief band that made them go mega-viral, you single-handedly saved the day when Tucker what's-his-face threw that beer bottle from The Stage's rooftop."

"I'm just doing my job," Eva said. "Besides, everyone knows my mom got me here."

"Yes, she did," Tara turned Eva's chair to face her with her foot, "but it's you that's put the work in ever since. Eva Coleman you are smart and capable. But hon' no one can see that when you let people walk all over you."

"It's fine!"

Her phone rang and Tara hopped off her desk shaking her head.

"Monarch Music, Eva Coleman speaking."

"Eva, it's Mom." The familiar drawl came through clear as a bell, as if Sandy Coleman were sitting right next to her instead of across town at her boutique 'The Silver Spur'. "Just checking you're all prepared for this evening and that you remembered to pack the blue sundress I got you. The one that makes your eyes pop."

"Yes, Mom. I am and it's packed."

"And your hair appointment? The highlights?"

"Done yesterday." Eva touched her hair.

"Good girl." A pause. "And you think tonight will be the night?"

"Mom," Eva whispered.

"Yes?" Sandy answered.

"I didn't get the promotion."

"Oh, honey," Sandy said, but there was no real sympathy in her voice. "Well, this job has never really been your passion anyway. Not like the way Lily is with her nursing degree or Maddie with her teaching. You know those practical careers are where the real security is."

Eva furrowed her brow but bit back a reply. Sandy had never understood her desire to be a writer, encouraging her instead towards a more 'sensible' path. This was typical of her mother, to dismiss the job she'd pushed Eva into when things hadn't gone her way. Originally, Sandy had been thrilled when her boutique and clothing line connection landed Eva the marketing job at Monarch. Now that the promotion was out of sight, so was her interest in Eva's career.

"But enough about that," Sandy continued. "What about tonight? Do you think Richard's going to propose?"

"I don't know that for sure, but . . . maybe."

"Well, if he does, you say yes, you hear me? Richard is a catch. A tax attorney with his own condo and no student loans? In this economy? And you're not getting any younger, Eva. Twenty-nine next month. I was married with a baby on the way at your age."

"I know, Mom."

"Call me the minute you get home. I don't care how late."

After they hung up, Eva stared at her computer screen, not really seeing the transcription she was supposed to be finishing. She pictured Richard down on one knee at Kayne Prime, the upscale steakhouse where everyone who was anyone in Nashville went to be seen. The ring—princess cut, she hoped, though she'd be happy with whatever he'd chosen—glinting under the soft lighting. Their flight to Cancún was in three days, where they'd celebrate their engagement with three weeks of sun and relaxation over the Christmas holiday.

Perfect. It was all going to be perfect.

Her email pinged with a message from the studio coordinator:

Need someone to sit in on the Brooks meeting. Glitter budget for the country tour costumes. Can you take notes? J

Eva sighed. Transcribing arguments about glitter wasn't exactly the career pinnacle she'd imagined for herself. Once, she'd dreamed of writing novels, creating worlds populated with characters brimming with passions and flaws. Not documenting debates about how much sparkle belonged on a cowboy hat. But it was fine. She had a steady pay check in a job her mother deemed acceptable, a boyfriend about to become a fiancé, and her family's approval. *What more could she want?*

A memory flashed across her mind in response—a worn leather notebook, pages filled with stories she'd written late into the night during high school. The summer she'd

11

spent crafting a novel about a girl who discovered a hidden door in an English garden. The acceptance letter to the writing program in Oxford.

Eva pushed the thought away. Those dreams belonged to a version of herself she'd outgrown—the messy, emotional girl who believed in magic and possibilities. That girl wasn't practical. She'd been dismissed by her mother. That girl would never have landed Richard.

She grabbed her notepad and headed for the conference room, passing the framed gold records lining the hallway, all decorated with tiny sprigs of holly for the season. She'd walked this corridor hundreds of times, but today she noticed something she usually tuned out—her reflection in the glass. When had she started wearing so much beige?

"Coming, Eva?" called Jacqueline, the studio coordinator, already holding the conference room door open.

"Of course," Eva replied, quickening her step. Tonight, Richard would propose. This weekend, they'd be in Cancún.

She had no idea the universe had other signs coming her way . . .

*   *   *

Later that evening, Kayne Prime glowed with low lighting and the quiet hum of very expensive wine lists. Eva had curled her hair, the way Richard liked and worn heels for the special occasion. She'd checked her reflection in the mirrored bar wall and tried to imagine what she'd look like with a diamond on her finger.

She spotted Richard at a corner table, already seated.

He didn't stand up when she approached. Which was fine. Modern men and all that.

He did, however, give her a long look. The kind of look you give a puppy you're about to return to the shelter. *What was that for, did he know about the missed promotion?*

"Hey," she said, smoothing her dress as she sat. "You look nice."

"Thanks," he said, adjusting his napkin. "You too."

The waiter appeared with menus. Richard waved him off. "We'll just do drinks for now. I'll have the watermelon vodka whammy, and she'll have . . ."

"Pinot Noir," Eva said.

They exchanged pleasantries for a moment, though something felt tense. *Was Richard nervous?*

After a few beats of silence, Richard leaned forward, his hair unmoving from the gel. He folded his hands on the table with the careful precision of someone who'd practiced this moment. Eva held her breath in anticipation. "I didn't want to do this at your apartment. Or in public, really. But you're busy this week, and we're supposed to be flying out soon, and . . . well, I didn't want to drag it out."

"Drag it out, what are you talking about?" Eva frowned with confusion.

The waiter returned with their drinks, setting a deep red wine in front of Richard and the hot pink watermelon cocktail before Eva.

"Actually, I had the watermelon vodka whammy," Richard said, barely glancing at the server.

"The wine is mine, please," Eva added, awkwardly raising her hand.

They switched glasses, Eva took a too-large sip, feeling the warmth spread through her chest.

"This just isn't working, Eva."

It was like someone pulled the tablecloth out from under their meal—only, there was no food, and Eva was left sitting in front of a very empty place setting with a man who looked more like a tax form than a person.

"I'm sorry?" she said.

"You're . . . great, Eva. You're really sweet. And you've been—" He stopped. "Look, I just think we want different things."

Eva felt her cheeks heat as her ears rang. It was impossible to tell if her hands were shaking or if the restaurant itself had started to vibrate.

"You were just on Tiffany's website," she said, almost dazed as the gravity of the situation hit her.

"What? Eva, I was browsing cufflinks," he shook his head.

He gave her a wimpy half-smile. "You're always . . . hoping. Overthinking and reading into things."

"Well, we've been dating for two years Richard. So yes, I guess I did think this was leading somewhere, how callous of me!" Eva banged her wine glass on the table, sloshing a drop over the edge.

"Please, be quiet. People are going to start staring. Eva, I need a woman with a sense of ambition, purpose. I know you're really into colour-coding and creating our schedules but I need more than that," Richard threw her the next insult.

As her ears continued to buzz, Eva found herself transfixed on Richard's shirt. The pale blue button-down from that boutique in Green Hills was clinging to his chest like it had separation anxiety. Had it shrunk in the wash? Or had he deliberately chosen to wear what appeared to be a size too small? Who wore a shirt this tight to break up with someone? More importantly, who wore a shirt like that period?

"You were literally sending me pictures of our villa in Cancún yesterday!" She managed to keep her voice steady, despite the earthquake happening inside her chest.

"I still think you should go," he said, like he was offering her the last slice of pie. "You could use some time away. It'll be good for you."

The absolute nerve of this man, telling her what *he* thought *she* needed right now! Eva felt the familiar sting behind her eyes, the treacherous pre-cry burning that had earned her the office nickname 'waterworks'. She'd overheard the junior A&R guys once: "Don't tell Eva. She'll cry." Followed by laughter.

Not today. She swallowed hard.

The waiter returned to check on whether the two would be ordering food. Richard handed him a credit card and eagerly asked for the bill.

Eva wanted to fling her wine in his face, to create the kind of scene that would be recounted by the waitstaff for years to come. To embarrass him to the level she was currently reaching.

Instead, she went quiet. She nodded along as Richard monologued about 'personal growth journeys' and 'fundamental incompatibilities'. She watched as he signed the credit card slip with a steady hand. Mortified by the evening's turn of events, that last bit of pride within her declined his offer to drive her home.

Outside the restaurant, the December air hit her flushed face. Nashville sparkled around her, all holiday lights and Christmas cheer. Lampposts were wrapped in garlands, shop windows displayed festive scenes, and somewhere a street musician was playing *Silent Night* on a saxophone. But Eva didn't see any of it. The twinkling lights blurred through unshed tears, the festive storefronts might as well have been empty, and the haunting saxophone notes only underscored the hollow feeling in her chest. It was as if someone had adjusted the contrast on the world.

Everything that had seemed bright and promising just hours before now looked flat and meaningless.

She stood on the sidewalk, hugging her coat to her chest despite the relatively mild Tennessee winter, and realised she had nowhere to go. Her apartment felt like the last place she wanted to be—filled with a half-packed suitcase and resort wear that now seemed to mock her with its cheerful tropical prints.

"Christmas is supposed to be magical!" She yelled into the night sky.

"No it ain't!" yelled a man on the ground in grubby sweats, holding an empty Coors bottle. "You gotta make your own magic. No one gonna do it fer ya. Follow the signs, Eva."

Did he just say my name? Eva wondered. *Surely not. He was slurring his words.*

Stomping off, Eva turned the corner so the man couldn't give her any more helpful tips.

Eva's phone buzzed in her purse.

Mom: How is dinner, sweetheart? Has he popped the question yet? I'm dying to know!

Eva stared at the text, her thumb hovering over the screen. Her mother had been dropping not-so-subtle hints about marriage since Eva turned twenty-four. Five years later, it had evolved into a full-blown campaign. Every Thanksgiving she was met with, "Eva you need to get it together and give me grandkids! Your sisters are making me a grandmother, when will it be your turn?" Sandy would say, as if motherhood were a relay race and Eva had dropped the baton.

Richard surprised me! Talk tomorrow xoxo

She tucked her phone back before she could think about the white lie she'd just told. It had been a surprise all right, just not the kind she'd wanted. Just another day of pretending everything was fine. She'd had plenty of practice. It was easier than dealing with her mother's disappointment or, worse, her immediate plan to fix everything.

Eva glanced at the street signs, calculating the distance to her apartment. Four miles. Technically walkable, but this was Nashville—a city designed for cars, not pedestrians. No sidewalks for half the journey, intersections built like death traps for anyone not surrounded by two tonnes of metal. And the never-ending construction. Another uniquely American problem: you can't even storm away dramatically after a breakup without calling an Uber.

Instead of heading home, Eva's feet led her towards the gym—open twenty-four hours, glowing sterile white under the cold December sky. The place was nearly empty at this hour, just a few dedicated fitness enthusiasts on treadmills and one guy grunting at his reflection as he curled what looked like small cars.

The attendant—a chipper blonde whose ponytail seemed to defy gravity—gave Eva's outfit a once-over. "A little over dressed for a workout, aren't we?" She laughed, then motioned her in. Eva was a regular now.

Reaching her locker, Eva prayed that there was something left in here from her last session. Result! Towards the back of the shelf she found a crumpled pair of black leggings and T-shirt that was so creased it could make an iron cry. No sneakers though, damn. Slipping out of her dress and into the leggings, Eva glanced down at her strapless bra and across to the heels she'd now have to put back on. "Just perfect," she sighed. Looking from her made up face, bedraggled outfit and down to her toes she took a deep breath, *screw it*. Shoulders back, she held her head high as her fancy strappy heels clicked against the tile floor on the walk up to the bike row. Today Eva was sporting a particular brand of determination that only arrives when your carefully constructed future has just imploded.

She climbed onto a stationary bike in the corner, the one facing a blank wall, and started pedalling. The clink of the half-done buckles against the pedals echoed in the cavernous room. She looked ridiculous. She didn't care.

Her phone buzzed in her hand: Courtney.

Eva answered, pressing the phone between her shoulder and ear while she pedalled miserably.

"What the hell are you doing over there, psychopath?" Courtney said by way of greeting.

"I'm at the gym."

"The GYM? On your big night? Where's Richard?" There was the sound of kitchen activity in the background—Courtney prepping for tomorrow's catering gig, always working.

"Richard . . ." Eva swallowed hard. "Richard just broke up with me."

"HE WHAT?" The background noise stopped abruptly. "That absolute rodent of a man. Where are you really?"

"I told you. I'm at the gym. On a bike. In heels, actually."

A pause. "Oh my God, you're serious. You're pedalling away your feelings in formalwear?"

"It seemed like a good idea at the time." Eva glanced down at her strappy sandals, clacking against the metal pedals with each rotation. "My apartment is filled with . . . him. I couldn't go home yet."

"What about Cancún? The tickets? The resort?"

18

Eva hadn't even thought that far ahead. "I'll cancel it, I guess."

"Hell no," Courtney said with such conviction that Eva sat up straighter on the bike. "Don't you dare cancel that trip."

"I can't exactly go to a couples resort alone."

"Not Cancún. Somewhere else. Move the tickets."

"To where?"

"I don't know. Paris? Bali? Literally anywhere that isn't Nashville or a place you planned to go with that walking tax deduction."

Eva pedalled slower, considering it. "I don't know . . ."

"Eva," Courtney's voice softened. "When was the last time you did something just because *you* wanted to? Not because your mom approved, or because it fitted into Richard's five-year plan?"

The question hung in the air like smoke. Eva couldn't remember. Every decision—college major, apartment, job, even her highlights (caramel, not too blonde) —had been guided by her mother's gentle but insistent hand or by what she thought a girlfriend of Richard's calibre should be. The last time she'd made a choice just for herself . . .

"I'd have to change the flights," Eva said finally.

"So change them. Tonight."

"I'll think about it."

"Don't think. That's all you do, Eva. You overthink until you talk yourself out of what you actually want. For once in your life, just do something impulsive."

Eva heard the telltale sound of a knife chopping in the background—Courtney multitasking even during an emergency call. Eva envied that about her friend—the absolute certainty she had about her path, because it was her passion. When had Eva lost that?

19

Had she ever really had it? Or had she always been this person? Safer, smaller, less than she could be, because that's what good girls do.

"Listen," Courtney continued, "I would have come and got you, but I've really got to finish this prep for tomorrow, I'm sorry Eves. But promise me you're gonna get off that stupid bike and go home. You'll tell me when you're back? At least consider changing the flights. Go somewhere that's just for you."

"I promise."

"Call me when you decide. And, Eva?"

"Yeah?"

"You deserve better than him. And better than the life you think you're supposed to want." Her friend sighed before hanging up.

Maybe it was time to stop pedalling in one place. Maybe it was time to move forward.

Chapter Two

Changing the Flight

Perspiration on her face and the heels still on, Eva stared at her suitcase—the one stuffed with resort wear that had maxed out her credit card.

The sight of it made her stomach turn. This wasn't just luggage anymore—it was a monument to her naivety, sitting in the middle of her apartment like evidence of how wrong she'd been about everything.

"No," she said aloud to the empty room. "Absolutely not."

She grabbed the suitcase handle and yanked it open, the zipper protesting. The swimsuits alone had cost more than her weekly grocery budget. She pulled them out one by one, each tropical print more offensive than the last.

She grabbed the sundress her mother had insisted would "make her eyes pop"—bright blue with tiny white flowers—and flung it across the room. Next to go was the wide-brimmed hat Richard had said made her look "sophisticated", and the sandals she'd spent an hour picking out because he hated when women wore "trashy flip-flops".

She was performing an exorcism on the things in her life. And it felt good.

Every item she touched felt contaminated by the future that wasn't going to happen. The white cover-up for romantic beach walks. The new lingerie still with its tags. The waterproof phone case for all those engagement ring photos she'd planned to take by the ocean.

Something inside her had snapped. She moved through her apartment like a hurricane, gathering every trace of Richard and throwing it into a pile in the middle of her living room floor. Photos in frames. The stupid little teddy bear he'd won at the state fair. The 'romantic' mix he'd made her that contained three Dave Matthews Band songs and something by the Plain White T's. His extra toothbrush. The books he'd loaned her—all biographies of 'successful people' with advice about 'maximising potential.'

She grabbed a garbage bag from under the kitchen sink and started shoving things in. She wanted anything that could be thrown away out of her safe space immediately. Then she found a cardboard box for the things that technically belonged to him: his Northwestern hoodie, a watch he'd left on her nightstand, that pretentious coffee table book about wine regions he'd insisted would 'class up' her apartment. God, what a tool.

Her phone buzzed again: Courtney.

"I've been awaiting your call woman! How's the packing slash unpacking going?" she asked without preamble.

"Oh I'm packing all right," Eva said, shoving the teddy bear into the garbage bag with particular venom. "Packing up every trace of Richard Andrew Henderson the Third."

"This is exactly what I wanted to hear. Screw him! I've literally just put the last bits in the dishwasher, so I am good to go! Want me to come over?"

"No, it's fi—" Eva paused, looking at the destruction around her and realised she needed to actually ask for what she wanted. "Actually, yes. And bring wine."

"Twenty minutes," Courtney promised.

She'd spent two years trying to be the right kind of girlfriend for a tax attorney. Before that, four years trying to be the right kind of employee at a job nobody thought she deserved. And before that, twenty-some years trying to be the right kind of daughter.

When was the last time she'd tried to be the right kind of Eva?

Her gaze landed on a dusty cardboard storage box tucked in the back corner of her closet shelf. It was labelled 'Hight School—Keepsakes' in her neat teenage handwriting, the ink faded to a ghost of its former self. She hadn't opened it in years, maybe not since college.

Eva pulled the box down, suddenly curious about the girl she used to be. What had she cared about? What had she wanted? Before Richard, before her mother's expectations had solidified into the walls of her life, who had she been?

She sat cross-legged on her bedroom floor, lifted the lid, and began sifting through the time capsule of her younger self. Dance recital programs. Honor Society certificates. A dried corsage from prom. Her old Lisa Frank diary tumbled out, rainbow unicorns faded against the purple background. It fell open to a December page, and something green caught her eye. A sprig of mistletoe lay pressed between the pages—but that couldn't be right. The mistletoe was fresh. Impossibly, vibrantly green with tiny droplets of moisture still clinging to the leaves, as if it had just been picked. Eva blinked hard. She'd pressed this mistletoe in here after her first kiss at the school Christmas dance fifteen years ago. It should be brown, crumbling, dead. But it wasn't. She touched it with a trembling finger— cool, slightly damp, smelling of winter mornings. Real. Fresh. Impossible. Her fourteen-year-old handwriting in glittery gel pen declared: *Magic is REAL if you look for it!!* Eva quickly shut the diary, her heart racing. She was overtired, emotional, seeing things. That had to be it. At the bottom, a manila envelope with 'ENGLAND' written across it in excited block letters.

The paper had yellowed at the edges, its metal clasp tarnished from years of neglect. Eva stared at it, memories flooding back. She flipped open the clasp with trembling fingers.

Inside: a crinkled brochure for a summer writing workshop in Oxford. The colours had faded, but the Gothic spires still reached skyward on the cover. Her name was printed on the acceptance letter, alongside words like 'exceptional talent' and 'full scholarship'. She ran her fingers over the embossed letterhead, remembering the day it had arrived. How her hands had shaken then, too, but with excitement rather than regret.

She'd won it in high school, the only student from Tennessee that year. She'd run into the kitchen, waving the letter, already imagining herself walking cobblestone streets between ancient buildings, notebook in hand.

And her mother had looked up from her cookbook, brow furrowed, lips pursed, and said:

"Writing? That's not a real job, honey. That's a fantasy. You need to focus on things that will get you somewhere. Plus, I need my girl with me to work at the boutique this summer!"

"Real careers," her mother had continued, setting down her spatula. "Like your cousin Jennifer in pharmaceutical sales. Or teaching, like the Morrison girl. Writing stories won't pay your bills, Eva. It won't give you stability."

She'd seen the genuine concern in her mother's eyes—Sandy Coleman had grown up with nothing and worked incredibly hard to build her boutique business. She only wanted security for her daughter, but in doing so she was crushing her. Her father, Robert, had been standing in the doorway, his expression caught between pride at Eva's accomplishment and deference to his wife's practical concerns. "Your mother might have a point, Evie," he'd finally said, though his eyes told a different story. "Maybe save the writing for weekends?"

And Eva had listened. Had folded the dream away, tucked it into this envelope, and buried it beneath yearbooks and graduation caps. Had let herself believe this version of her life—the one with the practical job and the suitable boyfriend and the designer bags and the beige furniture—was enough. That wanting more was somehow greedy or impractical. That disappointing her parents was worse than disappointing herself.

Something else slipped from the envelope. A notecard with loopy handwriting in faded purple ink—the kind of passionate scrawl that could only belong to the type of English teacher who wore flowing scarves and quoted William Wordsworth from memory:

"Promise me you'll go to England one day. I think that's where your story lives."

Ms Jensen, Senior Lit

Eva's throat tightened. She remembered Ms Jensen's face when she'd told her she wasn't going—the disappointment, yes, but something else too. Recognition. Like she'd seen this

25

story before, watched other young women fold their dreams into neat squares and tuck them away. Maybe even her own.

Like she knew what it meant to set aside a dream.

A laugh escaped Eva's lips, surprising her. And then came the tears—not the careful, contained ones she'd mastered for office disappointments or the quiet ones she'd perfected in bathroom stalls. These were torrential, body-shaking sobs that felt like they were coming from some long-sealed chamber inside her chest.

They weren't tears of sadness. They were tears of recognition. Of meeting a version of herself she'd almost forgotten existed. The girl who'd stayed up until 3 a.m. writing stories about women who solved mysteries and crossed oceans and followed their hearts. The girl who'd dreamed of a life beyond Nashville society expectations, who'd believed that words could build worlds.

The girl who had slowly disappeared beneath layers of sensible choices and careful compromises.

As her sobs subsided, Eva wiped her face with the back of her hand, not caring about her smeared mascara or puffy eyes. She looked down at the brochure again, at the promise of Gothic architecture and literary history and possibility.

She wasn't going to Cancún. She wasn't getting engaged.

But maybe, just maybe, she was finally going to start her story.

Eva's laptop glowed blue in the dimness of her apartment, casting shadows across walls she'd painted an agreeable grey because the name seemed like good advice at the time. She pulled up the airline website, fingers hovering over the keyboard. Change destination. Not cancel. Change.

But to where?

She brushed her fingers across the Oxford brochure, remembering how she'd dreamed of cobblestone streets and ancient bookshops, of afternoon tea and Gothic cathedrals. England had been her escape since she was twelve, devouring Jane Austen novels under her bedcovers with a flashlight.

She looked at Ms Jensen's note again. *I think that's where your story lives.*

Her fingers hovered over the keyboard for a moment, trembling slightly, before she navigated to 'Manage Booking' and selected 'Change Destination'. In the search field, she typed: London.

The screen filled with options, fees, and available flights. A flight leaving tomorrow night caught her eye—a red-eye that would land her in London just as the city was waking up. Before she could overthink it, before she could make a pro-con list, Eva clicked 'Select', paid the change fee, and confirmed the switch.

The confirmation email arrived seconds later, its cheerful subject line almost comically at odds with the seismic shift she felt inside:

Thank you for booking your flight to London Heathrow. Your adventure awaits!

She read it aloud in a British accent and watched her skin prick with goosebumps.

She did it. And it was surprisingly easy. Instead of a trip to Cancún with Richard, it was now a solo travel experience to London.

She stared at the screen, a strange mix of terror and exhilaration washing over her. She had just made a massive decision without consulting anyone. The thought was both terrifying and thrilling, like standing at the edge of a cliff and choosing to jump—not because she wanted to fall, but because she needed to know what it felt like to fly. She pictured that movie scene from *Pride and Prejudice* where Elizabeth Bennet stands on the edge of the cliff thinking about her choices. She did the same on the edge of her bed, laptop beside her.

For a brief moment, Eva wondered if this was another mistake. What if this grand gesture was just another way of running from the uncomfortable truth that maybe she didn't know who she really was anymore? What if she got to London and discovered that the dreamy, creative girl from her youth was truly gone?

But as she glanced down at Ms Jensen's note again, something settled inside her. The purple ink had faded over the years, but the conviction in those words hadn't. Maybe she didn't need to find herself. Maybe she just needed to remember who she'd been before she'd started letting other people define her.

Her phone came to life once more: Courtney.

"Okay so I know I said twenty minutes but there was a whole dishwasher overflow situation-don't even ask. I'm at the store now though, so red or white?"

Eva looked around her apartment—at the garbage bags, the box of Richard's things, the open suitcase spilling resort wear, the laptop still showing her London confirmation.

"Both."

True to her word, Courtney arrived shortly after, a bottle of wine in each hand and a bag of Cheez-Its tucked under her arm.

"Oh Eves," Courtney said, taking in the scene of destruction. "You've been busy."

"I booked a flight to London," Eva blurted out.

Courtney set the wine down carefully. "You did what now?"

"London. Tomorrow night. I changed my Cancún ticket." Eva held up the Oxford brochure. "I found this. From high school. Remember when I got into that writing programme"

"The one your mom wouldn't let you go to?" Courtney's eyes widened. "Holy shit, Eva. You're actually doing it."

"I'm doing something," Eva said. "What exactly that is I'm not one hundred percent sure."

Courtney pulled her into a fierce hug. "You're choosing yourself. Finally." She pulled back, surveying the apartment again. "Now, let's open this wine and I'll help you sort through Hurricane Richard. We can't have you thinking about that shallow idiot while you're away. You're having your European awakening."

* * *

The next morning, Eva stood in front of her mirror, applying a fresh coat of red lipstick that matched her nails. She picked up her blush and this time didn't even try to tone it down. Her reflection looked different somehow—there was a brightness in her dark brown eyes that hadn't been there yesterday, a slight lift to her chin that spoke of resolution rather than resignation.

Her phone buzzed with a text from her mother.

Mom: Still waiting to hear more about last night! Did he give you a ring or just promise it's coming?

Eva took a deep breath and typed rapidly:

Eva: Richard broke up with me last night. I'm okay. Going to take the vacation anyway—changed my Cancún ticket to London. Leaving tonight.

She hit send before she could second-guess herself, before the habitual need to soften the truth for her mother's benefit could take over. Her greatest fear had always been disappointing her parents—especially her mother, who had such clear ideas about what Eva's life should look like. Her dad would be more understanding, probably tell her to "follow her gut" like he always did, though he'd ultimately defer to Sandy's judgement on matters concerning their daughter.

The response was immediate, buzzing through with predictable alarm:

`London?!`

`In December?`

`By yourself?`

`At CHRISTMAS?`

`Call me right now.`

Her phone immediately started ringing. Eva stared at it, her mother's contact photo—taken at last year's Silver Spur boutique Christmas party—smiling up at her. She let it go to voicemail.

Another text: `Eva Ann Coleman, answer your phone this instant.`

Eva typed back: `Can't talk now. Packing. I'll call when I land.`

The phone rang again. This time Eva turned it to silent and flipped it face down.

Emergency "call me now" texts from her mom always meant she dropped absolutely everything and called. But not today. Instead, she opened a message to Courtney: `Flight's at 4:40p.m. We still on for airport drop off?`

Courtney: `All hail the queen!`

`Or the king. Whatever. YES!`

Eva: `Thank you! You're THE best.`

Another text came through from Courtney:

`Also I'll handle the Richard stuff. Leave the box and trash bags by the door. I know where he lives.😼`

She wasn't going to listen to all the reasons why this was impractical or ill-advised or potentially dangerous for a woman travelling alone. She wasn't going to justify, defend or apologise.

She was just going to go.

That afternoon, she packed her warmest sweaters, her best boots, and more books than was probably reasonable. This was Christmas, it called for thick knitted scarves and hot mulled wine, not bikinis and cocktails in Cancún. She tucked her passport into her wallet, checked her ticket for the tenth time, and waited for Courtney's text saying she was outside.

As she zipped up her carry-on, Eva hesitated. The Lisa Frank diary still sat on her bedroom floor where she'd left it, closed tight. She hadn't looked at it again since finding the Oxford envelope, but she couldn't stop thinking about what she'd seen. Or thought she'd seen. That mistletoe couldn't have been fresh. It was impossible. But . . . She walked back to her bedroom and picked up the diary, opening it carefully to that December page. The mistletoe was still there. Still green. Still dewy. Still impossible. She stared at it for a long moment, then made a decision. Gently, she lifted the sprig out—it felt real, substantial, alive—and wrapped it in tissue paper before tucking it into a small pocket of her purse. She didn't understand it. She didn't even fully believe it. But something told her it belonged on this journey. If she was chasing impossible dreams, maybe she needed impossible things.

She placed the garbage bags and Richard's box by the door as instructed. Courtney had already promised to document the delivery of his things with photos 'for posterity and potential blackmail'.

In her carry-on, she carefully placed Ms Jensen's note, now protected in a plastic sleeve—a talisman of the road not taken, and the one she was finally brave enough to walk down. It was time to write her own story. Courtney texted at exactly 4.00 p.m., punctual as always:

`Your carriage awaits, m'lady`

Eva hauled her black hard-sided rolling bag down to the street where Courtney's beat-up Subaru idled, hazards blinking. Her friend leaped out to help with the luggage, her curly hair piled in a messy bun on top of her head, flour still dusting her chef's jacket.

"You came straight from work?" Eva asked, touched.

"Are you kidding? My best friend is having an international crisis of self. I wouldn't miss it." Courtney slammed the trunk shut. "Plus, I have to hear the latest on your mother's reaction to saying goodbye to our not-so-golden boy Richard and of course your British escapades."

As they pulled away from Eva's apartment, Courtney turned down the radio. "Okay, spill."

"She's called seventeen times. I texted her that I was fine but needed space."

"Bold," Courtney nodded approvingly. "Very un-Eva-like. I'm here for it."

They rode in silence for a moment, the Nashville skyline glittering behind them in the low afternoon sun.

"You know what this means, right?" Courtney finally said.

"That I'm having a breakdown?"

"No. That you're finally having a break*through*." Courtney reached over to squeeze her hand. "You've spent your whole life trying to be what everyone else wanted. Maybe it's time you did what YOU want."

"That's the problem," Eva admitted. "I don't think I know what that is."

Courtney glanced at her, her expression softening. "You know, Eva, you think because everyone's got these boxes checked—a good career, a significant other—that that means their life is perfect. Life can still be very difficult even with those boxes checked."

Eva stared out the window, watching the airport signs approach.

"And furthermore," Courtney continued, "a wonderful life doesn't necessarily have to have those things. Life isn't a Jane Austen novel. Once you are betrothed, it doesn't simply mean that life is tied up in a perfect silver box with a ribbon. Shit happens. Because it's life. But hey, if you want that fairy tale then you're going to have to write the damn thing yourself."

Eva smiled despite herself. "When did you get so wise?"

"Around the same time I realised my catering business meant I'd be working every weekend for the rest of my life," Courtney laughed. "Just because I have the career box checked doesn't mean I don't sometimes look at normal people with their weekends off and feel jealous. Everyone's searching for something Eves, you're about to go find it."

* * *

As Courtney helped her with her suitcase at the curb, she pulled Eva into a fierce hug. "Text me when you land. And Eva?"

"Yeah?"

"Don't you dare come back until you've had at least one wild adventure. Preferably involving a sexy British man with an accent."

Eva laughed. "I'm going for self-discovery, not romance."

"Why not both?" Courtney winked. "Now go. Find yourself. I'll handle your mom if she shows up at your apartment with a search party. Don't waste another minute thinking about Richard either, I'll deal with that crap."

* * *

Inside the terminal, Eva immediately felt out of place. Nashville International was swarming with people who clearly weren't alone. There were families in matching Disney shirts, business travellers in crisp suits looking importantly at their watches, and then . . . the bachelorette parties.

Dear God, the bachelorette parties.

They travelled in packs, like bedazzled wildebeests migrating across the Nashville plains. Every group seemed to have followed the exact same Pinterest board: white cowboy boots, denim shorts (despite it being December), and rhinestone-encrusted cowboy hats. The brides were easy to spot with their white Stetsons and sashes proclaiming 'BRIDE Y'ALL!' and 'BOOTS, BOOZE & I DO'S' in glittery script. One group was already doing tequila shots at the airport bar at 2.45 p.m.

Eva had always found this charming before—the excited women coming to Nashville for a weekend of honky-tonks and pedal taverns, living out their country music fantasies. But today, it stung. All these women celebrating impending marriages while she couldn't even get Richard to stick around for a third Christmas together.

Everyone here was going *to* something.

She was going *away* from everything.

Near her gate, a bachelor party was in even worse shape. The guys wore matching tank tops with 'NASH BASH' emblazoned across the chest, and one—presumably the groom—was passed out at the bar, his head on the sticky counter while his friends took photos.

"That guy can't even stand up, and someone's marrying him," Eva muttered to herself. "What is wrong with me?"

She felt a twinge of guilt at her uncharacteristic cynicism. This wasn't her. She was usually the one defending

Nashville's tourism, explaining to eye-rolling locals how these visitors kept the economy going. But tonight, the sea of soon-to-be-married strangers felt like the universe rubbing salt in her very fresh wound.

*   *   *

As the plane lifted off the runway that evening, Eva pressed her forehead against the cool window and watched Nashville—now decorated with thousands of Christmas lights—shrink beneath her. The city looked beautiful from above, a grid of golden light pulsing with holiday spirit. But Eva wasn't sad to see it disappear, at least not tonight.

About an hour into the flight, the reality of what she'd done hit her like a physical force. She was on a plane. To London. Alone. With no plan beyond a note from her high school English teacher and a half-remembered dream.

Her breathing quickened. The cabin suddenly felt too small, too warm. The woman next to her was knitting, the repetitive click of needles somehow both soothing and maddening. What was she doing? She didn't know anyone in London. She hadn't even booked a hotel. She was about to blow a huge chunk of her savings on a last-minute international trip.

"First time to London?" the knitting woman asked kindly, apparently noticing Eva's death grip on the armrest.

"Yes," Eva managed.

"How exciting! Travelling alone?"

"Yes."

"Good for you," the woman said, her needles never pausing. "I didn't take my first solo trip until I was sixty-two. Divorced my husband, sold the house, and went to Italy for a month. Best decision I ever made."

"Really?" Eva's breathing slowed slightly.

"Oh yes. There's something about being alone in a new place. You can't hide behind anyone else's expectations. You have to figure out what you actually want." She glanced at Eva with knowing eyes. "Scary as hell, but worth it."

Eva nodded, feeling her panic subside. She looked down, eyes clearer now as the woman continued to knit a matching scarf to the Christmas jumper she was wrapped in. She was a complete stranger, but damn it she was right. This was scary. It was also exactly what she needed.

She pulled out her phone and typed a message to save for when she landed:

`Eva: Court, made it on the plane. Currently having a mild panic attack but the lady next to me says that's normal. Thank you for everything. Give Richard's teddy bear an extra aggressive toss for me.`

`Eva: Mom, I'm safe. I'm okay. I need this. Please try to understand. I'll call when I land. I love you.`

In her purse was her passport, her wallet, the mistletoe, and surprisingly, a small note Courtney must have slipped in when she wasn't looking: *Be brave. Find your story. Bring me back some British chocolate. C*

The plane banked gently, turning east towards the sunrise she'd meet halfway across the Atlantic. Below her, Nashville faded into darkness.

She was terrified. And for the first time in years, she was breathlessly, gloriously alive.

Chapter Three

The Discovery

Eva's first thought upon arriving in London was that nobody had properly explained English rain. It wasn't the dramatic downpours of Nashville thunderstorms or the gentle mist of movie-theatre London. It was persistent, determined and somehow horizontal. It had a quiet confidence, as if it had been perfecting its technique for centuries.

Because, of course, it had.

"You'll want a proper umbrella," the taxi driver had told her on the way from Heathrow, eyeing her flimsy travel-sized version with something between pity and amusement. "That thing's just going to cave in after an hour."

Regrettably, he was right. Eva's umbrella surrendered somewhere between Leicester Square and Piccadilly Circus—its metal spines twisting inside out with a sickening crack as a passing double-decker bus splashed gutter water onto her jeans. Three days in London, three umbrellas down. The rain here didn't fall so much as it hung suspended in the air, waiting for the perfect moment to slip down your collar or find that tiny gap between sleeve and glove.

She ducked beneath an awning, wiping droplets from her phone screen as she checked her map. The bright red buses and black cabs roared past, sending up sheets of water. Across the street, the billboard for *The Phantom of the Opera* glowed electric-white against the grey sky, while street performers dressed as gold-painted statues broke character long enough to shake the shower from their hats. A saxophonist in the Underground entrance played *Last Christmas* as commuters streamed past, somehow managing to never break stride or make eye contact. The smell of roasting chestnuts from a street vendor mingled with diesel fumes and the warm, yeasty scent of a nearby pub.

This wasn't the London of period dramas and royal weddings. This was louder, brighter, a sensory collision of old and new, where glass skyscrapers reflected in the windows of Tudor-era pubs.

Eva decided to walk towards Regent Street, where she'd heard the Christmas lights were spectacular. As she turned the corner, she saw them—enormous, illuminated angels suspended across the street. Their golden wings stretched from building to building and cast a warm glow over the shoppers below.

They were beautiful. Magical, even. She felt a warmth deep in her chest at the sight of them.

Until she spotted the couple and the frost quickly returned.

They stood directly beneath the largest angel, locked in an embrace that suggested they might be auditioning for a romance novel cover. The woman—blonde, gorgeous, wearing a coat that probably cost more than Eva's monthly rent—had one leg popped up behind her like she was in a 1950s movie. The man—tall, with the kind of jawline that seemed computer-generated—held her face so delicately between his gloved hands as if she were made of porcelain.

A photographer circled them with a professional camera, directing: "More passion! Pretend you're in *Love Actually*!"

Eva felt her lunch curdle. Three days post-breakup was apparently not enough time to witness this level of performative romance without her gag reflex kicking in.

"Just gorgeous!" the photographer squealed. "This is going to get so many likes!"

Eva pressed her lips together, willing her nausea to subside. The couple was now doing the thing where they touched foreheads and gazed into each other's eyes, laughing as if they'd just shared the most delightful secret. Eva briefly considered whether anyone would notice if she vomited directly into her now useless inside-out umbrella.

"Perfect! Now kiss under the angel wings!" the photographer directed.

"Oh God," Eva muttered, averting her eyes as the couple went in for what could only be described as a cinematic kiss—complete with the man actually lifting the woman slightly off her feet.

A passing businessman caught Eva's pained expression and followed her gaze to the romantic scene. "Been there," he said with a sympathetic grimace. "My advice? Pubs are that way." He pointed in the opposite direction.

Eva nodded gratefully and turned away from 'Love Actually: Regent Street Edition', feeling both vindicated by the stranger's understanding and pathetic for being so transparent in her misery.

"Mind the gap," blared from the station entrance, as if offering life advice rather than a transit warning.

Her phone buzzed.

Courtney: How's London? Is it magical?

Eva paused, looking up at the kaleidoscope of humanity rushing past. A woman in full Victorian dress complete with parasol passed a teenager with green hair clutching a vape pen. A man in a bespoke suit stepped carefully around a puddle while talking rapidly into his AirPods, cycling through at least three languages.

Eva: It's amazing. But different than I expected.

Courtney: Different good?

Eva: Different . . . still searching for something? If that makes sense

Courtney: Don't fall in love with any British men.

Eva: That's for Italy. No chance here. I'm neither eating, praying or loving.

Courtney: GOOD IDEA. NO SCRAP THAT ON THE LAST TWO. A GIRL'S GOTTA EAT.

Another notification dinged on the screen. Her bank. Funds were critically low and payment was due on her credit card.

But that was a problem for Nashville Eva. Not England Eva.

Now, on day three, she stood alone in the middle of Winter Wonderland at Hyde Park, sipping an £8 cup of mulled wine that tasted a little more like a melted down Yankee candle than 'Christmas in a cup' that she'd been sold on. Spices she couldn't identify swirled with sweetness that bordered on medicinal—not unpleasant, just unexpected.

The Christmas market sprawled across the park like a glitter explosion, every tree strung with enough lights to be visible from space. Eva wandered past rows of wooden chalets, where mass-produced ornaments dangled under hand-painted signs that still smelled faintly of fresh varnish. A nearby carnival ride screeched as it hurled teenagers skyward, tinny Christmas song audio competed with the metallic clang of arcade games.

In the middle stood a neon green, plastic, Christmas tree. The hard steel in the middle was visible and the branches looked like lasagne noodles stacked in a cone. These seemed to be a theme at London Christmas markets. All of them identical. With the same red and silver ornaments, topped with a gingerbread star. It was Christmas capitalism personified.

Eva took a sip from her paper cup of mulled wine. The cinnamon scent was cloying, too sweet, like Christmas had been boiled down, concentrated and bottled.

And why on Earth were there so many damn churro stands?!

Eva stood next to a carnival ride blasting Mariah Carey's *All I Want for Christmas* for what felt like the fortieth time that hour. It was time to go for a walk; she was here for the plot. She wanted something to happen in her life, no, she *needed* it to. And she wasn't going to have the transformative experience she'd been craving by staring through a neon ride that plummeted to the ground. There had been enough plummeting in her life recently. England was not supposed to remind her of the recent fall from grace.

Her phone buzzed again. A notification from Instagram—Richard had liked one of her London stories. The selfie of her at Tower Bridge from yesterday.

Eva stared at the alert, anger bubbling up. The audacity. He dumps her and then creeps on her social media? She swiped to Instagram, found his profile, and blocked him without hesitation. Then did the same on every other platform she could think of. He had no right looking into her business right now.

Another buzz. This time, her mother.

Mom: Eva, I've been very patient, but this is getting ridiculous. When are you coming home? Your father thinks I should give you space, but I know what's best for you. Call me immediately.

Eva typed back:

Eva: I'm staying a bit longer. I'm fine. I'll call when I'm ready.

She turned off read receipts preparing for the onslaught of messages to come. She didn't need her mother seeing that she'd read the messages. Then, feeling bold, she muted the conversation entirely.

Eva: Court, I don't know what I'm doing do you think I made a mistake? Maybe Mom's right . . .

Courtney: Hell no! You're just having a wobble, it's totally understandable but don't listen to those negative thoughts. If you don't like where you are just go find somewhere new, remember you can do that there!

The rain had settled into a mist fine enough to be almost invisible until you realised your hair was completely soaked. Eva's carefully straightened auburn waves had expanded into something that would have made an '80s rock band proud.

Courtney was right, Eva was searching for something but unfortunately, she hadn't found it here. With a deflated sigh, she walked away from Hyde Park, away from the crowds and the churros and the carnival music. Ahead, streets narrowed as if the city itself was inhaling. Buses couldn't squeeze down these lanes, and tourists thinned out with each block she walked.

The buildings grew older, their stone facades darkened with centuries of London soot. Gas lamps—converted to electric but maintaining their vintage charm—cast warm pools of light onto slick cobblestones. Here, Christmas looked different: simple wreaths hung on ancient wooden doors, sprigs of holly tucked into window frames, strings of white lights reflecting in leaded glass windows. No inflatable Santas, no animated reindeer—just quiet tradition that had survived hundreds of December twenty-fifths.

Courtney's words from the apartment echoed in her mind: "Go find yourself." But how did you find something you weren't even sure existed anymore?

She slipped through streets where shops sold single, specialized items: one sold only antique maps, another nothing but wooden jigsaw puzzles. A third displayed fountain pens in a window so small she had to stoop to peer inside. Each storefront seemed to exist in its own time zone, unconcerned with the digital world that Eva had left behind in Hyde Park. This felt much more like the haven she'd been seeking.

She turned down Marylebone Lane, where the street curved like a question mark. Her shoulders brushed brick walls on either side as a black cab somehow navigated the bend, its tyres slick on cobblestones that had been worn smooth by centuries of footsteps. The driver nodded at her with a smile.

Her Google Maps app had given up trying to tell her where she was, the blue dot jumping erratically between streets. But getting lost, Eva decided, was exactly what she needed.

A shop window caught her eye—not the gleaming displays of Oxford Street, but something altogether different. Behind rain-spotted glass, vintage teacups balanced in precarious towers, each one different from the last. The sign above read 'The Marylebone Curiosity Cabinet' in gold letters that had seen better decades.

Next door, a pub called The Golden Eagle looked as though it had been serving pints since before the USA was even a country. A Christmas garland framed its door, but not the shiny mass-produced stuff from Winter Wonderland—this was real pine, decorated with dried orange slices and cinnamon sticks. It was beautiful.

The rain picked up again, but here it felt different. Maybe it was the way it caught the light from the antique street lamps, or how it made the cobblestones gleam like black glass. Either way, something in Eva's heart told her she wasn't so lost anymore. Ready to escape the rain she ducked under a striped awning, brushing the droplets off her red jacket. In Nashville, she'd have been huddled in her car by now, cranking the heat and complaining about the weather. Here she was getting soaked and somehow enjoying it.

A sign pointed down a narrow passage: 'St. Christopher's Place'.

Eva hesitated. The alley was barely wider than her shoulders, and definitely not on any tourist map. She hesitated for a moment at the quietness of it all. *But wasn't this what she'd come for?* Not the London of guidebooks and Instagram, but the real city, with its secrets and stories? The Eva from last week would have kept walking, concerned about safety ratings and Yelp reviews. But that Eva had also believed Richard was going to propose and that she was a shoo-in for the promotion, so clearly her judgment wasn't infallible.

She took a deep breath and stepped into the passage.

What opened up before her was a scene like stepping through the wardrobe into Narnia. A hidden courtyard, strung with lights that danced in the rain. Small shops lined the square, their windows curved and glowing amber against the twilight. There was a chocolatier hand-dipping truffles in the window and a shop selling only flat cap hats and feathers. The kind of specialisation that suggested either extreme dedication or terrible business acumen.

That's when she saw it: a bookshop. The window display featured a stack of old books arranged like a Christmas tree, topped with a worn copy of *A Christmas Carol*. A brass bell tinkled softly as she pushed open the door, her boots squeaking against the worn wooden floor.

The smell hit her first—old paper, leather bindings, and something that might have been tea or possibly just centuries of British dampness. Books were stacked everywhere, creating narrow canyons barely wide enough to squeeze through. It was like someone had taken the concept of fire safety regulations, considered them thoughtfully, and then laughed deciding they were entirely optional.

"Looking for anything in particular?" asked a voice from somewhere behind a towering stack of worn British classics. Eva caught a glimpse of silver hair and wire-rimmed glasses perched on a man's crooked nose. Upon further investigation, she locked eyes with pools of blue that had clearly seen their fair share of books.

"Just browsing," Eva replied, running her fingers along the spines. They felt different from the books at Barnes & Noble back home—more lived in, like each one had character and a story deeper than just the words printed on their pages. They'd been held in bathtubs, at bedsides, in gardens, on trains, capturing a little of the lives they'd touched.

The shop seemed bigger on the inside than the outside suggested—a very British trait, Eva was learning. She wandered deeper, past shelves of Jane Austen editions with broken spines and dog-eared Agatha Christies that looked as though they'd been involved in more mysteries than they contained.

Her phone buzzed in her pocket. Another message from her mother, probably. But Eva didn't even check. For once, she was exactly where she wanted to be. She wanted to be present, with no distractions, when she reached to power it off, her elbow knocked a book from a high shelf.

At least, that's what she thought happened.

A soft thud at her feet made her jump. Eva glanced up instinctively—rows of books loomed, undisturbed. No gaps. No fallen volumes.

Yet there it was: a green book, resting squarely in front of her boots, its cover glistening faintly under the dusty shop lights.

The air around her shifted, almost imperceptibly, as if the room itself was holding its breath. Eva crouched down, fingertips brushing the worn leather. The book felt warm against her palm, unnervingly so, like it was responding to her touch and had been waiting just for her.

A draught curled around her ankles, cool and certain, nudging her forward.

Doubting herself, she looked up once more. But as before, there was no gap in the books above. No space where one might have fallen from.

In her grip was some sort of sign, Eva was convinced of it. With a faded green hardcover, no dust jacket protected the boards and the gold lettering had mostly worn away. Her fingers trembled slightly as she turned it over in her hands—something about it felt important, like finding a key before you know which door it opens. The tired leather notebook she'd brought from Nashville, one that was supposed to contain Eva's creative writing but had been resigned to shopping and to do lists, suddenly felt like a pretender in the presence of the real thing.

Inside was a handwritten note in faded ink:

If you find this, you're on the right path. Follow the signs.

Below it was an address in York, written in the same careful hand, and a name: Margaret Wells. The address indicated 'The Fairy Light Tea Room' on Stonegate.

"Excuse me," Eva called out, her voice barely above a whisper because something about the moment seemed to demand quiet. "Do you know anything about this book?"

The silver-haired man emerged from behind a shelf, adjusting his glasses. "Ah" he said, studying the green book in her hands. "You've found Margaret's book."

"Margaret Wells?" Eva asked, her heart beating faster.

The man smiled, his deeply lined face creasing further. "That book's been here longer than I have. Ten pounds if you'd like it."

Eva opened her purse and pulled out her wallet, extracting a crisp ten-pound note. "Can you tell me anything about Margaret Wells or this tea room in York?"

"Only that the book's been waiting for the right person," the man said, taking the money and placing it in an ancient-looking register.

Through the window, Eva could see the courtyard had grown darker, the Christmas lights reflecting off the wet cobblestones like an illuminated runway. This, she realised, was the magic she'd been looking for. Not in the bright lights of Winter Wonderland or the polished window displays of Oxford Street, but here in this hidden corner of London where mysterious books found their way into the hands of girls who were looking for . . . something.

Back in her room at the Resident Hotel, Eva sat cross-legged on the crisp white duvet, still wearing her damp socks because she couldn't quite figure out the radiator settings. It seemed to look at her, mockingly. British appliances appeared to operate on a principle of national solidarity—united in their resistance against American interference.

She held the green book in her hands, its worn cover almost glowing in the warm light of the dim lamp on the bedside table. Next to it lay her battered notebook from home, still waiting for the promised thoughts, important enough to deserve its pages. The contrast between them couldn't have been more stark—one alive with history and possibility, the other paralysed by perfectionism.

She carefully set down the book next to the lamp. The light flickered out.

"That's odd," Eva wondered aloud.

Eva fiddled with the brass switch, knocking the book to the ground. The light came back on, as if it had a mind of its own.

A draughtless shiver moved through the room; the book's pages fluttered of their own accord and settled on a heading written in looping script: *The Fairy Light Tea Room, York. Follow the signs.*

Eva felt goosebumps tickle her flesh. The signs? Eva laughed. No. No, she couldn't just suddenly change her plans.

She went to set the book down, but hesitated. *Just dive in, Eva.* She argued with herself on whether or not to keep reading. Who was she? This was crazy. A part of her felt weary, though she wasn't sure why. She shouldn't have watched *Harry Potter and the Chamber of Secrets* on the plane. The diary scene always freaked her out. Harry follows a diary and almost dies because of it. But that was just a story. And so was this. *Damn it, be brave, Eva. Open the cover* . . . Flipping to a third page, another handwritten note was revealed: *Sometimes the best stories start where you least expect them.* She flipped back to the page that had caught her eye in the bookshop—the one about the tea room in York. Reading more carefully, she saw the full address: *The Fairy Light Tea Room, Stonegate, York.* The ink looked strangely fresh, as if written moments ago.

Eva's MacBook Air glowed as she pulled up the National Rail website. York was only two hours away by train. The photos looked like something out of a movie she'd have watched with Courtney on a girl's night in, but . . . real. She leaned closer to the screen, heart lifting as photo after photo scrolled by—stone walls tangled with ivy, crooked timber houses leaning together like they were a team. It wasn't just a city. It was a storybook.

And then there was the Christmas Market—images showed wooden stalls dusted with snow, steam rising from cups of mulled wine, artisans selling handmade crafts.

Her phone buzzed.

Richard: Hey, saw your London pics on Instagram. Looks amazing.

Eva looked at the message, then at the mysterious book, then back at the message. She closed it without responding and clicked 'Purchase' on a train ticket instead. *She needed to block his ass.*

Her phone buzzed one more time. She glanced at it, expecting her mother next. But it was Courtney:

Courtney: How's the finding yourself going? Any magical epiphanies yet?

Eva looked at the mysterious book, then typed back:

Eva: Maybe. Following a lead to York tomorrow. Will explain later.

Courtney: That's my girl! Chase that adventure!

Eva smiled and closed her laptop. Outside her window, London sparkled in the rain. Yes, it was beautiful and grand and exactly what she'd thought she wanted. But maybe, just maybe, what she really needed was waiting in a tearoom in York. Like when Dorothy had realised the Emerald City wasn't home after all, Eva was finding that the London she'd dreamed of for so long was just one stop on a longer journey.

Eva packed her carry-on, carefully wrapping the green book in her favourite oversized cream sweater. For a moment, she held her untouched notebook from Nashville, considering whether to leave it behind. She packed it too—a reminder of who she'd been, even as she was becoming someone new.

Then she did something she hadn't done since she was a kid writing in her Lisa Frank diary—she made a wish.

Not on a star (London's light pollution took care of that), but on the book itself.

She felt a little bit ridiculous, standing there with her eyes closed, in damp socks, whispering a wish into the cold London air. But maybe that was the point. Maybe magic only found the people who still believed it might. Maybe change wasn't something you planned for—it was something you asked for, even when you weren't sure you deserved it.

"Please," she whispered, feeling only slightly ridiculous, "let this be something amazing. Something . . . real."

The next morning, she wheeled her suitcase through King's Cross Station, past the tourist crowds taking photos at Platform 9¾, and found her way to her train. As London's suburbs gave way to rolling countryside, Eva opened the book again.

She noticed something else written on the back of the note, in different handwriting:

P.S. - Don't forget to look up when you reach Stonegate. The best magic happens above the shop signs.

Eva smiled and settled back in her seat. Despite the fact that she didn't quite know where she was going, for the first time since leaving Nashville, she felt like she was exactly where she was supposed to be.

Chapter Four

Cobblestones and Confrontations

Perhaps the greatest miracle of Eva's trip so far was that the British transport system, despite their notorious reputation, had somehow been more reliable than her relationships. Outside the window, the landscape blurred past—patchworks of green and brown dusted with frost, stone walls slicing through fields like handwritten notes across parchment. Eva sat curled by the window, clutching her second cup of tea of the day.

She hadn't slept much the night before. The mysterious green book had sat on her nightstand like a visitor from another world, its presence somehow both comforting and unsettling. She'd found herself repeatedly reaching for it in the dark, running her fingers over the worn cover as if it might whisper secrets if she touched it just right.

Now, as the train rushed towards York, Eva held the book in her lap and tried to make sense of her own decision.

For once in her life, she was doing something purely for herself. Not because her mother approved, not because it looked good on her résumé and not even because it was the practical choice. She was following a thread of possibility, hoping it might lead her back to the girl who used to believe in magic. The girl who had written stories late into the night and dreamed of adventures beyond Nashville's city limits.

Maybe that girl was still in there somewhere, waiting to be rediscovered.

An elderly woman with a cloud of white hair and spectacles perched on the end of her nose watched Eva from across the aisle, setting down her Agatha Christie book.

"York's your stop, is it?" she asked, her accent softening the words into something musical.

"Yes," Eva replied.

The woman smiled. "You have that look. Like you're expecting something marvellous to happen."

"I'm not sure what I'm expecting," Eva admitted.

"That's the best way to arrive anywhere," the woman said, nodding approvingly. "York doesn't disappoint those who come with an open heart."

Eva's phone buzzed.

`Richard: I think I made a mistake. Can we talk?`

She stared at the message, feeling a familiar tug of obligation. The old Eva would have responded immediately, would have reassured him, would have made it easy for him to waltz back into her life. But sitting on this train, with the English countryside flowing past and Margaret Wells' mysterious book in her lap, Richard's message felt like an echo from a life she was no longer sure she wanted. She'd spent a considerable amount of time on her travels reflecting on their relationship. How there'd never been a true balance. Eva seemed to put in all the work. She'd compromised on what she'd wanted nearly all the time, she'd been polite to cover his rudeness in social scenarios, laughed at his frankly *terrible* jokes and excused his belittling comments. And for what?

Eva: We were never right for each other. You know that.

His response came immediately: That's not true. We worked well together.

Eva almost laughed. *Worked well together.* Like they were business partners, not lovers. Like their romance was a project he was managing rather than a feeling to be cherished. God, she'd never felt cherished by him at all.

Eva: Take care of yourself, Richard.

She typed her response, then did something she'd never done before in the (very brief) history of her dating life—she blocked his number. She'd already removed him from Instagram to tear away his prying eyes from her exciting adventures, this was now the final step. With a new sense of empowerment, she thought of a world free of Richard, his judgements and demands— damn it looked pretty good.

The elderly woman glanced up from her book. "Good for you, love. Nothing worse than someone who doesn't know when they've been properly dismissed."

Eva blushed, realising her internal monologue on 'blocking that jerk' hadn't been as in her head as she'd thought. "Do you think I did the right thing?"

"Of course you did. Look at your body language, I just know, love. You've relaxed, it's like you've just taken a proper deep breath for the first time in years."

* * *

54

The train announcement crackled overhead: "We will be arriving at York Station in approximately five minutes. Please ensure you take all your belongings with you when you leave the train."

As Eva pulled down her suitcase, a wave of uncertainty hit her. She had no hotel reservation, no concrete plan beyond finding the Fairy Light Tea Room. What if this was all a terrible mistake? What if she was just running away from her problems instead of solving them?

But as she stepped off the train onto the platform, the air felt different—crisper, somehow, as if the city had been preserving winter just for her arrival.

York Station itself was a marvel of Victorian engineering, a cathedral to the golden age of rail travel with its sweeping curved roof and intricate ironwork. Eva paused, gazing up at the vaulted ceiling, momentarily lost in its grandeur.

This was it, her chance to take on an adventure and outside, the city waited.

"Holy shit," she whispered, the words forming a small cloud in the cold air.

Ancient stone walls encircled the city like a protective embrace, standing sentry as they had for centuries. Within their protection, a tangle of medieval streets and crooked buildings created a skyline that looked like something from a fairy tale. And rising above it all, the magnificent York Minster, its twin Gothic towers reaching towards heaven.

Eva felt her breath catch. This wasn't just a city—it was a living storybook.

Following the signs towards the city centre, Eva found herself on narrow cobblestone streets that seemed untouched by time. The buildings leaned towards each other like old friends sharing secrets, their Tudor frames creating intricate patterns of dark timber against whitewashed walls.

She turned onto a street marked 'The Shambles' and immediately understood why this place had captured imaginations for centuries. The medieval buildings pressed so close together that Eva could nearly touch both sides of the street with her outstretched arms. Above her head, upper floors jutted out at impossible angles, creating a tunnel of ancient timber and stone. Shop signs hung from wrought-iron brackets, swaying gently in the winter breeze—a golden unicorn, a silver moon, a painted dragon that seemed to wink at her as she passed.

Following the address from Margaret's book, Eva found the Fairy Light Tea Room nestled between a jewellery shop and an antiquarian bookstore. Its windows were steamed up from within, offering glimpses of twinkling lights and the warm glow of candles through the condensation. The sign—a delicate wrought iron creation featuring a teapot with tiny stars emerging from its spout—swung gently in the winter breeze.

Eva pushed open the door, which announced her arrival with the gentle chime of a silver bell.

The interior was like stepping into someone's whimsical dream of what an English teashop should be. Mismatched vintage tables were arranged across a creaky wooden floor. Each was set with different china—some floral, some gilt-edged, no two alike. Fairy lights were strung across the ceiling, reflected in dozens of tiny mirrors that caught and multiplied their glow. The space smelled of cinnamon, cloves, and something buttery baking in the kitchen. Eva had overheard whispers on the train of scones that rivalled the King's personal bakes available here in York and her stomach grumbled at the thought of securing one.

"Just yourself?" asked a woman about Eva's age, her blonde hair twisted into a messy bun secured with what appeared to be a pencil. She wore a deep green apron over a floral dress, and round glasses that gave her a slightly bookish air.

"Yes," Eva said, suddenly conscious of her suitcase. "Sorry about this—I just arrived and wanted to come straight here."

"No need to apologise," the woman said with a laugh. "I once went straight from the airport to a castle in Scotland because I couldn't wait to see it. Twenty kilogrammes of luggage and all. I'm Jean, by the way."

"Eva. And thanks for understanding the impulsive tourist thing."

"The impulsive ones have the best adventures," Jean said, leading Eva to a table by the window. "Careful planners never find the hidden doors."

Eva settled in, ordering the 'full afternoon tea' without really knowing what that entailed, and arranged the green book on the table beside her. When Jean returned with a steaming teapot and the first tier of what would become a towering stand of treats, Eva took a chance.

"I'm—well, I'm following a sort of trail," she said, turning the book to show Jean the inscription. "Do you know anything about Margaret Wells?"

Jean's eyes lit up with recognition. "Margaret Wells! She used to come in here every Thursday at precisely four o'clock, rain or shine. That was before my time, mind you, but my aunt owned this place then. Everyone in York knew of Margaret. She was . . . well, she was special." Jean glanced at the book. "And you found one of her books? That's quite something."

"You mean there are others?"

"Oh, I believe so. Plus, Margaret was famous for leaving little treasures around York—notes in library books, messages tucked behind loose stones, that sort of thing. Like a treasure hunt for the heart, my aunt used to say."

Eva leaned forward eagerly. "Do you have anything of hers here?"

Jean's smile widened. "As a matter of fact . . ." She disappeared into the back room, returning with a small envelope. "This has been waiting for whoever might come asking about Margaret. My aunt always said it would find its way to the right person eventually."

Eva took the envelope with trembling fingers. Inside was a yellowing card with the same careful handwriting as the book:

York reveals its secrets to those who look beyond the surface. The gruffest exteriors often hide the kindest hearts.

Eva stared at the note, a shiver running down her spine. "She . . . she left this for someone she'd never met?"

"Margaret believed in serendipity," Jean explained. "She said the universe had a way of bringing the right people together at exactly the right time."

After finishing her tea and paying the bill, Eva asked, "You wouldn't happen to know of a good place to stay, would you? I was so eager to get here that I forgot to book anything."

"The Riddle & Quill Inn," Jean said without hesitation. "Florence runs it—she's a bit sharp around the edges, but she has a good heart. Tell her Jean sent you."

* * *

The address led her to a striking Tudor-style building nestled between two more modern structures. Its black timber frame created a dramatic geometric pattern against white-washed walls that had yellowed slightly with age. The steeply pitched roof featured two dormer windows that peered out like watchful eyes, and the distinctive hexagonal leaded glass windows glowed with warm light from within. A simple wreath hung on the black-painted door, and small box hedges, slightly overgrown, framed the entrance.

Eva paused to admire the building, which looked like it had been plucked straight from a storybook about medieval England. While the white paint was chipping slightly at the corners and one of the timber beams showed signs of recent repair, there was an undeniable charm to the place—the kind that came from centuries of history rather than careful decoration. This wasn't the polished, Instagram-ready version of England that tourists typically sought out, but something more authentic. It was unapologetically itself. Eva appreciated that.

She pressed the tarnished brass doorbell, hearing it ring somewhere deep within the house. A moment passed, then another. Eva was about to try again when she heard footsteps approaching from inside.

The door swung open to reveal a woman who seemed to Eva to be somewhere between seventy and infinity, with perfectly set silver hair, piercing blue eyes, and the kind of impeccable posture that came from a lifetime of being told to stand up straight. She was wearing a cardigan that appeared to have been knitted from actual clouds, and tartan slippers that looked like they'd weathered several monarchs.

"You all right?" the woman asked, her Yorkshire accent so thick that Eva had to lean in slightly to catch the words.

"Um, yes? I'm fine," Eva replied, confused.

The woman chuckled. "That's just how we say hello in Yorkshire, love. I'm Florence. Jean called ahead—you must be the American."

59

"Eva," she confirmed, adjusting her bag nervously. "Thank you for having me."

"Well, you'd better come in before we let all the heat out," Florence said, dropping her h's like they were unnecessary accessories. "Yorkshire doesn't warm itself, you know."

Florence led her up a narrow staircase that creaked with every step, past framed photographs spanning what appeared to be several decades. "You're in the room at the top. It has its own loo, thank the Lord. I'm too old to be sharing facilities with strangers."

The room was small but perfect—all vintage charm and surprising comfort. A wrought-iron bed was piled high with quilts, a small writing desk sat beneath a dormer window overlooking the street, and the sloped ceiling was crossed with ancient wooden beams that spoke of centuries of stories.

"Breakfast is from seven until nine," Florence said briskly. "I don't do special diets, but there's a vegan café down the street if you're one of those." She gave Eva an appraising look. "You'll be wanting to see the Christmas Market, I expect. That's where you'll find the real magic—not in the touristy bits, but in watching how the city comes alive when people gather."

After Florence left, Eva unpacked and freshened up, then ventured out into the early evening. The Christmas Market was everything she'd hoped for and more—wooden chalets adorned with pine garlands and twinkling lights lined the cobblestone streets, their roofs dusted with what might have been real snow. The air was intoxicating: warm clouds of cinnamon and nutmeg, sweet caramel scents of roasting chestnuts, rich chocolate mingling with buttery pastries.

Each stall was a small work of art. Hand-blown glass ornaments caught the light and projected magical rainbows. Intricately carved wooden figurines seemed to have personalities of their own. A cheese vendor offered samples that made Eva's eyes roll back in pleasure.

There were so many stands selling alcohol it made Eva giggle. She decided she needed to participate, a wrong from her earlier UK market experience had to be corrected. She was in the right place, spoiled for choice. She had to dive in now.

She found herself at a mulled wine stall, ordering without making a conscious decision, she picked the first option that her eyes landed on. The vendor—a rosy-cheeked man in a knitted hat—handed her a ceramic mug painted with holly leaves.

She stood allowing the swirl of the market atmosphere to envelope her. This was a Dicken's Christmas novel come to life.

She felt goosebumps on her arms, despite her warm coat, and smiled to herself. This risk was going to pay off, she could feel it.

Eva wandered deeper into the market, clutching her warm mug she was completely enchanted by the magical atmosphere around her. The mulled wine was nothing like anything she'd had in Nashville—complex and aromatic, warming her from the inside out.

She was so entranced by the sight of York Minster illuminated against the darkening sky that she didn't notice the uneven cobblestone beneath her feet. She stumbled slightly, and her mulled wine sloshed violently in its mug.

Time seemed to slow as she watched the hot liquid rise from her mug in a perfect crimson wave, arching through the air towards a display of what looked like hand-drawn maps. Eva's eyes followed the trajectory of the beverage to behind the prints. There stood a man in a thick wool coat and navy blue fisherman's beanie, his eyes widening as he watched disaster approach in slow motion.

The wine completed its graceful launch, landing with spectacular accuracy across both Eva's cream sweater and the stranger's coat. The ceramic mug tumbled from her grasp, bouncing once on the cobbles.

"Oh no, no, no!" Eva gasped, horror-struck. She frantically rummaged through her purse for tissues while backing into another of the map displays. Several carefully arranged prints fluttered to the ground.

"Oh my God, I'm so sorry!" she babbled, trying to blot the stranger's coat with one hand while attempting to rescue the maps with the other. "I'll pay for dry cleaning, I'll pay for everything, I just—"

"Stop," came a deep voice. Eva looked up to find herself staring into eyes that caught the winter light like sea glass—distant and definitely not amused. The man's dark curls escaped from beneath his beanie, and his expression suggested he was calculating exactly how much damage one American tourist could inflict in a single evening.

"You're dripping wine on a fifteenth-century street plan," he said, his voice clipped with barely controlled irritation.

Eva immediately stepped back, clutching her soggy tissues. "I'm really, really sorry. These are so beautiful— did you make them?"

"I did." He crouched to examine the maps, checking for damage with the careful attention of someone whose work meant everything to him. "They're historically accurate reproductions of York's development through the centuries."

Eva leaned closer, examining the detail. "It's like a Disney version of medieval England," she said, then immediately regretted it when his expression hardened.

"It's historically accurate," he said, his voice clipped. "Not sanitised for American tastes."

"Oh, I didn't mean—" Eva stumbled over her words. "I just meant it's magical. Like something from a storybook. Or Harry Potter."

His jaw tightened. "York has been here for two thousand years. It doesn't need fictional wizards or fairy tales to make it special."

"They're incredible," Eva said earnestly, trying to recover. "Like artwork you'd want to frame and—"

"They're not decorations," he cut her off. "They're educational tools. Historical documents."

"Of course," Eva said quickly, stung by his tone. "I didn't mean to minimise—"

"Americans," he muttered, not quite under his breath, as he carefully straightened a damp corner. "Turn everything into a photo opportunity."

Eva felt her cheeks burn. "I wasn't trying to—"

"No, you were just wandering around a crowded market drinking mulled wine while gawking at buildings instead of watching where you're going, like any sensible person would do."

"You know what?" Eva said, her embarrassment flaring into indignation. "I said I was sorry. Multiple times. I offered to pay for damages. I complimented your work. I'm not sure what else you want from me."

He looked up from the maps, his expression unchanged. "I want you to be more careful. This isn't Disneyland."

"I know it's not Disneyland," Eva snapped. "I came here because I thought British people were supposed to be polite." She couldn't believe she'd said it, this wasn't careful and controlled Eva. This wasn't the girl who always made a good first impression, the one who tried to mould herself into what people wanted her to be. But now she'd leant in, she had to admit: it felt good.

"We're polite to people who deserve it."

Eva stared at him, momentarily speechless at his bluntness. A movement in the corner of her eye caught her attention—a black and white spaniel with floppy ears trotted towards the stall, looking between them with what seemed like canine concern.

The man's expression softened instantly as he crouched to greet the dog. "There you are, Tilly," he said, his voice completely transformed—warm, gentle, tender. He scratched behind the spaniel's ears with obvious affection.

The contrast was so stark that Eva felt even more annoyed. "You're nicer to your dog than you are to people."

"Dogs don't knock over displays or spill wine on historical documents," he replied, but there was less edge to his voice now.

Tilly approached Eva cautiously, sniffing her wine-stained sweater before resting her head against Eva's knee with surprising gentleness.

"Well, at least one of you has manners," Eva said, stroking the spaniel's silky ears. The dog's warmth against her leg was oddly comforting after the man's coldness.

He watched this interaction with wide eyes but narrowed them once again, "She likes everyone, so don't feel special."

"Maybe she can sense that I'm not actually trying to destroy your city," Eva said pointedly.

For just a moment, something that might have been amusement flickered across his face. But then he stood, all business again. "You should watch where you're going before you cause any more accidents."

Rolling her eyes, she turned her back to him and walked away with as much dignity as she could muster. Careful of spotting the cobbles, she felt the heat of his gaze upon her neck. Or maybe that was just wishful thinking after such a thoroughly unpleasant first impression.

But as she moved deeper into the market, the magic gradually worked its way back into her mood. The fairy lights strung between medieval buildings created a canopy of stars overhead. Carol singers gathered around the enormous Christmas tree, their voices lifting into the cold air. Children raced past in colourful scarves, their laughter ringing like bells.

At a chocolate stall, Eva bought a small bag of truffles dusted with cocoa powder that melted on her tongue like velvet. The vendor—a woman with kind eyes—chatted about how her grandmother had run a sweet shop on this very spot.

"First time in York?" she asked, and when Eva nodded, added, "You picked the perfect time. Christmas Market brings out the best in everyone."

Everyone except grumpy stall owners, Eva thought, but found herself smiling anyway.

As she wandered through the glowing stalls, past artisans crafting everything from pottery to jewellery, past the warm scents of mulled cider and roasted almonds, Eva felt something shift inside her chest. This was why she'd come to England—not for the London she'd first imagined, but for this unexpected magic. For narrow streets that had witnessed centuries of Christmas celebrations. For the possibility that around any corner, she might find exactly what she didn't know she was looking for.

Even if that corner also happened to contain the rudest mapmaker in Yorkshire.

Eva finished the last of her truffles and made her way back through the winding streets towards The Riddle & Quill Inn. Tomorrow, she would continue following Margaret Wells' trail. Tonight, she would write in her own scruffy notebook—because sometimes the most important stories began with the most unexpected encounters.

Even the infuriating ones.

Chapter Five

A City of Stories

The sound of church bells and birdsong broke Eva's sleep. The windows were thin enough to hear nearly every noise outside, including what seemed to be an extremely passionate argument between two seagulls over what was probably a discarded chip. She pulled open the heavy curtains and watched as the weaker winter sun battled against dense, grey clouds.

She stretched, relishing the unexpected luxury of waking without an alarm. Back in Nashville, her mornings followed a precise routine: alarm at 6.15, scrolling through emails by 6.20, in the shower for 7.10, breakfast tracked on MyFitnessPal by 7.30. Life measured in fifteen-minute increments, recorded in her planner with colour-coded precision.

But here? She had no idea what time it was, and for once, it didn't matter.

The floor was ice-cold beneath her feet as she padded to the bathroom. The radiator in her room made occasional alarming clanking sounds, like something was trying to escape from the pipes, but it did a valiant job of keeping the bedroom warm. The bathroom, however, was an arctic temperature.

After a shower that involved a complex dance of keeping various body parts under the hot water while washing others, Eva wrapped herself in a towel printed with bright green frogs. The shower itself had been a uniquely British experience—an electric box on the wall that seemed to offer two temperature settings: 'surface of the sun' or 'ice bucket challenge'. The water pressure alternated between a gentle mist that wouldn't disturb a butterfly and a blast that could strip paint. She'd finally found a sweet spot by standing at exactly the right angle, but only if she didn't breathe too hard or think incorrect thoughts about the water temperature. *Positive vibes only*.

She pushed her wet hair back from her face and opened the bathroom door. Releasing a cloud of steam into the hallway, she stepped onto the patterned carpet that had probably been rolled out there since the Victorian era.

Through blurred vision, she walked directly into a firm surface. Looking up to clear her vision her eyes were met with a familiar scowling face. *The mapmaker*.

"Oh!" Eva yelped, clutching the towel tighter as she stumbled backward. "What are you—why are you—"

The seemingly permanent scowl slipped from him suddenly as the scene unfolded. The man looked as startled as she felt, his eyes wide, a toolbox dangling from one hand and what appeared to be a wrench in the other. His mouth opened and closed soundlessly for a moment like a fish before he managed, "Radiator. Florence said it was making noise."

In hearing his voice Eva became acutely aware of several things at once: her wet hair dripping down her neck, her bare feet on the well-trodden carpet, and the way the stranger's eyes seemed to be determinedly fixed on a point somewhere above her left ear.

"A little warning would have been nice," she said, trying to sound dignified.

"I thought you were out," he replied, his usual gruffness replaced by something that sounded almost like panic. "Florence said the guest upstairs was early riser. Always up with the birds."

"I am. Usually. Back home." Eva shifted uncomfortably. "Different time zone."

"Right. Of course." He shifted the toolbox from one hand to the other, the metal tools clanking loudly in the quiet hallway. "I'm Charlie, by the way. Charlie Blackwood. Florence is my aunt, well not exactly, but she's as good as."

"Eva," she managed, acutely aware that this was possibly the worst first impression she'd ever made. "Eva Coleman. The American in the frog towel."

"Right." Charlie's mouth twitched slightly. "Well, Eva Coleman, I should—" He gestured vaguely with the wrench. "Florence will be wondering—the radiator—"

"Are you having a stroke? Also, my eyes are up here buddy." Eva asked, surprised by his flustered rambling but finding it slightly amusing nonetheless.

That seemed to snap him back to himself. His expression shifted back to its usual studied indifference, though his ears remained suspiciously pink. "Excuse you! Look, Florence likes to meddle," he muttered. "She probably knew exactly where you were. Thinks this is funny, sending me up here now."

"Meddle how?"

"She's been trying to set me up with half of York for the past year. Says I need someone 'steady' in my life. Last month it was the post office clerk. Month before that, the baker's daughter." He shook his head. "She'll definitely read into this."

"Read into what? You fixing a radiator while I happen to be getting out of the shower?"

"You don't know Florence," Charlie said darkly. "She once tried to lock me in the storage closet with the dental hygienist during a Christmas party. Said it was an accident, but that closet locks from the inside. Make that make sense."

Despite trying, Eva found herself fighting a smile. "That's . . . dedicated."

"That's Florence." Charlie gestured vaguely with the wrench. "I should actually fix that radiator before she comes up here and finds us talking in the hallway. She'll have us married by teatime."

Eva's eyes widened in mock horror. "By teatime? But I haven't even seen your tax returns yet. In America, we at least wait until the second date before planning the wedding."

"Bold of you to assume this counts as a first date," Charlie shot back, then immediately looked like he wanted to swallow the words.

Eva stepped aside to let him pass, pressing herself against the wall. As he squeezed by in the narrow hallway, she caught a whiff of his scent—wood shavings and something like old books.

"For what it's worth," she called after him, "I promise not to let Florence marry us off."

Charlie paused at her door, glancing back. "Appreciated. Though fair warning—she's very persuasive. She once convinced me that plaid and stripes could work together."

"And did they?"

"I looked like a vintage sofa that had lost a fight with a circus tent."

Eva surprised herself by laughing. Charlie's mouth twitched in what might have been the beginning of a smile before he disappeared into another room, presumably to wage war with another clanking radiator.

Twenty minutes later, Eva descended to find Florence pushing a cheerful red vacuum cleaner across the dining room carpet. The machine had a painted-on face that made it look like a rotund, smiling cartoon character.

"Morning!" Florence called over the noise, switching off what Eva now saw was labelled 'Henry'. "Sorry about the racket. Henry and I like to get an early start on Saturdays."

"Henry?" Eva asked, amused by the idea of naming a vacuum cleaner.

"Best help I've got around here, besides Charlie when he shows up." Florence gave Henry an affectionate pat on his red dome. "Been with me fifteen years and never complains. Can't say that about most men."

She wheeled Henry to the corner and gestured for Eva to sit at a table already set with a cheerful yellow cloth. "Full English this morning—none of that continental nonsense."

Florence disappeared into the kitchen and returned with a plate that could have fed three people: eggs, bacon, sausages, grilled tomatoes, mushrooms, baked beans, and toast. A pot of tea appeared next, in a China teapot painted with forget-me-nots.

"This is amazing," Eva said, overwhelmed by the sheer volume of food.

"Can't have you wandering York on an empty stomach," Florence said, finally sitting down with her own cup of tea. "Speaking of which, what are your plans for the day?"

"I'm not sure. I was thinking of exploring more of the city, maybe trying to find more of Margaret Wells' notes?"

Florence's eyes sharpened with interest. "Persistent, aren't you? Well, if you want to know about York—the real York, not just the tourist bits—you should take Trinkett's tour."

"Trinkett?"

"Mister John Trinkett. Bit of an odd duck, dresses like he's escaped from a Dickens novel, but he knows every stone in this city. Does a walking tour every morning at ten, starts at The Shambles. Tell him I sent you."

Eva took a bite of bacon—perfectly crispy—and asked, "Has he lived here long?"

"All his life. His family's been in York since before America was even a twinkle in King George's eye." Florence poured more tea. "If anyone would know about Margaret's hiding spots, it'd be Trinkett. Though he does tend to go on about the plague pits."

"The what now?"

"Never mind. You'll find out soon enough." Florence's smile was mischievous. "Just don't let him scare you off with his ghost stories. Half of them he makes up on the spot."

John Trinkett was exactly where Florence had said he'd be, impossible to miss in his top hat adorned with what appeared to be several decades' worth of tour badges. A small group had already gathered around him.

"Gather 'round, gather 'round!" he called. "The Trinkett Tour of Truth and Tales is about to commence!"

For the next two hours, Trinkett led them through York's hidden corners, his theatrical delivery making even drainage systems sound fascinating.

As they squeezed through The Shambles, Trinkett had to raise his voice over the crowd. "And there—" he pointed to a shop with Gothic lettering: York Ghost Merchants, where a queue of tourists snaked halfway down the narrow street, "—is proof that people will wait an hour in Yorkshire rain for a good ghost story. York is filled with all kinds of experiences, that place over there, they've got some sort of interactive experience. I think they act out séances or some such nonsense." He sniffed disdainfully. "Though I'll admit, whatever they're doing in there, people come out looking properly spooked. See that couple?" He nodded towards a pair emerging from the shop, eyes wide and clutching each other. "That's the look of folk who've paid twenty quid to be scared by someone in a Victorian nightgown."

But it was when they stopped at The Golden Fleece pub that his tone grew serious.

"One of York's oldest watering holes, dating back to 1503. And now—" his voice dropped dramatically, "—threatened with closure. New owners want to turn it into luxury flats."

"That's terrible," Eva said, thinking of The Riddle & Quill and Florence's worried expression.

"It's progress, apparently," Trinkett said bitterly. "Though what's progressive about destroying five hundred years of history is beyond me."

As the tour wound down, Eva approached Trinkett privately. "Do you know anything about someone named Margaret Wells?"

His bushy eyebrows shot up. "Margaret Wells! Now there's a name I haven't heard in a while. Local legend, she was. Used to leave little notes around York for visitors to find—tucked in library books, behind loose stones, that sort of thing. Always encouraging words, bits of poetry."

"Do you know why she did it?"

Trinkett's expression grew thoughtful. "Started during the war, they say. She was a nurse, saw terrible things, God love her. The notes were her way of putting beauty back into the world. She wrote the most heartwarming stories but never published them. Whenever anyone asked her about it she'd just say she was saving them for the right time." He shook his head sadly. "Poor woman never found it."

Eva turned heading away from Trinkett when she heard a small voice, "Excuse me, dear," the woman said, her voice papery but warm. "I couldn't help overhearing you asking about Margaret Wells on Mister John Trinkett's tour."

"Yes," Eva said, steadying the woman as she navigated the uneven cobbles. "Did you know her?"

"She saved my father's life." The woman's rheumy eyes grew distant. "Not quite in the medical sense—she was his nurse, yes, but that's not what I mean. He came back from the war unable to speak, just sat in our front room staring at nothing. Mum was beside herself."

Eva waited, sensing the weight of the memory.

"Then one day, he came home from the library with a book. Tucked inside was a note—I still have it. It said, 'The words will come back when you're ready. Until then, let these borrowed words speak for you.' It was signed 'M.W.'"

"What happened?"

"He started reading aloud to us every night. Children's books at first, then poetry, then proper novels. Took six months, but one evening he stopped mid-sentence in *The Wind in the Willows* and said, 'That reminds me of . . .' and told us about a river he'd seen in France. First words of his own in over a year." The woman dabbed at her eyes. "Mum tried to find Margaret to thank her, but she'd only say she was glad the books helped. That was her way—plant the seed and disappear before the bloom."

Eva wandered back through The Shambles, lost in thought. Margaret Wells, a nurse during the war who left notes of hope around the city. Who never published her stories. Who—

"Getting the full tourist experience, I see."

Eva looked up to find Charlie Blackwood leaning against a shop doorway, arms crossed. Without his toolbox, in just jeans and a wool sweater, he looked younger, more relaxed.

"Mr Trinkett is very . . . thorough," Eva said.

"That's one word for it." Charlie pushed off from the wall. "He tell you about the ghost of Mad Alice?"

"In graphic detail."

"The plague victims?"

"Complete with sound effects."

"The—"

"I now know more about medieval sewage systems than any person needs to," Eva interrupted.

This time Charlie definitely smiled, just a quick flash before he caught himself. "Yeah, that's Trinkett. Comes from a long line of town criers. The theatrical gene runs strong."

They fell into step together, Charlie's long strides forcing Eva to quicken her pace.

"Actually," Eva said, trying to sound casual, "I asked him about Margaret Wells."

Charlie's step slowed slightly. "Did you?"

"He said she was quite famous locally. For her notes."

"Trinkett likes to exaggerate and make more of things for his stories," Charlie said shortly. "She was just . . . well, she just helped people during the war. That's all."

"That's all? He made it sound like she was some kind of local hero."

"People need heroes," Charlie said, his tone carefully neutral. "Especially in places like this, at a time like that. Sometimes we can make the past out to be more glorious than the present."

Eva studied his profile, noting the tension in his jaw. "You know more than you're saying."

"It's just local history," he said, but his voice lacked conviction.

"Local history that you seem to take personally."

Charlie stopped walking, turning to face her. "Why are you so interested in Margaret Wells?"

Eva held up the green book. "I found this in London. It led me here."

Charlie stared at the book, something flickering across his face but too quick for Eva to read. "You came all the way to York because of a book?"

"When you put it like that, it sounds crazy."

"No," Charlie said quietly. "It sounds like something she would have wanted."

Before Eva could ask what he meant, Charlie seemed to realise he'd said too much. His expression shuttered again.

"I'm actually quite the York expert now," Eva said, trying to lighten the moment. "I know about the ghosts, the plague pits, the Victorian sewers . . ."

"But have you seen the real Minster?" Charlie asked. "Not the tourist version. The hidden bits."

"I didn't know there were hidden bits."

"Everything in York has hidden bits," Charlie said with a flicker in his eye. "That's what makes it interesting."

Was he flirting with her? Eva couldn't tell. His expression remained studiously neutral, but there was something in his voice . . .

"Show me," she said impulsively.

Charlie looked surprised, then checked his watch. "Now?"

"Unless you have more radiators to fix."

"Florence's radiators have survived centuries without me. They can manage another afternoon." He paused, then added, "But this isn't . . . I'm not trying to . . ."

"Relax," Eva said. "Florence isn't here to read anything into it. You're just showing a tourist around. Civic duty and all that."

"Right. Civic duty." Charlie looked relieved. "Follow me then. And try not to destroy anything sacred. You're only allowed mulled wine when *leaving* the market from now on."

"That was one time!"

"Once was enough," Charlie said, but his tone was lighter now, almost teasing.

York Minster in the late afternoon was a different creature than the morning tourist attraction. The crowds had thinned, and long shadows stretched across the stone floor. Charlie led her away from the main nave, through a door marked 'Private'.

"Are we allowed back here?" Eva whispered.

"I help with restoration work sometimes," Charlie said. "Comes with certain privileges."

He led her up a narrow spiral staircase that seemed to go on forever. Eva's legs burned by the time they emerged onto a hidden balcony overlooking the main cathedral.

"Oh," she breathed.

From here, the Minster's vastness was even more apparent. The stained-glass windows caught the late afternoon sun, throwing jewelled light across the stone. Far below, people moved like ants, their voices a distant murmur.

"Three hundred years to complete," Charlie said softly. "Countless craftsmen, most of them nameless now. All that work, all that beauty, and they knew they'd never see it finished."

"That's either depressing or inspiring," Eva said. "I can't decide which."

"Both," Charlie said. "That's what makes it human."

They stood in comfortable silence, watching the light change. Then Charlie pointed to a section of the wall. "There. See that angel?"

Eva followed his gesture to a carved angel, different from the others. While most celestial beings in the Minster looked serene, this one seemed almost mischievous.

"The apprentice who carved it got in trouble," Charlie explained. "It was too 'worldly', they said. But the master mason fought to keep it. Said even angels should be allowed to smile."

"I like that story."

"It's one of the better ones," Charlie said. "This place is full of stories, if you know where to look."

He showed her more hidden details—a mason's mark tucked behind a pillar, graffiti from the English Civil War, a small carving of a mouse that the Victorian restoration workers had added as a signature.

"How do you know all this?" Eva asked.

"Spent a lot of time here as a kid," Charlie said, his voice carefully neutral. "Good place to hide from the world."

As they made their way back down to the main floor, Eva remembered what she'd found in the green book. "Actually, there's something I wanted to check. The north transept— Mr Trinkett mentioned something about angels there?"

Charlie's expression shifted slightly. "The Angel Choir. Yeah, it's worth seeing."

They made their way to the north transept, where carved angels lined the walls at eye level. Eva studied them, remembering the note from the green book about looking beneath an angel's wing.

"Looking for something specific?" Charlie asked, watching her closely.

"Just . . . exploring," Eva said, examining the intricate carvings. Each angel was unique—some played instruments, others held scrolls or flowers.

She paused at one angel set slightly apart from the others, its wings spread protectively. There, at the base, she spotted a small brass plaque that looked much newer than the medieval stonework:

In memory of those who came to heal but found home instead. For the American who left his heart in York, 1945-1946.

"Oh," Eva said softly. "Charlie, look at this."

Charlie crouched beside her, and she noticed his jaw tighten when he read the inscription. "Interesting," he said, his voice too casual.

"An American, just after the war," Eva mused. "I wonder who he was."

"Could be anyone," Charlie said, standing abruptly. "Lots of Americans came through York during the war. Bases nearby."

79

"But this sounds personal," Eva pressed. "'Left his heart in York'. That's not just about being stationed here."

"Maybe," Charlie said, already moving away. "Or maybe someone just thought it sounded poetic."

"Why are you being so dismissive of this? What do you know Charlie?" Eva said, studying his profile.

"I know that we should go," Charlie said, not meeting her eyes. "Florence will wonder where you've got to."

As they walked back through the darkening streets, Eva couldn't shake the feeling that the plaque was important. The reference to healing, to finding home—it connected somehow to Margaret Wells, the nurse who helped wounded soldiers. But for some unknown reason, Charlie clearly didn't want to talk about it.

* * *

"Thank you," she said as they reached the inn. "For showing me the Minster."

Charlie nodded, his hands shoved deep in his pockets. "York has a way of revealing its secrets slowly. Just . . . don't be in too much of a hurry to uncover them all."

He left before she could ask what he meant.

That evening, after a quiet dinner in the inn's small dining room, Eva climbed the stairs to her room. She opened the desk drawer and found a small stack of Riddle & Quill stationery—cream coloured paper with the inn's logo embossed at the top.

She sat at the small desk, pen poised, thinking about the day. About Charlie's careful deflections, about the hidden corners of the Minster, about the American who left his heart in York. Then she began to write:

There are stories that live in the spaces between stones, in the silence after church bells stop ringing. York keeps

80

them all—the nurse who wrote love into a broken world, the American soldier who never quite made it home, the people who make up the tapestry of this ancient city.

Today a man showed me hidden angels in ancient walls. He spoke of craftsmen who built beauty they'd never see completed.

In the north transept of York Minster, there's a plaque that reads: 'For the American who left his heart in York.' The brass has worn smooth from touching, as if people come here to remember their own lost loves, their own unfinished stories.

Charlie knows who the American was. I saw it in the way his hands tightened, the way he turned away. Some pain runs so deep it becomes part of the architecture of a family, passed down like brown eyes or stubborn chins.

I came to York following a stranger's breadcrumbs, but I'm beginning to understand that Margaret Wells wasn't leaving clues—she was leaving a confession, scattered across the city in pieces small enough to bear.

She folded the letter carefully and tucked it into the green book. Through her window, York glowed under the streetlights, and somewhere out there were more pieces of Margaret Wells' story, waiting patiently to be found.

Chapter Six

Fish, Chips and Friction

Eva hadn't planned on having dinner at the local pub. In fact, she hadn't planned much of anything beyond following a quest sparked by a mysterious green book. Planning had once been her superpower—the Eva Coleman specialty. Now she was following breadcrumbs through an ancient city, and strangely, it felt more right than any carefully plotted course she'd ever charted.

Earlier that day, she'd made what she considered a brilliant discovery at the local Tesco Express. The meal deal—a sandwich, snack, and drink for £3.50—had seemed like the pinnacle of British efficiency and value. She'd chosen an egg and cress sandwich (because when in England), salt and vinegar crisps (also very British), and a bottle of Ribena (which she'd never heard of but the purple colour looked appealing).

"Florence, you'll never guess what I discovered today," Eva had announced upon returning to the inn, holding up her Tesco bag like a trophy. "Have you ever had a meal deal? It's genius. Three items, one price. And this egg and cress sandwich—I mean, who knew cress could be so good?"

Florence had looked up from her book, eyebrows climbing towards her hairline. "You had a meal deal for lunch?"

"Yes! And these chips—sorry, crisps—that's right isn't it? Anyway, they're so vinegary they make your eyes water. It's fantastic. Is this what British people eat every day?"

"Oh, love," Florence had said, closing the covers together with a definitive boom. "That's not a proper meal. That's what office workers grab when they've got five minutes between meetings. You can't experience British food through a plastic triangle sandwich."

"But it was so convenient—"

"Convenient?" Florence had looked personally offended. "You're in York, not some motorway service station. Tonight, you're going to The Horse and Hound for a proper meal. Fish and chips, done right. None of this meal deal nonsense."

"I don't know, the sandwich was pretty good—"

"I won't hear it, that is a sorry excuse for a meal. The Horse and Hound—that's where you'll find real British cooking. Tell Oliver I sent you. And for heaven's sake, don't mention the meal deal. He'll bar you for life."

Which was how Eva found herself at The Horse and Hound, discovering again that Florence had been absolutely right. The pub was the kind of place that seemed to have been marinating in beer for centuries, the dark oak floors were sticky underfoot and the low ceiling was stained a deep amber from decades of tobacco smoke before the ban. Brass fixtures glowed dully in the warm light. The whole place smelled of beer, chips, and history.

The wooden beams overhead were so low that a sign at the entrance warned 'DUCK OR GROUSE'—which Eva initially thought was a drink option until she nearly concussed herself on a particularly treacherous beam. A string of Christmas lights had been half-heartedly tacked around the bar, blinking erratically as if they were trying to send a coded distress signal.

"You all right, love?" the bartender asked when she approached.

"Yes, thanks," Eva said, rubbing her forehead. "Just getting acquainted with British architecture."

"First rule," he said, "everything's shorter than you think it'll be. Except the history. That's longer."

"Florence sent me," Eva added. "She said I needed a proper meal."

Oliver's face lit up. "Ah, she's saved another one from the tyranny of supermarket sandwiches, has she? Good woman, Florence. You'll be wanting the fish and chips then."

Eva noticed Charlie sitting at the bar when she arrived, nursing what she assumed was a whiskey, his back to the door. He wore the same navy beanie from their market encounter, but had swapped the wool coat for a worn flannel shirt. Tilly lay curled at his feet, occasionally lifting her head when the door opened.

Charlie had nodded briefly when Eva entered but made no move to join her, which suited her fine. After their moment at the Minster earlier, she wasn't sure where they stood. He blew between hot and cold far more erratically than the inn's shower and she didn't need to concern herself with a man's mood any time soon.

The menu was a laminated sheet listing items that sounded simultaneously familiar and alien: Toad in the Hole, Ploughman's Lunch, Spotted Dick. A chalkboard by the bar announced daily specials like 'Proper Pie & Mash' and 'Gran's Sunday Roast', alongside a note that read 'No, we don't have bloody sriracha.' Eva ordered the fish and chips, as instructed, although she wasn't entirely sure what 'mushy peas' were and whether she should be excited or concerned about them.

"With scraps?" the bartender asked when she ordered.

Eva blinked. "What?"

"Scraps," he repeated, as if saying it louder would translate the term into American. "The crispy bits from the fryer."

"Oh," Eva said, trying to sound like she understood perfectly. "Yes, please."

"Good lass," he said approvingly. "Can't have proper fish and chips without scraps. Criminal, that would be." Eva nodded solemnly, as if she hadn't just learned a new culinary term that sounded like something you'd feed to particularly fortunate dogs.

Eva excused herself to the bathroom and noticed a painting of a horse on the toilet seat and paintings of little hounds trotting all over the bathroom walls. So the pub name made perfect sense. Eva giggled. She washed her hands under the two taps of the sink, furiously bobbing her hands from hot to cold.

She settled herself into a worn booth in the corner, the dark red vinyl seat patched in at least three places with duct tape. The table wobbled when she leaned on it, steadied by what appeared to be a folded coaster under one leg.

The wall beside her was covered in black and white photographs of York from bygone eras—flooded streets from the 1950s, celebrations from the end of the war, serious-faced men standing outside this very pub when it was still lit by gas lamps.

Eva sipped a half-pint of something amber the bartender had recommended when she'd requested "something not too beer-ish." It tasted like bread in liquid form, but in a pleasant way that grew on you, like a first date that starts awkwardly but improves after appetisers arrive.

The pub was filled with locals—not the pressed-khaki tourists from the Christmas Market, but people who looked like they might argue about football (so, soccer) scores and know each other's grandparents. An old man in the corner was explaining something passionately to an audience of two, his hands tracing shapes in the air with the precision of someone who has told this particular story many times and has perfected the choreography. Behind the bar, a shelf displayed dozens of local gin varieties and hand-labelled jars of what appeared to be home-infused spirits.

A pair of men in their sixties were playing dominoes near the fireplace with the intense concentration of chess grandmasters, slapping each tile down with a theatrical flourish and occasional exclamations of "Gerrin!" or "You're having a laugh!" Two middle-aged women at the next table were deeply engaged in what Eva could only assume was top-tier gossip, their conversation punctuated with "I'm not being funny, but . . ." and hushed "No, she never did!"

The door to the pub opened periodically, letting in gusts of cold air and a chorus of greetings. Each new arrival seemed to warrant a series of nods, nicknames, and inside jokes, creating a symphony of "All right, Dave?" and "Evening, all" and "Look what the cat dragged in!"

While waiting for her food, Eva took in the room. There, right by the fireplace where she sat she noticed a small brass plaque on the wall, partially hidden behind a Christmas wreath. She moved the greenery aside to read:

The Veterans' Corner Established 1946 by M. Wells *"Every soldier needs a home fire"*

"See you've found our bit of history," Oliver the bartender said, appearing at her elbow. "That's from Margaret Wells, she set up a fund after the war. Any veteran could come here for a hot meal and a pint, no questions asked, no payment needed."

"That's lovely," Eva said, tracing the worn letters.

"Still going, too," Oliver said proudly. "The fund ran dry years ago, but we keep it up. Got three regulars who come in under Margaret's Promise, we call it. Old Dennis there—" he nodded towards a man nursing a half-pint by the window, "—he's been coming since the sixties. Says this place saved him when he had nowhere else to go."

Eva looked at the elderly man, who raised his glass slightly in her direction.

"She understood," Oliver continued, polishing a glass that was already clean. "Some hurts can't be fixed with medicine. Sometimes you just need a place where nobody asks questions and the fire's always lit."

Oliver handed her the huge platter of fish and chips, sitting on top of a sheet of newspaper print that sucked in the grease. The chips were thick and golden, nothing like the skinny fries from home, and the promised "scraps" turned out to be deliciously crispy fragments of batter scattered across the top like savoury confetti. The mushy peas were exactly what they sounded like—a vibrant green mash that tasted better than their appearance suggested, especially when mixed with the sharp malt vinegar she'd been instructed to apply "generously, love, not like you're paying for it."

This was definitely not a meal deal. This was an experience. Florence had been right—again. Damnit, that woman knew what she was talking about.

She was halfway through her meal, lost in the simple pleasure of proper comfort food and mentally composing her apology to Florence for ever thinking a triangle sandwich could compare, when the pub door swung open, letting in a gust of cold air and a man who could only be described as the kind of handsome that belongs in glossy magazines—the type whose eyebrows appear to have their own stylist and whose five o'clock shadow arrives precisely at five, perfectly distributed like it was applied by a mathematical algorithm.

He was tall and lean, with dark hair styled deliberately rather than simply existing. He wore a camel coat over a blue sweater that looked so much like cashmere Eva could practically feel it from across the room. His smile, when he flashed it at the bartender, was the work of orthodontics that someone had paid dearly for.

"Oliver! How are you, mate? Gin and tonic, double lime," he called, his accent more London than Yorkshire.

"Aidan! As I live and breathe," the bartender replied. "Haven't seen you since summer. What brings you up from London?"

At the bar, Charlie straightened, his shoulders tensing visibly. He drained his whiskey in one swallow but didn't immediately leave.

"Business, unfortunately. Though it's always good to be home. How's Nancy?"

"Pregnant. Again."

"Congratulations! Or condolences. Whichever's more appropriate."

Eva watched the exchange with interest, trying not to be obvious about it. The new arrival—Aidan—had the easy charm of someone accustomed to being welcome anywhere. He scanned the pub as Oliver prepared his drink, and his eyes landed first on Charlie, then on Eva.

Recognition, followed by something else—curiosity, maybe—flashed across his face. He collected his drink and, rather than acknowledging Charlie, headed straight for Eva's table.

"You must be the American staying at Florence's," he said, his smile turning up a notch. "I'm Aidan. May I?" He gestured to the empty seat across from her.

God, word does travel fast around here, doesn't it? Eva thought to herself. Suddenly conscious of having vinegar and grease on her fingers and probably her face, she wiped her hands hurriedly on a napkin. Eva wondered if she had tartar sauce on her chin, but quickly realised that if she did it was far too late to try to save the situation. Nothing like meeting an impossibly polished man while you're mid-bite into fried food.

"Eva," she said, making a quick calculation that refusing him would be awkward in a place this small. "Please, sit."

He slid into the booth with the kind of grace that suggested he'd never awkwardly bumped a table or knocked over a saltshaker in his life. "So, what brings you to our little corner of England? Most Americans stick to London and Edinburgh."

"I needed a change of scenery," Eva said, which wasn't exactly a lie. "York seemed . . . interesting."

"Interesting is one word for it," Aidan said, sipping his drink. "I'd go with 'stubbornly resistant to the passage of time.'"

"You don't like it here?"

"I grew up here. It's complicated." He gestured around the pub. "Places like this—they've got charm, history, atmosphere. But they're dying. They can't adapt, can't compete."

"With what?" Eva asked.

"Progress. Chain hotels. Modern amenities." He leaned forward slightly. "Most people say they want authentic experiences until they realise authentic means draughty rooms, weird plumbing, and Wi-Fi that works when it feels like it."

Eva thought of the Riddle & Quill, with its creaking floors and temperamental radiators. "Some people might find that charming."

"Some people," Aidan agreed. "But not enough to keep places like this profitable."

There was something familiar about him—not his face, but his manner. The easy confidence. The subtle assessment. He reminded her of Richard, or at least what Richard aspired to be.

"So what do you do?" she asked, taking another bite of her fish. She knew this was a classic American line of questioning, but she had no idea what else to say. What do people talk about?

"I'm in real property development. Historic properties, mainly." He said it casually, but there was a careful watching in his eyes, as if gauging her reaction. "We restore old buildings, convert them into usable spaces for today's market."

"Like turning pubs into luxury flats?" Eva couldn't help asking, thinking of Trinkett's tour.

Aidan's smile tightened slightly at the edges. "Sometimes. Though I prefer to think of it as giving these buildings a new life. Better renovated than falling apart, right?"

"I'm not sure everyone would agree," Eva said. "There's something irreplaceable about these old places—the community they create, the history they preserve."

"You sound like someone I used to know," Aidan said with a dry laugh. "Always going on about 'preservation' and 'heritage.'"

"Maybe they have a point," Eva said, surprising herself with her conviction. "Places like this are more than just buildings. They're living history."

"What about you?" he asked, shifting the conversation. "Tell me about where you're from and what you do."

"Nashville born and raised. I work in the music industry." Eva started off boldly, but faltered slightly. "It's . . . different from what people imagine," she said carefully. "A lot of spreadsheets and marketing meetings. Not as glamorous as it sounds to be honest."

"But surely you love it? The energy of a big American city? The opportunities?" Aidan leaned forward, genuinely curious. "I've always wondered what it would be like to live somewhere so . . . modern. So forward-thinking."

Eva found it odd how eager he was to hear about anywhere that wasn't York. While Charlie had shown her hidden corners of the Minster with reverent attention, Aidan seemed to want to look everywhere but here.

"Nashville has its charms," she said. "But I'm actually enjoying the history here. The layers of stories within every building."

Aidan waved a hand dismissively. "Stories don't pay mortgages. But tell me more about your work. You must travel a lot? See other cities?"

Before Eva could respond, Charlie appeared at their table, Tilly at his heels. His expression was carefully neutral, but Eva caught the tension in his shoulders.

"Aidan," Charlie said flatly.

"Well, well. Charlie Blackwood." Aidan's smile sharpened. "Still haunting the same old places, I see."

"Some of us appreciate consistency," Charlie replied. His eyes flicked to Eva. "Not everyone needs to run off to London to prove something."

"And not everyone needs to hide in the past to avoid facing reality," Aidan shot back. He turned to Eva with that practiced smile. "Charlie and I were at school together. Back in the day."

Eva sensed layers of history between them that went beyond a casual acquaintance. The way they stood—Charlie rigid, Aidan lounging—spoke of old rivalries and unresolved tensions.

"Charlie's still playing with his doodles and clinging to the past, I see," Aidan said dismissively.

Eva felt her spine straighten. "He's not playing. And they're not just doodles, they're historically accurate reproduction maps. They're preserving history."

She surprised herself with the vehemence of her defense. Charlie looked equally surprised, something flickering across his face before he masked it.

Aidan laughed, but there was no warmth in it. "Preserving history. That's one way to put it. I prefer to think of it as refusing to move forward." He looked at Charlie. "I build the future; he clings to the past. That's always been our difference."

"Your 'future' tends to come with eviction notices for whoever gets in the way," Charlie said quietly.

"My future comes with jobs and investment. But we've had this argument before." Aidan sipped his drink. "No point rehashing old debates in front of company. Eva doesn't want to hear this crap does she?"

Eva watched the exchange, wondering about their history. They clearly knew each other well enough to know exactly which buttons to push, but there was something deeper here than a silly schoolboy rivalry. There was a fundamental disagreement about what York should be.

Charlie's jaw worked for a moment. Then he looked at Eva. "Be careful," he said simply, before turning and heading back to the bar.

"Don't mind Charlie," Aidan said once he was out of earshot. "We've never seen eye to eye. Different values, different visions. He thinks I'm destroying York's soul. I think he's keeping it trapped in amber."

"How long have you known each other?" Eva asked, watching Charlie's rigid back at the bar.

"Since we were boys. Went to the same school, ran in the same circles for a while." Aidan's expression grew thoughtful. "We were even interested in the same things once upon a time. But that was a long time ago."

Eva wondered what—or who—they'd been interested in. If only she knew what they competed for, maybe she'd understand more. She didn't dare to ask.

"Anyway," Aidan said, brightening again. "I actually wanted to ask—I'm having drinks with some investors later in the week. Nothing formal, just a nice wine bar. I'd love to show you the parts of York that might actually have a future. If you're interested?"

Eva looked at him carefully. In Nashville, this would be simple—a good-looking and successful man asking her out. She'd jumped when Richard had looked her way. He'd been exactly what her mom had said she needed. But here, everything felt different. She wasn't the same Eva who'd dated Richard, who'd planned her outfits around his preferences, who'd laughed at jokes that weren't funny.

"Just to be clear, this isn't a date, right?" she said finally.

Aidan looked taken aback for a moment, then laughed. "Hey, I was offering you a networking opportunity, but it can be whatever you want it to be Eva," he said smoothly. "No pressure. Just a local showing a visitor the best of York. The real York."

"The real York," Eva repeated, glancing towards where Charlie sat hunched at the bar. "Everyone seems to have a different definition of that."

"Well, my version comes with decent wine and heating that actually works," Aidan said. "What do you say?"

"Why not?" Eva said, surprising herself. "I've got to be upfront with you though, I recently got out of a relationship, and I'm not looking to—"

"Say no more," Aidan held up his hands. "Like I said, you'll be amongst friends. No pressure."

They chatted a bit more, with Aidan asking about her travel plans, whether she'd been to London, if she'd visited Paris or Rome—anywhere, it seemed, but here. When Eva mentioned she was researching local history, specifically someone named Margaret Wells, Aidan's response was tellingly brief.

"Margaret Wells," he repeated with a slight shrug, swirling his drink. "Oh yes, one of those local stories. York's full of them—everyone's got a tale about someone who did something once upon a time." He glanced at his watch. "Now, have you been to the Met in New York? That's real culture."

As they finished their drinks, Eva couldn't help wondering what Florence might say about Aidan and his development projects. The way Trinkett had spoken about developers turning pubs into luxury flats, she suspected she might have strong opinions.

"Well, I should get going," Aidan said, sliding gracefully from the booth. "Meetings with investors wait for no man." He pulled out his wallet and dropped enough money on the table to cover both their bills, waving away Eva's protest. "Please. It's the least I can do to welcome you to York."

"Thank you," Eva said, still feeling off-balance. "For the drink and the conversation."

As Aidan prepared to leave, he paused by Charlie's spot at the bar. Eva couldn't hear what was said, but she saw Charlie's knuckles whiten around his glass. Aidan clapped him on the shoulder—a gesture that looked friendly from a distance but made Charlie flinch—then strode out into the night.

Eva waited a moment, then found herself walking to the bar. "Are you okay?"

Charlie didn't look at her. "You should be careful around him."

"Because he's a developer?"

"Because he's very good at making people think he cares about what they care about." Charlie finally met her eyes. "Right up until he doesn't need them anymore."

"You two have history," Eva said softly. It wasn't a question.

"Ancient history." Charlie's laugh was bitter. "The kind that's well and truly buried. I'd appreciate it if you just dropped it." He stood abruptly, Tilly immediately at attention. "Enjoy your evening, Eva. Try not to let him sell you any bridges."

After he left, Eva lingered at the table, finishing her drink. Aidan was certainly charming. Polished. Professional. Everything Richard had aspired to be, down to the cashmere sweater and perfect teeth.

And yet.

There was something about Charlie—gruff, difficult Charlie with his ink-stained hands and disdain for tourists—that felt more genuine. More real. The way he'd looked when she'd defended his maps, like she'd handed him something precious he'd thought lost.

The green book sat in her bag, a constant reminder of why she was really here. Tomorrow evening, Aidan would show her what he considered to be the 'real York'— whatever that meant.

But watching the two men interact, Eva wondered if she'd just witnessed something more real than either intended to show. Old wounds, old competitions, different visions for the same beloved city. And she wondered why being caught between them felt like being asked to choose between two different versions of the same story.

She paid for her own meal (leaving the money Aidan had set down for the bartender as a generous tip) and stepped out into the cold night air. York was beautiful at night, the medieval buildings lit with a soft glow that blurred their edges against the dark sky. The sound of laughter and music drifted from pubs and restaurants, and the Christmas lights strung across the narrow streets cast star-like reflections in puddles.

Eva walked slowly, in no hurry to return to the inn. Here, in this moment, she felt oddly free—not Eva Coleman, daughter of Sandy, ex-girlfriend of Richard, passed-over employee of Monarch Music. Just Eva, following a mystery through an ancient city, with no expectations other than her own.

And definitely not the Eva who'd thought a meal deal counted as experiencing British cuisine. Florence would never let her live that down and neither would Courtney (she regretted texting her friend that update now).

But she was also no longer the Eva who would have automatically sided with the polished, professional man, with the voice of her mother in the back of her mind. Something in York was changing her, helping her see past surfaces to what lay beneath.

For now, that was enough.

Chapter Seven

Florence's Wisdom

The walk back from The Horse and Hound should have taken ten minutes. Eva managed to stretch it to twenty, partly because she kept stopping to peer into shop windows (closed, but prettily lit), and partly because she wasn't quite ready to face the empty room at the inn. The conversation with Aidan had left her feeling unsettled, like she'd accidentally picked up someone else's coat—it fit, but it wasn't quite right.

York at night was a different creature than its daytime self. The tourist crowds had thinned to nothing, leaving only locals hurrying home and the occasional ghost tour group huddled around their guide's lantern. The narrow streets created wind tunnels that sent her scarf flapping like a banner, and the cobblestones gleamed wet under the streetlights despite no recent rain.

She paused at a corner where three streets met at impossible angles—the kind of intersection that only made sense in a city that had grown organically over two millennia. A brass plaque on the wall caught her eye, barely visible in the amber light. She stepped closer, using her phone's flashlight to read it.

The plaque itself was unremarkable—something about a merchant's house from 1487. But tucked behind it, wedged between the brass and the stone, was a folded piece of paper.

Eva's heart quickened. Another of Margaret's notes?

She carefully extracted the paper, her cold fingers fumbling with the folds. But instead of a note, something small and metallic tumbled out, hitting the cobbles with a bright ping.

A key.

Eva crouched, searching in the dim light until she spotted it—a small brass key, ornate and old-fashioned, the kind that belonged to a music box or a diary. She picked it up, feeling its surprising weight in her palm.

The paper, when unfolded, revealed not a cheerful note but what appeared to be a page torn from a manuscript. The handwriting was definitely Margaret's—Eva recognised it from the green book—but the tone was entirely different:

We tell ourselves that duty is noble, that sacrifice is beautiful. But what if duty is just fear dressed in respectable clothing? What if the greatest betrayal is not of others, but of our own hearts?

I chose what was expected. I chose what was safe. I chose everyone's happiness but my own, and now I sit in this room full of other people's love stories, wondering if the heroine of my own story simply gave up too soon.

The cruellest lies are the ones we tell ourselves in the early hours, when the house is quiet and our hearts are loud.

Eva read it twice, then a third time. This wasn't the Margaret Wells who left hopeful notes for strangers. This was someone wrestling with regret, with choices that couldn't be undone.

She tucked the key and paper carefully into her bag and hurried the rest of the way to the inn, suddenly eager for its warmth and light.

Back in her room, Eva sat on the bed and pulled out her phone. Seventeen unread messages from her mother. She'd been ignoring them all day, but Sandy Coleman was nothing if not persistent.

Mom: Eva, this is getting ridiculous.

Mom: You can't just disappear to England without a plan.

Mom: Your father thinks I should give you space but this is INSANE.

Mom: What about your job? What about Christmas?

Mom: Call me. NOW.

The messages grew increasingly capitalised as they progressed. Eva could practically hear her mother's voice rising with each text.

She pulled up Courtney's messages instead—a palate cleanser of friendship:

Courtney: How's the British adventure? Meet any Mr Darcys yet?

Courtney: Your mom called me FOUR TIMES today

Courtney: I told her you joined a convent

Courtney: She didn't find that as funny as I did

Eva smiled despite herself and typed back:

Eva: No Darcys. Did meet two guys who hate each other though. Very Shakespearean.

Eva: Also I'm extending my time in York.

Courtney's response was immediate:

Courtney: DO IT

Courtney: Your mom will literally explode but DO IT

Courtney: Also guys??? SPILL . . .

Eva: One's charming and wants to develop real estate. The other makes maps and scowls a lot.

Courtney: Let me guess which one you like

Eva: I don't like either of them. I'm here for self-discovery, remember?

Courtney: Sure

Courtney: It's the scowly map guy isn't it

Courtney: You always had a thing for the difficult ones

Eva was composing a defensive response when another text from her mother arrived:

Mom: If you don't call me in the next hour I'm flying to London myself.

Eva sighed. She couldn't put it off any longer. But she could control the medium. She typed carefully:

Eva: Mom, I'm safe and I'm okay. I'm extending my trip by another week. I still have vacation time and this is important to me. I'll call you tomorrow. Love you.

She hit send before she could second guess herself, then immediately turned off her phone. She'd deal with the explosion tomorrow.

*   *   *

The next morning, Eva woke to the sound of rain pattering against her window. Real showering rain this time, not just York's perpetual mist. She dressed in her warmest sweater and made her way downstairs, where Florence was already bustling around the dining room.

"Morning, love," Florence said, not looking up from where she was arranging fresh flowers in a vase. "Full English again, or are you wanting something lighter? I've got some lovely porridge if you're feeling delicate."

"I'm actually feeling pretty good," Eva said, settling at her usual table. "But I need to ask you something. I'm supposed to fly home tomorrow, but I'd like to stay longer. Would that be possible?"

Florence's hands stilled on the flowers. She turned, studying Eva with those sharp blue eyes. "Found something worth staying for, have you?"

"Maybe," Eva said. "I'm not sure yet. But I'm not ready to leave."

Florence nodded slowly. "The room's yours as long as you need it. You know Eva, York's full of stories, if you're willing to read into them a little bit more. They might just help you re-write your own."

There was something in the way she said it—a weight to the words that suggested she wasn't just talking about tourist attractions.

"Actually," Eva said, pulling the brass key from her pocket, "I found this last night. Behind a plaque on Stonegate. With a page from what looks like a manuscript."

Florence's reaction was immediate. She set down the flower she was holding and crossed to Eva's table, her eyes fixed on the key. "May I?"

Eva handed it over. Florence turned it carefully in her fingers, examining it from every angle.

"Where exactly did you find this?" Florence asked, her voice carefully controlled.

"Corner of Stonegate and Little Stonegate. Behind a merchants' plaque. It was with this." Eva showed her the manuscript page.

Florence read it, her expression growing more complex with each line. When she finished, she sat down heavily in the chair across from Eva.

"So you've been pursuing Margaret Wells," Florence said. It wasn't a question.

"Mr Trinkett told me a little about her. How she left notes around York during the war, trying to spread hope."

"That's how it started," Florence agreed. "She worked at the military hospital, saw terrible things. Young men who'd never walk again, who'd lost their friends, their futures. She began leaving notes in library books—little bits of encouragement for the wounded soldiers to find."

"That's beautiful," Eva said.

"It was." Florence was still turning the key in her fingers. "But some notes became more than that. More personal. There was—" She stopped herself, shaking her head. "Well, that's not my story to tell."

"But you know more," Eva pressed gently.

Florence gave her a long look. "I believe Margaret felt that if she helped enough people find love, maybe she'd forgive herself for giving up her own."

"What do you mean?"

But Florence was already standing, bustling back to her flowers with renewed energy. "Now then, enough of the past. What you need is some proper Yorkshire company. You can't understand York by sitting outside our attractions and just reading plaques."

"I've been doing okay on my own," Eva said, slightly defensive.

"Have you now?" Florence's tone was sceptical. "Been out to the Dales yet? Seen Haworth where the Brontës lived? Walked the moors that inspired Wuthering Heights?"

"Well, no, but—"

"Charlie will take you," Florence announced, as if it were already decided.

Eva laughed. "Charlie? The man barely tolerates me, Florence. Something tells me he's not really my biggest fan."

"Nonsense. He's just guarded, careful with people. That's what happens when you've been hurt before." Florence's expression softened. "Besides, Tilly likes you, and that dog's never wrong about people."

"Florence, really, I can't ask him to—"

"You're not asking. I am." Florence's tone brooked no argument. "Tomorrow morning, bright and early. Well, maybe not too early. Traditionally, Charlie's not what you'd call a morning person."

Eva wanted to protest further, but something in Florence's expression stopped her. There was the mischief Charlie had warned her about there, certainly, but also genuine concern.

* * *

After breakfast, Eva retreated to her room. The rain had intensified, streaming down her window in sheets that blurred the outside world into watercolour impressions. She pulled out her phone, bracing herself for the onslaught.

Twenty-three texts from her mother. Four missed calls. Two voicemails.

She scrolled past them all and opened Courtney's messages instead:

Courtney: Your mom just called me AGAIN

Courtney: I told her you were taking a vow of silence

Courtney: She didn't believe me

Courtney: How's the self-discovery going?

Courtney: Any news with the two guys?

Courtney: This is better than Netflix

Courtney: PLEASE tell me you're writing this down

Eva glanced at the desk where sheets of Riddle & Quill stationery lay scattered, already filled with her observations and fragments of Margaret Wells' story.

Eva: Actually, I am. First time in years.

Courtney: 🙌🙌🙌🙌🙌

Courtney: What about the grumpy map guy?

Eva considered how to answer. Something about Charlie felt familiar, like a book she'd read before but couldn't quite place. The way he'd shown her the hidden corners of the Minster, how he'd tensed when she'd mentioned Margaret, the unexpected vulnerability when he'd talked about people leaving . . .

Eva: He's complicated. Apparently taking me on a road trip to the moors tomorrow. Don't get excited though, it'll be out of obligation to Florence.

Courtney: Or maybe he likes you

Eva: He literally told me I was basically destroying British heritage with my tourist ways

Courtney: That's probably flirting in British

Eva was saved from responding by a knock at her door. "Come in," she called.

Florence peered around the door. "Charlie's agreed to tomorrow. Nine o'clock. Wear something warm and waterproof—Yorkshire weather doesn't care about cutesy matching ensembles."

After she left, Eva sat at the desk and pulled out a fresh sheet of the inn's stationery. The cream-coloured paper felt substantial under her fingers, the embossed logo at the top lending weight to whatever words she might write. She thought about Margaret Wells, leaving notes for wounded soldiers, trying to heal others when she couldn't heal herself.

She began to write:

There are women who write love stories for everyone but themselves. They leave trails of happy endings in their wake— matchmaking friends, penning perfect proposals for tongue-tied suitors, crafting the words others cannot find. They become cartographers of the heart, mapping routes to joy they never take themselves.

Margaret Wells was one of these women.

I think I might be one too.

We are the architects of other people's happiness, building beautiful structures we never inhabit. We choose duty's grey uniform over passion's red dress. We tell ourselves that sacrifice is noble, that putting others first is love's highest form.

But what if we're wrong?

What if the greatest betrayal isn't breaking someone else's heart, but ignoring our own? What if all our careful kindnesses are just elaborate ways to avoid the terrifying possibility of our own joy?

Margaret wrote: 'The cruellest lies are the ones we tell ourselves in the early hours, when the house is quiet and our hearts are loud.'

I'm beginning to understand what she meant. In the daylight, we can pretend our choices were noble. But at night, when the world strips away its pretenses, we know the truth: we were afraid. Afraid to want. Afraid to reach. Afraid to fail at our own happiness after succeeding so brilliantly at arranging everyone else's.

Tomorrow, I'll follow her footsteps to the moors. Not to solve her mystery, but to understand my own. Because maybe—just maybe—it's not too late to stop writing other people's happy endings and start writing my own.

She set down the pen and picked up the brass key, looking over it beneath the lamplight. Whatever it opened, Margaret had wanted it found. But not easily, not by just anyone. By someone willing to look behind things, to see past the surface.

Through her rain-blurred window, York continued its ancient business of existing, indifferent to the mysteries it harboured. Somewhere out there, Charlie was probably bent over his maps, adding careful details to streets that had been walked for centuries. Florence was downstairs, creating her own small kingdom of warmth and belonging.

Eva sat with the brass key, turning it over and over in her hands. The more she did so the more soothing it became. Deep in her chest she felt a growing certainty that she was exactly where she needed to be, even if she couldn't say why.

Tomorrow, the moors. Tonight, the surprisingly comfortable unknown of a story still being written.

She placed the key carefully in the desk drawer, next to the green book that had started it all, and the growing stack of stationery pages that had become something more than a journal—perhaps the beginning of the book she'd always meant to write. Whatever door the key opened could wait. She was learning, slowly, that not every mystery needed to be solved immediately. This wasn't just one of the methodical to do lists she was so good at clearing through quickly. Some stories were better for the waiting.

Outside, the rain continued, turning York's streets into rivers of reflected Christmas lights. And somewhere in the city, the rest of Margaret Wells' story waited patiently, as it had for decades, for someone ready to understand not just what happened, but why it still mattered.

Chapter Eight

Dales and Doubts

Eva woke to the sound of paper sliding under her door. Not the violent shove of a pizza menu or the aggressive thwack of a noise complaint she was used to back home, but a gentle whisper of movement that somehow managed to be more intrusive for its politeness.

She stumbled out of bed, her feet finding the perpetually cold floor, and picked up the folded note. The handwriting was Florence's—neat, no-nonsense cursive that looked like the standard to teach penmanship lessons.

Be ready at 9. Wear sensible shoes. Charlie's taking you to see the real Yorkshire.

Eva checked her phone. 7.47 a.m. She had just over an hour to make herself presentable for a day with a man who seemed to regard her existence as a personal affront to British heritage.

"Fantastic," she muttered, heading for the shower.

By 8.55 a.m., she was downstairs in her thick cable-knit cardigan she'd bought in London, jeans, and the only 'sensible' shoes she'd brought—a pair of ankle boots that were more fashionable than functional but would have to do. Florence was at her usual post in the dining room, arranging the breakfast buffet with military precision.

"Ah, good, you're ready," Florence said, not looking up from the perfectly aligned croissants.

"Quiet morning," Eva observed carefully.

"Oh, it's always peaceful this time of year," Florence said, her tone determinedly bright. "People busy with their Christmas shopping, you know. January will pick up. Always does." She moved a jam pot three millimetres to the left. "Besides, gives me more time to look after my special guests properly, doesn't it?"

Eva suspected 'special guests' meant 'only guest', but didn't say so.

"Charlie will be here any moment. I told him he needs to stop by Kilnsey to get fresh milk from the vending machine. You absolutely must see it—it's one of Yorkshire's hidden treasures."

"A milk vending machine?" Eva's voice rose with unexpected delight. "Like, actual fresh milk? Straight from cows? In a vending machine?"

"Everything's a treasure if you look at it the right way," Florence said cryptically. "Besides, Charlie needs to get out more. All he does is work on those maps and brood. You'll be good company for him."

"I don't think Charlie wants—"

The front door opened, cutting off her protest. Charlie stood in the doorway, looking like he'd rather be anywhere else but here. He wore a thick green jumper that had seen better decades and jeans with suspicious stains that could have been ink or mud or both. Tilly bounded in ahead of him, tail wagging enthusiastically at the sight of Eva.

"Morning," he said to the air somewhere over Eva's left shoulder.

"Charlie!" Florence bustled over. "Perfect timing. You'll take the scenic route, won't you? And stop at—"

"The milk machine, yes, you've mentioned it seventeen times," Charlie interrupted. He glanced at Eva, taking in her outfit. "You're not bringing a rain jacket?"

"It's not supposed to rain," Eva said, gesturing at the relatively clear morning sky visible through the window.

Charlie gave her a look that suggested she'd just announced plans to wrestle a bear. "It's Yorkshire. It's always supposed to rain."

"I'll be fine," Eva said confidently. "The weather app says partly cloudy."

"The weather app," Charlie repeated, still not looking at her. "Right. Are you coming?"

Eva grabbed her coat and bag, giving Florence a look that said *I'm doing this for you, not him.* Florence just smiled serenely and made shooing motions towards the door.

Charlie's Land Rover was exactly what Eva expected— ancient, mud-splattered, and held together by what appeared to be equal parts rust and stubbornness. The inside smelled of wet dog, old leather, and something earthy that might have been peat or just accumulated Yorkshire.

"Sorry about the . . ." Charlie gestured vaguely at the interior as Eva climbed in. "I don't usually have passengers. Human ones, anyway."

Tilly had already claimed the middle seat, her warm weight pressed against Eva's thigh. The dog looked up at

111

her with liquid brown eyes that seemed to say *Don't mind him, he's always like this*.

"It's fine," Eva said, buckling herself in with a seat belt that might have been original to the vehicle. "I appreciate you taking me. I know Florence probably strong-armed you into it."

Charlie's hands tightened on the steering wheel. "Florence has her ways," he said carefully. "She seems to think I need more . . . social interaction."

"And I'm social interaction?"

"Apparently." He started the engine, which coughed to life with the enthusiasm of someone forced to work on their day off. "She also genuinely believes you need to see a milk vending machine, so I'm not sure how much we should trust her judgement."

Despite herself, Eva smiled. "Maybe she knows something we don't."

"Florence usually does," Charlie admitted, pulling out into the narrow street. "It's tremendously annoying."

They drove in silence through York's morning streets, the city still waking up around them. Eva tried not to stare at the way Charlie's hands moved on the steering wheel—confident, careful, with the same precision he probably used on his maps. Tilly dozed between them, occasionally sighing with deep canine contentment.

As they left the city behind, the roads narrowed dramatically. Eva found herself pressing against the door as stone walls seemed to close in on both sides.

"Are these roads built for actual cars?" she gasped as Charlie swerved slightly to avoid an approaching delivery van, the vehicles passing with what seemed like mere inches between them. "How do you not have accidents every ten feet?"

Charlie navigated the tight spaces with relaxed confidence. "You get used to it. The roads were designed for horse carts, not Land Rovers. Some are a thousand years old."

"And what's with all the walls of bushes?" Eva asked, gesturing at the dense greenery lining both sides of the lane, occasionally brushing against the Land Rover. "It's like driving through a very narrow green tunnel."

"Hedgerows," Charlie corrected. "They're living fences, basically. Some are hundreds of years old—they mark ancient property lines, parish boundaries. Did you know there are enough hedgerows in England to wrap around the world ten times?"

"That's . . . fascinating," Eva admitted, her death grip on the arm rest relaxing slightly. "They're beautiful."

They drove for what felt like hours. Eva was unsure of what to say or how to present herself. Usually, she would tell someone exactly what they wanted to hear. But for some reason, in England, or maybe, around Charlie, she didn't want to do that anymore.

"So," Eva said when the silence became too heavy, "what exactly makes this milk vending machine so special?"

"It's fresh milk," Charlie stated simply, as if this explained everything. When Eva's blank look persisted, he added, "Straight from the farm. You put your pound in, or credit card, whatever, place your bottle and fresh milk comes out. Still warm sometimes."

"That's actually kind of amazing," Eva said. "Very un-American. We like our milk to travel at least a thousand miles and have a shelf life of several weeks."

"Explains a lot about your cheese, you know it's not meant to come out of a can." Charlie muttered.

"Hey! We have excellent cheese in America."

"You have orange cheese. That's not the same thing."

"Wisconsin would like a word with you."

"Wisconsin can take it up with Wensleydale."

Eva found herself grinning. Grumpy Charlie was actually kind of fun when he wasn't actively trying to make her feel like a culturally insensitive tourist.

As the city gradually gave way to countryside, dry stone walls replaced shop fronts, and sheep replaced pedestrians. The landscape opened up like a book, each hill and valley a new chapter. Morning mist clung to the hollows, and the weak winter sun painted everything in shades of pearl and silver.

Eva couldn't help but imagine Mr Darcy striding out of the mist, making his way across the moors towards Elizabeth Bennet in *Pride and Prejudice*. Though knowing her luck lately, she'd probably get Collins instead.

"It's beautiful," Eva breathed, pressing her face closer to the window.

"Wait until you see the Dales proper," Charlie said, and there was something in his voice—pride, maybe, or possession. "This is just the preview."

They stopped at Kilnsey, where the promised milk vending machine sat like a small technological miracle next to a traditional stone barn. Charlie demonstrated the process with the seriousness of someone explaining nuclear physics, while Eva tried not to laugh at the absurdity of getting a tourism lesson about fresh milk.

"You try," he said, handing her a glass bottle that he'd produced from somewhere in the Land Rover's cluttered back.

Eva inserted her pound, placed the bottle, and watched in genuine delight as fresh milk poured out. "This is the best thing I've seen in England," she declared.

"Better than the Tower of London?"

"Infinitely. The Tower of London doesn't give you fresh milk."

"Fair point," Charlie conceded. "Though that would improve the tourist experience considerably."

They continued north, the landscape growing more dramatic with each mile. The Dales unfolded around them—vast moorlands stretching to the horizon, limestone cliffs catching the light, valleys carved by ancient rivers. It was beautiful in a way that made Eva's chest tight, like the landscape was too big for her heart to hold.

Charlie pulled into a small car park beside a weathered sign marking a public footpath. "Come on," he said, "you can't see the Dales properly from the car."

They set off along a well-marked trail, Tilly racing ahead then circling back, her tail a constant flag of joy. The path wound along a river, following the water between ancient trees and younger saplings. The water moved swiftly, dark and mysterious, catching occasional glints of sunlight that broke through the cloud cover.

"What about tea time?" Eva asked, remembering Florence's comment about British traditions. "Is that as sacred as they say?"

"Absolutely," Charlie nodded gravely. "Missing tea time is a criminal offence punishable by public tutting and disapproving glances. Last year, a man in Leeds forgot to offer his visitor a cuppa, and they exiled him to France."

"Now you're definitely making fun of me."

"Maybe a little," Charlie admitted, that almost-smile appearing again. "But tea is important. It's not just the beverage—it's the pause, the ritual. Everything stops for tea."

They reached a bend in the river where a fallen tree created a natural bench. By unspoken agreement, they sat down, Tilly immediately flopping at their feet with a contented sigh.

"I thought British people were supposed to be reserved and formal," Eva said. "You're surprisingly sarcastic."

"We're not reserved," Charlie corrected. "We're private. There's a difference."

"And what does Charlie Blackwood keep private?" Eva asked, immediately regretting her boldness when his expression closed again.

Scared of the painful silence that was sure to follow, she filled it. "I can see why the Brontës wrote such dramatic novels," she said, gesturing at the dramatic scenery around them. "This landscape demands it. All that passion and tragedy—it fits here."

Charlie glanced at her sideways. "You've read them?"

"Multiple times. *Wuthering Heights* was my favourite in high school. All that doomed love and drama on the moors." She pointed at the landscape. "Though I pictured it differently. More . . . I don't know, purple? Gothic? This is beautiful but in a quieter way."

"Life's usually quieter than books," Charlie said. "Less dramatic. More disappointing."

"That's a cheerful worldview."

"It's a realistic one." His tone had shifted, becoming closed and defensive. Or as Charlie would say: 'private'.

"Don't you love the worlds that books invite you into? They are exciting and comforting and encouraging!" Eva could feel herself becoming aggravated.

"Books sell you stories about destiny and soulmates and love conquering all. Real life is more like people leaving. People choosing easier options. People forgetting you the moment something shinier comes along."

Eva studied his profile, noting the tension in his jaw. "God, Blackwood, who left you?" she attempted to draw some humour from him.

"Everyone, eventually." He said it matter-of-factly, but his hands tensed at the red worn leash in his hand. "That's what people do. They leave."

Before Eva could respond, the sky, which had been merely overcast this morning, suddenly opened. Rain hammered down with the enthusiasm of a percussion section, turning the path into a stream.

"Shit," Charlie muttered, pulling his collar up uselessly against the deluge. "So much for your weather forecast."

Eva was too frustrated to muster a response and could only manage a huffed exhale. They were in the middle of the moors, the car park at least twenty minutes behind them. There was no point turning back on themselves, they had to dash forwards. Charlie spotted what appeared to be the only building for miles— luckily it was a pub. Although, it looked like it had grown out of the landscape itself, all weathered stone and tiny windows.

"Run for it," he said, and so they did, Tilly leading the charge with the confidence of a dog who knew exactly where the warm fires and potential food scraps were.

They burst through the pub door in a spray of rain and Yorkshire mud, gasping and dripping onto worn flagstones. The pub—The Shepherd's Rest, according to a crooked sign—was exactly what Eva would have imagined if someone had asked her to design the perfect countryside pub. Low beamed ceilings, a fire crackling in an enormous stone hearth, the smell of woodsmoke and ale and something cooking that made her stomach rumble.

Eva looked down at her filthy boots, then spotted the sign that read 'muddy boots welcome'.

"Charlie Blackwood!" The bartender—a middle-aged woman beamed at them. "Haven't seen you in donkey's years. And you brought company!"

"Hello, Mags," Charlie said, looking slightly embarrassed. "Just escaping the rain."

"Course you are, love. Get yourselves by the fire. I'll bring the blankets."

They claimed a table near the fireplace, Tilly immediately curling up on the hearth rug like she owned the place. Eva peeled off her soaked coat, acutely aware of how her wet hair was plastering itself to her head in what was definitely not an attractive way.

"Here," Charlie said gruffly, handing her his jumper. "You're shivering."

"Won't you be cold?"

"I'm a Yorkshireman. We don't feel the cold."

The jumper was warm and soft and smelled like him— that mix of old books and wood shavings she'd noticed before. It was also enormous on her, the sleeves hanging past her hands, she looked like a child dressed in their parent's clothing. But it was blissfully warm.

"Thanks," she said softly.

Mags re-appeared with the fleece blankets. Tilly accepted one with the dignity of a duchess, allowing herself to be dried while maintaining eye contact with Eva the entire time, as if sharing some secret female solidarity about the silliness of men. Mags offered a knowing look that made Charlie scowl. "I'll bring you both something to warm up with," she said. "The usual, Charlie?"

"Please."

When she'd gone, Eva asked, "The usual?"

"Tea," Charlie said. "Properly made. None of that microwave nonsense you Americans do."

"I don't microwave tea!"

"You tried to once. I can tell."

The horrible thing was, he was right. Eva had definitely microwaved water for tea in her college days. "That was years ago. I've evolved."

"Have you?" He was almost smiling. "Next you'll tell me you've stopped putting ice in everything."

"Now you're just being culturally insensitive."

"Am I?"

The tea arrived, along with what Mags called 'a little something to keep you going'—which turned out to be enormous slabs of fruit cake that could have doubled as building materials.

Eva bit into hers and made an involuntary sound of pleasure. "Oh my God. This is incredible."

"Mags makes it herself," Charlie said. "Family recipe going back generations."

"Everything here goes back generations," Eva observed. "It's like the whole country is built on layers of history."

"That's exactly what it is," Charlie said holding his hands up to the firelight. "Layer upon layer, each generation building on the last. Sometimes it feels like the weight of all that history will crush us."

"Is that why you make maps? To document it all?"

Charlie was quiet for a moment, staring into his tea. "I make maps because there's a permanency about them that's pretty comforting, to be honest. Streets don't just pack up and move to London. Buildings don't decide they've found something better. They stay where you put them."

The pain in his voice was so raw that Eva reached out instinctively, her hand covering his on the table. He looked down at their hands with a slightly crumpled brow, like he never had someone try to connect to him in this way before.

"People leave," he said quietly. "It's what they do. My parents couldn't wait to get out of York. Important jobs, important lives somewhere else. Left me with Gran when I was seven. Came back for Christmas sometimes, when they remembered."

"Charlie . . ."

"My ex-fiancée left too. Sophie. Said York was too small, too limiting. Said I was too focused on the past, not ambitious enough." He laughed bitterly. "She's in New York now. Marketing executive. Probably has the life she always wanted."

Eva squeezed his hand. "I'm sorry."

"Gran was the only one who at least tried to stay. And even she . . ." He trailed off, then seemed to shake himself. "Anyway. That's why I don't believe in fairy tales. The happy endings from those books you were swooning over earlier. People don't stay. They don't choose love over opportunity. They leave, and you learn to be okay with that."

"Your grandmother must have loved you very much," Eva said carefully.

"She did. But she understood the weight of leaving too. She never got over someone who abandoned her." Charlie pulled his hand away, wrapping it around his mug. "She waited for him. He was supposed to come back to her. He never did. She married someone else eventually, had my Dad, made a life. But she never forgot him."

"Maybe he tried—"

"Don't," Charlie cut her off. "Don't romanticise it. He left. She spent the rest of her life telling stories about love while never believing she deserved it herself. That's not romantic. It's just sad."

Charlie turned himself away from her, avoiding her gaze. Music drifted from the pub's ancient sound system— something that sounded distinctly American. Charlie's demeanour appeared to soften slightly, and he hummed along under his breath.

"Is that . . . country music?" Eva asked, grateful for the change of subject.

Charlie flushed slightly. "Maybe."

"You like country music?"

"The old stuff. Real country. Johnny Cash, Patsy Cline."

"Those are the only two country artists British people ever name," Eva teased. "Like when Americans say they like British music and only mention The Beatles and The Rolling Stones."

"Fine," Charlie said, sitting up straighter. "Willie Nelson. Merle Haggard. Loretta Lynn. Gram Parsons. Emmylou Harris."

Eva stared at him. "How do you know Gram Parsons?"

"Gran loved him. Said his music understood heartbreak." Charlie was definitely smiling now. "Used to play *Grievous Angel* on repeat after too much sherry."

"Your Yorkshire grandmother listened to cosmic American music?"

"She contained multitudes." The smile faded. "She always said she should have been braver. Should have chased what she wanted instead of just accepting what was expected."

The song changed, and Charlie hummed louder, actually tapping his fingers on the table.

"What is this?" Eva asked.

"Ray Charles," Charlie said. "*I Can't Stop Loving You.* Pure country heartbreak."

"Ray Charles isn't country!"

"This song is. Don Henley wrote it. Pure Nashville heartbreak." He was grinning now, actually grinning.

"Americans. You don't even know your own music history."

He started singing along, quietly at first, then louder when Eva laughed. His voice was surprisingly good—rough around the edges but with real feeling.

"You're ridiculous," Eva said, but she was smiling so hard her cheeks hurt.

"I'm from Yorkshire, Eva" Charlie corrected. "We're never ridiculous. We're 'characters'."

Eva smirked at his remark, laughing and rolling her eyes. It was then that Eva noticed the sprig of mistletoe hanging from the beam above their table. Her laughter died in her throat. Charlie followed her gaze and went very still.

"Ah," he said.

"Yep," Eva agreed.

They stared at each other across the table. The fire crackled. Ray Charles crooned about heartbreak in the background. The rain hammered against the windows like it was trying to get in.

"Well, rules are rules," Charlie said finally.

Eva's heart was doing something complicated in her chest. "What? I mean, I know it's tradition but come on Charlie don't be ridiculous . . ."

Charlie stood slowly and came around to her side of the table. Eva tilted her face up as he approached her. *Shit, this is happening then.* Anticipating his lean in, her eyes fluttering closed, and—

He kissed her forehead. Gently, sweetly, like a blessing.

Eva's eyes flew open. Charlie was grinning again, that rare, transformative expression that made him look years younger.

"Technical compliance, tick," he said. "I'll get us a fresh pot of tea."

He headed to the bar, leaving Eva touching her forehead and trying to remember how to breathe. Tilly looked up from her spot by the fire with what Eva could swear was amusement. "What the hell just happened Tills?" she whispered at the dog. The dog's tail thumped once, twice, in what was definitely approval, and she made a soft 'hmmph' sound that seemed to say 'well, it's a start, I suppose'.

When Charlie returned, teapot in hand, the awkwardness Eva expected didn't materialise. Instead, something had shifted between them, like a door opening just a crack to let light through.

"So," he said, settling back into his chair. "Your turn. What are you *running* from?"

Eva laughed, but it came out shaky. "What makes you think I'm running?"

"You changed your holiday destination last minute, came to York alone with no plan, and you're following the trail of a woman who died years ago. That's not exactly typical tourist behaviour."

Eva stared into her tea, trying to gather courage. Her go-to reaction here would be to deflect. She didn't like being the centre of attention, having any kind of focus solely on her. People say 'a problem shared is a problem halved' but somehow Eva had never felt that way. Sharing felt like being a burden. She never wanted to put herself on anyone or cause any problems. Taking a moment to reflect on how Charlie had opened up earlier about the darkest parts of himself, she sighed. Then, surprising herself, she felt the words she'd been bottling up inside spill from her lips. She told him everything. About Richard, about the promotion she didn't get, about a life that looked perfect on paper but felt like wearing someone else's clothes.

About her mother's expectations and her own fear that she'd never be enough.

"I've spent my whole life being what other people wanted," she said. "Good daughter, good girlfriend, good employee. And where did it get me? Dumped in a steakhouse by a man who thinks my dreams are too dreamy, while simultaneously thinking I'm not ambitious enough."

"Sounds like a tosser," Charlie said with feeling.

"He was. Is. But I chose him, didn't I? Because he fit the image. Because my mother approved. Because on the surface he looked right for the life I was supposed to want." She pulled Charlie's jumper tighter around herself. "I've got to this point in my life and I don't even know what I actually want. How pathetic is that?"

"It's not pathetic," Charlie said quietly. "It's human. We all do it—build lives based on other people's blueprints. Then we wonder why they never quite fit."

"Is that what you did?"

"In a way." He considered his words. "I stayed in York because it's safe. Because things are consistent, predictable and secure I guess. But maybe that's just another kind of running, isn't it?"

They sat, watching the fire, the perfect excuse for things left unsaid. The rain had softened to a steady patter, less violent but still insistent.

"Your grandmother," Eva said eventually. "She sounds like she was amazing."

"She was," Charlie agreed. "Complicated and sad and brilliant. She used to say that love wasn't about grand gestures or perfect moments. It was about choosing to stay and stick it out when leaving would be easier."

"But the man she loved left."

124

"Yeah." Charlie's voice was soft. "I think she never forgave herself for not going after him. For choosing duty over love. She made peace with her life, I think, but she never forgot him."

"But—"

"We should probably head back," Charlie broke her off, clearly done talking on the subject for now. "Florence will send out a search party if we're gone too long."

* * *

The rain had finally stopped, leaving the world washed clean and gleaming. They made their way back to the Land Rover, Tilly bounding ahead to claim her spot in the middle.

"Thank you," Eva said as they drove back through the transformed landscape. "For telling me about your grandmother. And for the terrible country music education."

"Ray Charles is a genius," Charlie insisted. "And you're going to admit it eventually."

"Oh he is, I agree there."

He glanced at her, then back at the road. "Listen, I have some friends."

"That's nice," Eva cut in, before she could help herself.

"Yeah well," Charlie continued, staring straight at the road. "A Christmas dinner. Just friends, nothing fancy. You should come."

Eva had to pause. Did he just ask her to meet his friends? For dinner?

"Are you inviting me out of pity?"

"I'm inviting you because Tilly insists," Charlie said. At her name, the dog's tail thumped against the seat. "See? She's very persuasive."

"Well, if Tilly insists . . ."

"She does. Vehemently."

125

The drive back was quieter but not uncomfortable. Eva found herself getting drowsy, the warmth of the car, Charlie's jumper and the emotional weight of the day all catching up with her. Tilly had migrated mostly onto her lap, a warm, breathing blanket.

She must have dozed off, because she woke to the sensation of Charlie's fingers gently moving a strand of hair from her face. His hand lingered for just a moment, and she kept her breathing steady, not wanting to break whatever spell had allowed this tenderness. She felt Tilly's tail give the slightest wag, as if the dog was awake too, in approval of this development.

"It's always best not to get too close," he murmured, so quietly she almost missed it. "She was right about that. You can't rely on people to hang around, no matter how you feel. No matter how much you want them to."

Eva wanted to open her eyes, to tell him he was wrong, that some people did stay. But something in his voice—the raw honesty of someone speaking to themselves—kept her still.

They drove the rest of the way in silence, Eva pretending to sleep while her mind raced. Charlie Blackwood was a man built of defences, each one carefully constructed from the disappointments of people who'd left. But today, in a pub in the middle of nowhere, she'd seen through the cracks.

And despite all her resolutions about self-discovery and not needing a man, Eva Coleman was beginning to suspect she was in trouble. The kind of trouble that came with grumpy mapmakers who sang country music and kissed foreheads under mistletoe and looked at their dogs like they'd had no greater best friend.

The kind of trouble that felt dangerously like coming home.

Chapter Nine

Mates and Mince Pies

A bomb had not, in fact, gone off in Eva's room at The Riddle & Quill, despite all evidence to the contrary. Her suitcase lay defeated and empty on the floor, having vomited its entire contents across every available surface. Sweaters draped from lampshades, jeans hung from the wardrobe door like surrendered flags, and a particularly optimistic sundress—*what had she been thinking?*—lay crumpled in the corner like a tropical casualty of Yorkshire winter.

Eva stood in the centre of the chaos, wearing only her underwear and an expression of pure desperation, her phone propped against the mirror with the selfie camera on. The ancient mirror only showed her from the shoulders up, but her phone's screen revealed the full catastrophe of her seventeenth outfit attempt.

"This is hopeless," she muttered, pulling off yet another sweater—too formal? Too casual? Too American? She tossed it onto the bed, where it joined its rejected brethren in a soft mountain of knitwear. "Why do I own so many beige things?"

She reached for a deep green cashmere sweater, pulling it on and studying her phone screen critically. Dark jeans—safe choice. The green sweater—nice but not trying too hard. She did a slow turn, checking every angle like she was preparing for a red carpet instead of a pub dinner with people she'd never met.

"Ridiculous," she told her reflection, both in the mirror and on the phone screen. "It's just dinner. With strangers. Who happen to be Charlie's friends. Who will definitely judge the American who destroyed his Christmas market stall with mulled wine."

But something about the evening felt important—like a door opening to a part of Charlie's life he kept carefully guarded. And Eva, much to her own surprise, very much wanted to step through that door without looking like she had got dressed in the dark. Or in a bomb site.

She grabbed a scarf—no, too much. Earrings—too fancy. Simple studs—better. One final check on the phone camera, then she surveyed the destruction around her. The room looked like a discount clothing store had got into a fight with her suitcase, and both had lost. This was a problem for late evening Eva.

The sound of muted mumbling voices from the floor below caught her attention and she froze. With one last mirror-twirl Eva was spiralling into panic mode. Charlie was right on time, of course. She grabbed her coat and started frantically shoving clothes under the bed, into drawers, anywhere they wouldn't be immediately visible if Florence happened to walk by her open door.

"On my way down now!" she called, jamming the sundress into her suitcase and kicking it under the bed. One last glance at the room—still a disaster, but a somewhat contained disaster— she hurried downstairs, where Florence had already let Charlie in out of the cold, Tilly wagging her tail beside him and seeming to give Eva an approving eyebrow.

"Don't you both look nice," Florence observed, looking to each of them with a barely concealed smile. "The Crown and Anchor tonight, is it?"

Eva couldn't help herself. "From The Horse and Hound to The Crown and Anchor. Are all British pubs just random noun combinations? What's next, The Sceptre and Spaniel? The Throne and Terrier?"

Charlie's mouth twitched. "The Duke and Dachshund is actually quite nice. Great Sunday roast."

Eva couldn't tell if he was joking until Florence chimed in, "Oh, you mean The Viscount and Vizsla on Micklegate? They changed the name last year."

Now Eva was completely lost, and both Charlie and Florence were clearly enjoying it.

"Yes, the Crown and Anchor," Charlie replied. "They've reserved the back room."

"Tell them I said hello," Florence said, shooing them towards the door. "And don't let Eva drink whatever concoction Ben's calling his 'Christmas Special' this year. Last time someone ordered it, they woke up feeling like one of Santa's reindeer after the Christmas Eve shift."

They walked through York's narrow streets, the Christmas lights creating a canopy of stars overhead. Charlie seemed tenser than usual, his shoulders rigid beneath his coat.

Tilly trotted alongside them, her tail high and confident.

"Wait, we're bringing Tilly into the pub?" Eva asked as they approached The Crown and Anchor.

Charlie looked at her like she'd suggested leaving a child in the car. "Of course we're bringing her. Where else would she go?"

"But . . . it's a restaurant. Won't they—"

"It's a *pub*," Charlie corrected. "This is England. Dogs have been welcome in pubs since before America was even a thought. Half the regulars probably come for the dogs more than the beer."

"In America, that would be a health code violation."

"In England, NOT allowing dogs would be a violation of basic decency," Charlie replied. "Tilly knows the drill—she'll find her spot by the fire and hold court like the queen she is."

"So," Eva ventured, still processing this cultural revelation, "anything I should know about your friends before we get there?"

Charlie glanced at her sideways. "They're . . . enthusiastic. And they haven't seen me at one of these dinners in years, so they might be a bit—"

"Charlie!"

They'd just entered The Crown and Anchor when a woman with short dark hair and an infectious grin spotted them from across the pub. She weaved through the crowd, dragging a tall man with kind eyes behind her.

"I told Tom you'd bail!" she exclaimed, throwing her arms around Charlie in a hug that he tolerated with surprising grace. "But here you are, and you must be Eva!"

"Charlotte," the woman introduced herself, pumping Eva's hand enthusiastically. "This is Tom, my long-suffering boyfriend. Come on, everyone's in the back room going through their third round already."

130

The back room of The Crown and Anchor was in full swing with decorations that looked like they'd been accumulated over decades rather than carefully curated. A long wooden table dominated the space, already laden with drinks and dishes of nuts and crisps. Buttery yellow walls softly turned orange from the firelight.

"Look who actually showed!" Charlotte announced to the room.

Three faces turned towards them, and Eva saw the moment Charlie's expression shuttered completely.

"Charlie." A stunning woman with long blonde hair rose from her seat, a smile playing at her lips. "I thought you'd be hiding away with your maps."

"Sophie." Charlie's voice was carefully neutral. "I thought you were in Manhattan."

"I was. I am." Sophie's smile widened, and Eva recognised the look of someone who knew the exact effect they had on their ex. "Home for the holidays. Couldn't miss the annual Crown and Anchor Christmas 'do, could I?"

An uncomfortable silence stretched until a man with intricate tattoos covering both arms cleared his throat. "Well, this is sufficiently awkward. I'm Marcus, by the way," he said to Eva. "The one who has to open up his home and live with Miss Manhattan over here when she's in town."

"Shut up, Marcus," Sophie said without heat, finally breaking eye contact with Charlie to look at Eva. "You must be the American everyone's talking about. How . . . interesting."

"Right then!" Charlotte intervened with aggressive cheer. "Drinks! Eva, what's your poison?"

The next hour was a masterclass in British social dynamics. Eva found herself seated between Charlotte and a friendly

131

woman named Priya who worked at the university, while Charlie ended up at the opposite end of the table—though whether by design or accident, Eva couldn't tell.

Eva noticed the intricate ritual of buying rounds—everyone mentally tracking whose turn it was with the precision of accountants, the subtle shame that fell on anyone who tried to skip their round, and the way Marcus loudly announced "This one's on me!" as if he were bestowing a great gift rather than fulfilling a sacred obligation. When Eva tried to buy a round out of turn, Tom actually looked offended. "You bought the last one," he said firmly, as if she'd violated some ancient law.

"It's the system," Priya explained quietly. "You can't mess with the system. We've fought wars over less."

Sophie held court from the middle, regaling the group with stories of New York that seemed specifically chosen to highlight how provincial York was by comparison. It was almost ironic that she never bothered to try and involve Eva in the conversation, the only attendee who could authentically vouch for Sophie's claims if she actually wanted to.

"The energy there is just incomparable," Sophie was saying, gesturing with her wine glass. "Everything happens so fast. Not like here, where the biggest news is whether they'll approve the new Costa on Goodramgate."

"Some of us like that the biggest news is about coffee shops," Tom said mildly. "Not everyone needs to live at Manhattan pace."

"No," Sophie agreed, her eyes finding Charlie. "Some people are perfectly content never changing, never growing, never taking risks."

Charlie, who had been quietly nursing his pint, set it down with a deliberate thunk. "And some people think living their life by what will get them more Instagram likes is the same as growth."

"Children, children," Marcus interjected. "It's Christmas. Save the philosophical debates for Boxing Day when we're all too full of turkey to argue properly."

"Speaking of Christmas," Charlotte said, producing a box of Christmas crackers with a flourish. "Tradition time!"

Eva watched in bewilderment as everyone crossed arms and reached for the brightly wrapped tubes. A clearly well-practiced tradition.

"You pull them," Charlotte explained, offering one end to Eva. "Like this—one, two, three!"

The crack was satisfying, and Eva found herself holding the larger piece along with a paper crown, a plastic puzzle, and a slip of paper.

"Crown goes on," Priya instructed, already wearing a purple one. "It's the law."

"Is it really?" Eva asked.

"Absolutely," Tom said solemnly. "Section 4, Subsection C of the Christmas Act of 1847."

Eva placed the flimsy, paper, orange crown on her head, catching Charlie's eye as she did. He was wearing a green one, and for just a moment, his expression softened with what might have been amusement.

"What's your joke?" Charlotte demanded.

Eva unfolded the paper. "What do you call a sleeping bull? A bulldozer."

The collective groan was impressive.

"Still better than mine," Marcus said. "Mine's just a statement: 'I used to hate facial hair, but then it grew on me.' That's not even trying."

*   *   *

Food arrived in waves of food that Eva had learned to appreciate. Fish and chips, shepherd's pie, bangers and mash, and mince pies for dessert.

"They're not actually meat," Charlotte whispered to Eva as she bit into one, "despite the name. Americans always think we're feeding them minced beef in a sweet pie."

"I may have had that concern," Eva admitted, savouring the spiced fruit filling.

As the evening wore on and the drinks continued to flow, Eva noticed how Sophie's attempts to monopolise Charlie's attention were becoming more obvious. Whether that was down to Sophie's boldness, or her own inability to stop staring down the table at them, she wasn't fully sure. Either way, Eva was becoming irritated by it. Sophie kept finding reasons to touch his arm, to lean in close when speaking to him, to reference shared memories that excluded everyone else.

"Remember that Christmas when we went to Edinburgh?" Sophie was saying. "That tiny hotel in the Old Town? The power went out and we had to—"

"I'm sure no one wants to hear about that," Charlie cut her off, his jaw tight.

"Oh, come on," Sophie laughed, a tinkling sound that seemed practiced. "We're all old friends here." Her gaze swept over Eva, taking in the green sweater and dark jeans with an appraising look that made Eva suddenly conscious of every thread on her cashmere, every crease in her denim. "Though I guess we have adopted a stray tonight."

Charlotte caught Eva's eye and made an apologetic grimace on her friend's behalf.

134

"Jesus Sophie, you're more of a stranger than anyone these days," Marcus said dryly. "Get off your high horse, now that you've come home for your one visit of the year."

"Shut up Marcus," Sophie murmured, adjusting herself in her seat. "It's not my fault I've been so busy overseas. I'm here now aren't I? Don't say you haven't missed me." She smirked raising her glass and sending Charlie a wink.

Eva felt her cheeks burn. After all that agonising over how Charlie's friends would perceive her, she felt the coldness of being shoved into Sophie's shadow. Clearly, she didn't want her here.

"Speaking of overseas," Charlotte said warmly, opening the floor for Eva to speak, "tell us about home Eva."

"Dolly wannabes and rhinestone honky-tonks, right?" Sophie said with a smile that didn't reach her eyes. "Personally, I've never felt the pull to Nashville, the class and progress of New York always called more to m—"

"So Eva," Priya intervened, clearly practiced at overriding Sophie's barbs, "Charlotte mentioned you're investigating some local history?"

"Just following a trail of interesting places I've found," Eva said, still recovering from the volatility of the conversation. "York has so many hidden stories," she continued trying to remain lighthearted.

"That's what Charlie's always saying," Tom mused. "He's always going on about preserving the city's history with those maps of his."

"Still playing with your little drawings, Charlie?" Sophie asked syrupy sweet. "I thought you'd have moved on to something more . . . substantial by now."

"They're historically accurate reproductions," Eva heard herself say. "They're important. They preserve things that might otherwise be lost."

The table went quiet. Sophie's perfectly shaped eyebrows rose slightly.

"How sweet," she said. "The American tourist defending our local mapmaker. Though I suppose you haven't been here long enough to understand how . . . limiting such devotion to the past can be."

"Sophie," Charlotte warned.

"What? I'm just saying, some of us believe in moving things along. In making something of ourselves beyond what our grandmothers might have wanted." Sophie's eyes never left Charlie's face. "Not everyone can live in the shadow of the dead forever."

Charlie stood abruptly. "I need some air."

He left through the back door that led to the pub's small garden. After a moment's hesitation, Eva followed.

She found him leaning against the brick wall, looking up at the narrow slice of sky visible between buildings. The night was cold, their breath forming clouds in the air.

"You don't have to check on me," he said without looking at her.

"I'm not checking on you," Eva replied. "I needed air too. Sophie's perfume is . . . aggressive."

That surprised a short laugh out of him. "It's new. She used to wear something subtler."

They stood in silence for a moment, the muffled sounds of the pub creating a comfortable backdrop.

"How long were you together?" Eva asked gently.

"Six years. Engaged for one." Charlie's voice was carefully neutral. "She got a job offer in New York. I had the shop here, my grandmother needed me . . . I thought we'd work it out long distance. She thought I was holding us back."

"I'm sorry."

"Don't be. She was right, in a way. I wasn't willing to leave York. She wasn't willing to stay. Simple as that."

"Nothing about that sounds simple," Eva observed.

Charlie finally looked at her, and Eva was struck by the vulnerability in his expression. "You'd have gone, wouldn't you? If someone you loved asked you to choose between them and everything you'd built?"

Eva considered this honestly. "A month ago? Yes. I'd have gone without question. I spent years being what Richard wanted, living where he wanted, dreaming his dreams instead of mine." She pulled her coat tighter. "Now? I don't know. Maybe the right person wouldn't ask you to choose."

"Maybe," Charlie said softly.

The mention of his grandmother intrigued Eva, but before she could ask more, the back door burst open, and Charlotte's head appeared.

"There you are! We're doing the annual terrible Christmas karaoke. Marcus is murdering *Fairytale of New York* and it's spectacular in all the wrong ways."

"We should go back in," Charlie said, but Eva caught his arm.

"We don't have to. We could leave, if you want."

He looked down at where her hand rested on his sleeve, then back at her face. "No. I'm not giving her the satisfaction. Besides," a small smile tugged at his mouth, "you haven't experienced Christmas until you've heard Tom's rendition of *I Wish It Could Be Christmas Every Day*. It's been known to make grown men weep. In horror."

137

They returned to find the back room transformed into a makeshift karaoke stage. Sophie had claimed a seat closer to the 'stage', seemingly absorbed in Marcus's enthusiastic destruction of The Pogues' classic.

"Eva!" Charlotte waved her over. "You're up after Tom. What's your go-to karaoke song?"

"Oh no," Eva protested. "I don't sing. At all. Dogs howl when I sing."

"Perfect!" Priya said. "That's the whole point. It's meant to be terrible."

What followed was an hour of spectacular musical carnage. Tom's performance was indeed tear inducing, though from laughter rather than emotion. Priya and Charlotte duetted on *Last Christmas* with choreography that seemed to have been invented on the spot. Even Charlie was convinced to join Marcus for *Merry Christmas Everyone*, which they performed with surprising competence.

"Your turn, Eva!" Charlotte insisted, pressing the microphone into her hand. "What'll it be?"

Eva scrolled through the options, her finger stopping on *All I Want for Christmas Is You*. She caught Charlie's eye and winked. "This is for anyone who's ever judged American contributions to Christmas music."

Her performance was, as predicted, terrible. But she threw herself into it with abandon, complete with pointing at random audience members during the chorus and attempting Mariah's notorious high notes. By the end, everyone was singing along, even Sophie, though she looked pained by the entire experience.

"Brilliant!" Tom declared when she finished. "Absolutely dreadful, but brilliant!"

As the evening wound down, people began making their farewells. Sophie approached Charlie while he was getting his coat, placing a proprietorial hand on his arm.

"We should catch up properly while I'm in town," she said, loud enough for Eva to hear. "Maybe dinner? For old times' sake?"

"I don't think that's a good idea," Charlie replied, gently but firmly removing her hand.

"Oh, come on. We're adults. We can have a civilised meal." Her smile was sharp. "Unless your new American *friend* has issues with that?"

"Eva has nothing to do with this," Charlie said quietly. "You made your choice, Sophie. You chose New York. I've made peace with that. You should too."

Sophie's perfectly composed mask slipped for just a moment, revealing something that might have been genuine hurt. Then it was back, sealed tight. "Of course. Well, if you change your mind, you know where to find me. I'll be here through New Year's. Plenty of time."

She swept out with the practiced exit of someone used to having the last word. Marcus followed, throwing an apologetic look over his shoulder.

"Right," Charlotte said into the sudden silence.

"We should go," Charlie said. "It's getting late."

The remaining goodbyes were warm, with Charlotte hugging Eva fiercely and whispering, "He's never brought anyone here before. Not since her. That means something."

Eva surprised herself and smiled, feeling oddly proud.

"There's something about you that speaks to him, I think. His gran was a storyteller you know? A beautiful writer who helped so many people after the war. Charlie says she died with dozens of stories in her desk drawer, unpublished. I reckon he's terrified of suffering a similar fate — creating beautiful things that no one ever sees." Charlotte sighed, "maybe you guys will help each other discover the things you're both looking for."

*　*　*

Outside, the cold air was a relief after the warmth of the pub. They walked slowly, in no hurry to end the evening despite its complications.

"Your friends are lovely," Eva said. "Charlotte especially."

"They liked you," Charlie replied. "Even Marcus, and he's suspicious of anyone who doesn't pronounce 'herbs' with the H."

"I noticed he kept asking me to say 'schedule.'"

"He finds American pronunciation hilarious. Simple pleasures."

They turned down a narrow alley that Eva didn't recognise.

"One more stop," Charlie said. "If you're not too tired?"

"Lead the way."

The alley opened onto a small square dominated by an ancient church. Charlie led her around the side to a low wall that overlooked the river. Beyond it, York Minster rose illuminated against the night sky, its reflection shimmering in the dark water below.

"This is beautiful," Eva breathed.

"My favourite view in the city," Charlie admitted. "I used to come here when things got . . . complicated. After my grandmother died. After Sophie left." He paused. "Tonight."

"I'm sorry about Sophie," Eva said. "That couldn't have been easy."

"It was . . . unexpected. I knew she was in town for Christmas, but I didn't think she'd show up tonight." He leaned against the wall. "She always did like a dramatic entrance."

"Can I ask what happened? Really happened?"

Charlie was quiet for so long Eva thought he wouldn't answer. When he spoke, his voice was low, contemplative.

"We met at university. She was brilliant, ambitious, going places. I was . . . well, I was still figuring out who I was after Gran died. She made me feel like I could be more than just the grandson left behind."

He picked up a small stone, turning it over in his fingers. "For a while, it worked. We were good together. But Sophie always wanted more—bigger cities, better opportunities. York was too small, too limiting. When the New York job came up, she couldn't understand why I wouldn't jump at the chance to leave with her."

"But you had the shop. Your work."

"It wasn't just that." Charlie tossed the stone into the water below. "York is . . . it's home. It's where Gran's buried. Where her stories live. Florence. The Inn. Where every street holds memories. I couldn't leave all that behind, not even for Sophie."

"That must have been an impossible choice," Eva said softly.

"The thing is, it wasn't. Not really. That's what told me everything I needed to know." He turned to look at her. "When you love someone—really love them—you find a way to make it work. You don't issue ultimatums. You don't make them choose between you and everything else they care about."

Eva thought about Richard, about all the small ways he'd tried to reshape her into someone more suitable for his vision of their future. "No," she agreed. "You don't."

They stood in silence, watching the lit windows of the Minster. Somewhere in the distance, church bells chimed midnight.

"Charlotte mentioned your grandmother was a writer," Eva said carefully, testing the waters. "She must have been quite something."

Charlie's expression closed slightly. "She was. Complicated, but brilliant."

"Charlotte said she helped a lot of people after the war?"

"She did." His voice was clipped, clearly not wanting to elaborate. "She had her own way of doing things."

Eva sensed she was approaching something delicate and decided not to push further.

"Thank you for tonight," Charlie said eventually, changing the subject. "For coming. For . . . handling Sophie with grace."

"Thank you for inviting me. Even if your ex-fiancée thinks I'm nothing more than a bedazzled line dancer."

Charlie laughed, a real laugh that transformed his face. "You handled yourself well. Better than I did the first time I met her friends. I told one of them I thought contemporary art was a load of rubbish. In front of her artist flat mate who specialised in it."

"Oh no."

"Oh yes. Sophie didn't speak to me for three days."

They began walking back towards the inn, taking the long way through the quiet streets. Tilly had been taken home by Charlotte earlier—"She can have a sleepover with our Rex," she'd insisted—so it was just the two of them under the occasional streetlight.

"Can I ask you something?" Eva said as they turned onto Stonegate.

"Hmm?"

"Why haven't you been going to those dinners? Charlotte said it had been years."

Charlie considered his answer. "At first, it was because Sophie would be there. Then it became easier to just . . . not. To keep to myself. Safer."

"What changed?"

He glanced at her, then away. "Florence is very persuasive."

"Ah."

"And . . ." he hesitated. "Maybe I was tired of safe."

They'd reached the Riddle & Quill. The windows were dark except for the porch light Florence always left burning.

"I should tell you," Charlie said suddenly, then stopped himself. "Never mind. It's late."

"Charlie?"

"It's nothing. Just . . . my grandmother, she had strong opinions about things. About people. I inherited some of them, I think. Not always the good ones."

Eva waited, but he didn't elaborate.

"Goodnight, Eva."

"Goodnight, Charlie."

She watched him disappear into the shadows of the narrow street before letting herself into the inn. Florence had left a note on the hall table: *Cocoa in the kitchen if you need it. Hope the karaoke wasn't too scarring. F x*

Up in her room, Eva sat on the bed and pulled out her phone to text Courtney:

Eva: Just survived British pub karaoke and meeting the ex-fiancée. She's basically

a blonde version of Richard with better
cheekbones.

Courtney's response was immediate:

Courtney: TELL ME EVERYTHING. Is she
awful? She's awful, isn't she?

Eva: Sophisticated. Beautiful. Kept
mentioning their shared past. Made me feel
like a naive American tourist.

Courtney: But???

Eva smiled at how well her friend knew her.

Eva: But Charlie chose staying here over
leaving with her. And tonight he chose to
show me his favourite view of the city.

Courtney: OH MY GOD HE'S SHOWING YOU HIS
SPECIAL PLACES. That's basically a British
marriage proposal.

Eva: Stop it.

Courtney: I'm serious! Next he'll be
making you tea without asking how you take
it because he's memorized your preference.

Eva: How is that romantic?

Courtney: Trust me. British romance is
all about small gestures and repressed
feelings. It's like Pride and Prejudice
but with worse weather.

Eva laughed, then typed:

Eva: His friends mentioned his grandmother
was a writer who helped people after the
war. Sound familiar?

Courtney: Wait . . . do you think . . .?

Eva: I don't know. He clams up whenever
she's mentioned.

144

Courtney: This is getting very mysterious. I love it.

Eva: I just wish I knew what the connection was. If there even is one.

Courtney: Patience, grasshopper. You can't force these things.

Eva: Since when are you the voice of patience?

Courtney: Since you're living in a real-life mystery novel and I don't want you to rush the plot.

Eva was composing a response when another text arrived, this time from her mother:

Mom: Just saw Linda Patterson at the club. She says Richard is dating someone new already. A paralegal from his firm. I hope you're satisfied. You could have had a nice life.

Eva stared at the message, waiting for the sting. Instead, she felt . . . nothing. Or rather, she felt free. Richard had moved on to someone more suitable, someone who would fit neatly into his five-year plan. And Eva was in York, following mysterious books and singing bad karaoke and maybe—just maybe—falling for someone who showed his affection through hidden viewpoints and rescued Christmas dinners.

She deleted her mother's message without responding and returned to Courtney's text thread:

Eva: You know what? I think I might be falling for him a little.

Courtney: FINALLY. Was that so hard to admit?

Eva: Terrifying, actually.

Courtney: Good. The best things usually are.

Eva plugged in her phone and got ready for bed, her mind replaying the evening. Sophie's polished perfection. Charlotte's warm acceptance. Charlie's quiet bravery in facing his past. The way he'd looked at her by the river, like she was something unexpected but not unwelcome in his carefully ordered world.

Tomorrow she would continue following Margaret's trail, wherever it led. She still hadn't found the lock to her key. Maybe she'd find more answers about Charlie's grandmother, about the connection all her evidence hinted at. But tonight, she fell asleep thinking about hidden viewpoints and paper crowns and the particular shade of green Charlie's eyes turned when he really laughed.

Chapter Ten

Cracks in the Façade

Eva whispered to herself, as if speaking too loudly might disturb old ghosts. "Margaret Wells . . . who were you really?"

The morning after the Christmas dinner had arrived grey and drizzly. This was the kind of Yorkshire weather that seemed to seep through windows and into your bones. Her experience so far of the British countryside now allowed her extra layers of vision on her favourite novels. Eva sat hunched over her laptop in the inn's small pub/ dining area, which smelled of last night's wood fire. The faint, yeasty ghost of centuries of spilled ale lingered. The room was dim despite it being mid-morning—heavy clouds outside filtered the light to a pewter glow that made the dark wood panelling seem to absorb rather than reflect illumination.

Florence had taken pity on her obvious hangover, bringing tea in a pot covered with a knitted cosy shaped like a sheep, and a plate of thick-cut, steaming, buttered crumpets. "To soak up whatever damage Tom's karaoke caused," she'd said with a wink.

The pub wasn't officially open yet, giving Eva the peculiar intimacy of being in a usually public space when it was private. Chairs were still stacked on most tables, their legs pointing skyward like a wooden forest. The mirror behind the bar reflected her solitary figure, making her look like a character in a painting—isolated, contemplative, searching for something just out of reach. Eva had noticed during her stay how quiet the inn appeared. However, this morning she welcomed the peacefulness of it all as she wrote.

She'd spread her research across the scarred wooden table: the green book opened to Margaret's cryptic note, her phone propped against a pewter tankard, notebook pages covered in her increasingly frantic handwriting. But Google, it turned out, was spectacularly unhelpful when it came to Margaret Wells. A few mentions in local history forums, a brief reference in a post-war nursing memorial, and that was it. For someone who'd apparently touched so many lives, Margaret had left surprisingly little digital footprint.

"Come on," Eva muttered, squinting at a blurry photograph from a 1946 Yorkshire Post article. "You can't just disappear."

The pub door opened with a cheerful chime that seemed too bright for the morning, bringing with it a gust of cold air that smelled of rain and diesel fumes from the tourist buses already circling the city walls. Aidan Finchley stepped inside, somehow immaculate despite the drizzle, his coat repelling water as if it had been personally offended by Yorkshire weather.

"Eva! What a pleasant surprise." His smile was warm and immediate as he spotted her in the corner. "I was just coming to see if Florence was around, but this is even better."

"Oh, um, hi," Eva said, suddenly conscious of her messy bun, held together by a pencil she'd forgotten was there, and the fact that she was wearing the same sweater from last night because everything else was in various stages of laundry. The pub's unforgiving morning light wasn't doing her any favours either, she was sure.

"Working on something?" Aidan asked, sliding uninvited into the seat across from her. The old chair creaked in protest, and Eva caught a whiff of his cologne—something expensive and vaguely Mediterranean that seemed at odds with the pub's earthy atmosphere.

"Just some research," Eva said, instinctively closing the green book.

"Let me guess," Aidan leaned back, the chair groaning again. "You've been asking about Margaret Wells around town again."

Eva's surprise must have shown on her face because his smile widened, his teeth flashing like fangs.

"Small city," he explained. "Word travels. Jean at the tea room mentioned you were interested in her. Then Trinkett was going on about it at the Conservative Club." He paused, studying her with those sharp blue eyes that seemed to catalogue everything. "I might have some information that interests you."

"I thought you knew nothing about Margaret Wells?" Eva couldn't hide her suspicion but she was eager to hear what he had to tell her nonetheless.

"I've been researching the inn's history," Aidan said smoothly. "For my work. Property development requires understanding the heritage of buildings, their stories.

Margaret Wells' name comes up quite a bit in the old documents."

"What kind of documents? Wait, for this inn?"

"Deeds, letters, council record," he waved his hand dismissively. "She was quite involved with the inn, apparently. Regular visitor, helped Florence's . . . predecessor during difficult times." He glanced at his expensive watch—the kind that probably cost more than Eva's car. "Actually, I have copies at my office. Remember you still owe me for drinks we talked about the other night at the Horse and Hound. The Vaults has an excellent wine list, and I can show you what I've found."

Eva hesitated. Something about Aidan set off small alarm bells in her head—not danger exactly, but a kind of calculated charm that reminded her too much of Richard. But if he had information about Margaret . . .

"Just drinks," she said finally. "Wait. I thought it was supposed to be with your investor people, how are we going to look at the documents?"

"Don't worry about that," Aidan dismissed her concerns easily. "Shall we say seven tonight? I'll meet you here."

Before Eva could grill him further, he had already got up and exited the pub. After he left, trailing expensive cologne and confidence, Eva tried to return to her research. But concentration eluded her. She gathered her papers, the sound of shuffling documents echoing in the empty room, and headed upstairs.

"Oh!" Eva said, grabbing the banister to steady herself. "Sorry, I didn't see you there."

There was Charlie. He was crouched over an old wooden window frame, carefully working putty into the gaps where December draughts had been sneaking through. The hallway smelled of linseed oil and sawdust, with that particular mustiness that came from carpets that had absorbed decades of footsteps.

"My fault," Charlie muttered, not looking up. His fingers worked the putty with practiced precision. "These windows have been letting in rain. Florence asked me to seal them up before winter really sets in."

"You're very handy," Eva observed, then immediately wanted to crawl under the floorboards. "I mean, with fixing things. Around the inn."

Charlie's mouth twitched slightly as he looked up at her. "Someone has to be. These old buildings need constant attention."

Eva shifted her weight, papers crinkling in her arms. The silence stretched, filled only by the radiator's occasional gurgle and the rain pattering against the window at the end of the hall. Just long enough to become uncomfortable before she blurted out, "I've been researching Margaret Wells!"

Charlie's hands stilled on the radiator valve. The wrench slipped, clanging loudly on the floor.

"I know we talked about her a little before," Eva continued, excitement overcoming awkwardness. "But I've been piecing together her story. She was extraordinary, Charlie. The things she did for people, the hope she spread during such a dark time. And the notes she left—they weren't just random acts of kindness. There was purpose to them, patterns. I think she was trying to—"

"Stop." Charlie's voice was rough. He stood slowly, wiping his hands on his jeans, leaving dark smudges. When he finally looked at her, his expression cycled through something like pain, recognition, and then fear before settling into careful blankness. "You're romanticising her whole story."

"What?"

"Margaret Wells." He said the name like it hurt, like each syllable was glass in his throat. "You're turning her into some tragic heroine from one of your books. She wasn't that. She was just . . . a broken woman in the end."

Eva felt like she'd been slapped. The papers in her arms suddenly felt heavier. "How can you say that? She helped so many people—"

"She helped everyone but herself," Charlie cut her off. The words came faster now, like a dam breaking. "Spent her whole life writing other people's love stories while her own life fell apart. That's not romantic, Eva. That's not brave. It's just sad."

"Or maybe she was brave in the only way she knew how," Eva shot back, clutching her papers tighter. "Maybe writing those stories for others was her way of—"

"Of what?" Charlie's laugh was bitter, echoing harshly in the narrow hallway. "Torturing herself? Living through other people because she couldn't face her own choices? She died alone, Eva. In that house on Micklegate, surrounded by unfinished manuscripts and letters she never sent. That's not brave. That's just . . . tragic."

The vehemence in his voice made Eva step back. The wall was cold against her shoulders. "How do you know where she lived? How do you know any of this?"

Charlie's jaw worked for a moment. The rain outside intensified, drumming against the window like impatient fingers. Then, the words escaped him so quietly she almost missed them: "Because she was my grandmother."

The words hung in the air between them like a physical presence. Eva felt her mouth drop open, the papers in her arms threatening to spill across the worn carpet. She'd suspected it, just for a moment, but hearing Charlie confirm her suspicions almost knocked the wind out of her.

152

"Your . . . what?"

"Margaret Wells was my grandmother," Charlie repeated, each word seeming to cost him something. His knuckles were white where he gripped the wrench. "So yes, I know exactly how her story ended. I was the one who found her unfinished manuscripts. I was the one who sorted through her letters, her regrets, her careful documentation of everyone else's happiness while she withered away in that house."

"Charlie, I—"

"You want to know what's in those notes she left around York?" His voice was rising now, years of suppressed emotion breaking through. "Regret. That's what. Regret dressed up as hope, spreading it around because she had none left for herself. She chose duty over love, chose what was expected over what she wanted, and spent the rest of her life helping other people avoid her mistakes while never forgiving herself for making them."

Eva's mind raced, trying to reconcile the Margaret she'd been building in her imagination with this broken woman Charlie was describing. "But the people I've talked to, they all said—"

"They saw what she wanted them to see," Charlie said flatly. "The kind nurse, the generous soul, the local character who made their lives a little brighter. They didn't see her at three in the morning, writing stories about love she'd never have again. They didn't watch her flinch every time someone mentioned America, or find her crying over a box of old photographs she couldn't bear to throw away."

"She sounds like she was in pain," Eva said softly. "That doesn't make her broken. It makes her human."

"Human?" Charlie laughed again, that harsh sound that seemed to come from somewhere deep and wounded.

153

"You want to talk about human? She couldn't even tell me about the man she *wished* was my grandfather. Instead, she married a man out of obligation. I had to piece it together from her letters after she died. An American soldier she fell in love with during the war. She let him go, never told him how she felt, and spent the next sixty years regretting it."

Eva thought of the plaque in the Minster—*For the American who left his heart in York*. Her breath caught. "The American soldier . . ."

"Now you're getting it," Charlie said bitterly. "My whole life, she told me stories about being brave, about following your heart, about not letting fear make your choices. And the whole time, she was the biggest coward of all."

"That's not fair—"

"Fair?" Charlie's eyes blazed. "You know what's not fair? Growing up thinking your grandmother was this pillar of strength and wisdom, only to find out her whole life was built on a lie. That every piece of advice she gave me came from her own failures. That when she told me to be brave, what she really meant was 'don't be like me'."

He grabbed his toolbox, metal clanking angrily. "So no, Eva, I don't think she was brave. I think she was a woman who made a choice and couldn't live with it, so she spent the rest of her life playing fairy godmother to everyone else's love story. And you sitting here, turning her into some kind of romantic legend . . . it's exactly what she would have wanted. Another pretty story to cover up the ugly truth."

"Life isn't a fairy tale," Eva said quietly, remembering their conversation in the Dales. "That's what you keep telling me."

"No," Charlie agreed. "It's not."

"But fairy tales and stories allow us a glimpse at paradise," Eva continued, meeting his gaze steadily. "Or the alternative. Maybe that's why she wrote them. Not to torture herself, but to imagine different endings. To give other people the chances she didn't take."

Something flickered across Charlie's face—vulnerability, maybe, or recognition. But then his walls slammed back up, higher than ever.

"Believe whatever makes you feel better," he said, turning away. "Just . . . leave me out of it."

This is it. This is why you think everyone leaves. Because he left her. The American soldier left Margaret Wells. This is why you were so harsh when we first met. Sophie isn't the reason you're so negative towards America – it's this. Eva thought.

He was halfway down the stairs when Eva called after him. "Charlie, wait—"

"I have work to do," he said without turning around. "Oh yeah, also, enjoy your drinks with Aidan tonight. I'm sure he'll tell you exactly what you want to hear. He's good at that."

The front door closed behind him with a decisive thud that seemed to shake the old building. Eva stood on the landing, arms full of research about a woman she apparently hadn't understood at all, while the window Charlie had been fixing gave one last shift and squeak, then fell silent.

* * *

By seven o'clock, Eva had showered, changed, and spent a good hour staring at the brass key on her bedside table. Margaret Wells. Charlie's grandmother. It all made horrible, perfect sense now—his defensiveness about the past, his reaction to her research, the pain in his eyes when he talked about people leaving.

She'd texted Courtney the revelation, receiving a string of shocked emojis and a voice note that just said "WHAT?!" repeatedly at increasing volumes.

The Vaults was exactly the kind of place Eva expected Aidan to choose—all exposed brick and Edison bulbs, with cocktails that cost more than her entire meal at The Horse and Hound. It smelled of small-batch gin and leather furniture, with none of the comfortable mustiness of a proper pub. The clientele looked like they'd rather be in London but were making the best of York's offerings, all careful beards and statement glasses.

"So," Aidan said once they were settled with glasses of red wine, "Margaret Wells."

He produced a leather folder from his bag, sliding it across the polished concrete table. Eva opened it to find photocopies of old documents—property deeds, council meeting minutes, a few photographs that smelled faintly of the archives they'd been pulled from.

"She was quite the local figure," Aidan explained, leaning back in his chair. "Very involved with the inn, helped arrange financing when it was in trouble after the war. There are records of her organising fundraising events, Christmas markets, all sorts of community activities centred around the Riddle & Quill."

Eva studied a photograph of Margaret standing outside the inn. She was younger than Eva had imagined, with dark hair pinned back and a smile that didn't quite reach her eyes. There was something familiar about the set of her jaw, the way she held her shoulders . . .

"She looks like Charlie," Eva murmured without thinking.

"Ah," Aidan said, his tone suggesting this wasn't news to him. "You've made the connection then. Yes, Margaret Wells was Charlie Blackwood's grandmother. I thought you knew."

"I just found out today."

"That must have been . . . interesting. Charlie's rather protective of her memory." Aidan sipped his wine thoughtfully. "Though I've never understood why. The woman was clearly remarkable—look at all she accomplished. But Charlie acts like her story is some kind of shameful secret."

"Maybe because he knew her as more than just a local legend," Eva suggested, thinking of Charlie's raw pain that morning, the way his voice had broken on his grandmother's name.

"Perhaps," Aidan agreed. "Though I think there's more to it. Margaret Wells had connections throughout York, influence that went beyond just charity work. The inn, for instance—she essentially saved it from closure in 1947. Arranged private financing, negotiated with the council. Quite progressive for a woman of that era."

"Why are you so interested in her involvement with the inn?" Eva asked, something about his tone made her wary. Aidan clearly wasn't the type of man who paid attention to something unless it served him in some way.

"Historical context," Aidan said smoothly. "When you're proposing developments for heritage buildings, you need to understand their significance to the community. Margaret Wells is part of the Riddle & Quill's story, which makes her part of my research."

"Development?" Eva's stomach sank. "You're planning to develop the inn?"

Aidan's smile didn't waver. "Nothing's finalised. I'm simply exploring options. The inn is a beautiful building,

157

but it's struggling financially. And honestly it's falling off a bit, how many people are you sitting across from at breakfast, hmm? Sometimes the kindest thing is to preserve what matters while adapting to modern needs."

"Like turning it into luxury flats?" Eva couldn't hide her dismay.

"Possibly. Or a boutique hotel that maintains the historic character while actually turning a profit." He leaned forward, and Eva caught another wave of that expensive cologne. "Florence is a lovely woman, but she can't run that place forever. And Charlie's maps, while admirable, aren't going to save it. Sometimes progress requires difficult choices."

Eva thought of Florence's warm kitchen that always smelled of baking bread, of Charlie fixing radiators with patient care, of Tilly sprawled before the fire. "Some things are worth more than profit."

"Spoken like someone who's never had to make payroll," Aidan said, not unkindly. "But I admire your idealism. It's refreshing."

The rest of the evening passed in a blur of expensive wine and Aidan's smooth conversation. He was knowledgeable about many things—art, travel, business—but Eva noticed how he deflected whenever she tried to steer the conversation back to York itself. He seemed more interested in where she'd travelled, what her life was like in Nashville, whether she'd ever considered living abroad.

"You're clearly a woman of intelligence and taste," he said as they finished their second bottle. "Have you thought about what you'll do when your holiday ends?"

"Not really," Eva admitted. "I'm taking things day by day."

"Very zen," Aidan smiled. "Though if you're interested, I have connections in London. Publishing, marketing, that sort of thing. Someone with your background could find interesting opportunities there."

Warning bells chimed in Eva's wine-fuzzy brain. This felt familiar—too familiar. Richard had done the same thing, painted pictures of a future that suited his vision of what Eva ought to be while assuming she'd gratefully go along with it. Or even her mother, steering Eva down the path *she* felt was best rather than the one her daughter actually hoped to follow.

"That's kind of you," she said carefully, "but I'm quite happy just being a tourist for now."

"Of course," Aidan agreed easily. "Just something to think about."

When they finally left, Eva politely declined his offer to take her back to the inn via cab. Instead, she insisted that she needed the fresh air. The wine bar's warmth gave way to York's crisp December night, and she found herself walking towards the Christmas market almost without thinking. There was no place that felt more magical.

The market was quieter at this hour, most families having gone home, leaving couples and groups of friends warming themselves with mulled wine. The air smelled of cinnamon and roasting chestnuts, with an undertone of damp wool from all the scarves and coats. Eva wandered past the stalls, many of which were closing up for the night, their owners packing away hand-crafted goods with practiced efficiency.

She stopped at a stall she'd noticed before—a leatherworker selling hand-bound journals. One in particular caught her eye: deep green leather with a brass clasp, its pages thick and cream-coloured. It smelled of leather and possibility, the kind of notebook that demanded important thoughts, meaningful words and creativity.

"That's a special one," the vendor said, noticing her interest. His hands were stained with dye, and he smelled faintly of the oils used to treat leather.

Eva picked it up, running her fingers over the smooth leather. It felt significant somehow, like it was meant for something more than shopping lists or journalling your latest crush updates. But when she checked her phone to see her credit card balance, reality intruded.

She'd extended her trip without thinking about the financial implications. The hotel in London, meals, trains, the wine Aidan had ordered tonight that she refused to let him pay for—it all added up. Her credit card was dangerously close to its limit, and she still had to solidify her flight home eventually.

"Maybe next time," she said reluctantly, setting the journal down.

She pulled out her phone to text Courtney:

Eva: Did you manage to mail those returns for my Cancún clothes? My credit card is having a nervous breakdown.

Courtney's response was prompt as usual.

Courtney: Mailed them in yesterday 😊 Should get your refunds in a few days, sorry been up the wall with food prep! How was wine with Mr Smooth?

Eva: Educational. He's planning to develop the inn.

Courtney: WHAT?! No! We must protect Florence at all costs!

Eva: I know. I just don't know how.

Eva was so absorbed in her phone that she didn't notice Charlie until Tilly bounded up to her, tail wagging enthusiastically.

"Oh!" Eva knelt to greet the spaniel, grateful for the excuse to avoid looking at Charlie. "Hello, beautiful girl. What are you doing out so late?"

"Market's closing up."

"I was just browsing," Eva said, standing awkwardly. "After drinks. With Aidan. Which you already knew I was doing . . ."

"How was it?" His tone was carefully neutral.

"Informative. He showed me documents about your . . . about Margaret. Her work with the inn."

Charlie's jaw tightened. "I'm sure he did."

They stood there, the weight of the morning's revelation hanging between them. Around them, vendors called goodnight to each other, the comfortable sounds of a community ending another day. Eva wanted to apologise, to explain that she hadn't known, that she would never have pushed if she'd understood. But the words tangled in her throat.

"I should go," she said finally. "It's late."

"Eva—" Charlie started, then stopped. "Never mind. Get back safe."

She walked back to the inn alone, her heels clicking on cobblestones that had probably known Margaret Wells' footsteps. The building loomed before her, windows glowing warmly against the night, and Eva heard something that made her pause—the unmistakable sound of papers rustling and quiet cursing from the parlour.

Eva crept closer, peering through the crack in the door. Florence sat at a desk covered in papers, her usually cheerful face creased with worry. The lamp cast harsh shadows, making her look older, more fragile. She was punching numbers into an ancient calculator that clicked and whirred with each entry.

"Bloody hell," Florence muttered. "How did it get this bad?"

Eva could see bills spread across the desk, red numbers glaring accusingly from bank statements. Florence rubbed her temples, and for the first time, Eva noticed how thin her hands were, how tired she looked beneath the usual bustle.

Eva backed away quietly, not wanting to intrude. But her heart sank. First Charlie's revelation about Margaret, then Aidan's plans for the inn and now this. It seemed like every story in York ended with loss—love lost, history lost, homes lost to progress and profit.

In her room, she sat on the bed and picked up the brass key again, turning it over in her hands. It felt warm from sitting on her nightstand beneath the lamplight, as if it had been waiting for her return. Margaret Wells' key led to something that had stayed locked away for decades. Charlie's grandmother, who'd loved and lost and spent her life helping others find what she couldn't keep.

Eva thought about fairy tales and their alternatives, about paradise glimpsed but not grasped. Maybe Charlie was right. Maybe turning Margaret into a romantic figure was just another way of avoiding the truth: that sometimes love wasn't enough, that sometimes being brave meant living with your choices even when they broke your heart.

But as she lay in bed, staring at the ceiling with its ancient cracks that looked like a map of everywhere and nowhere, Eva couldn't shake the feeling that the story wasn't over. That Margaret had left more than regrets scattered around York. That somewhere in this city of layers and legends, there was still truth waiting to be uncovered—not the pretty truth of fairy tales, but the messy, human truth of real lives and real choices.

The key now sat on her bedside table, catching the moonlight through thin curtains. But tomorrow would be different, she decided. Tomorrow she would find out what it opened, with or without Charlie's help. Because Margaret Wells—broken, brave, human Margaret— deserved to have her whole story told, not just the parts that were comfortable to remember.

Outside her window, York slept under its blanket of history, keeping its secrets close. But secrets, Eva was learning, had a way of surfacing when the right person came looking—even if that person was just a lost American, following breadcrumbs through an ancient city, trying to understand her own heart by decoding someone else's.

Eva felt a sense of sadness in all she had discovered. But another part of her felt purpose. For the first time in years, she felt she was actually on a quest that meant something. She just wasn't sure exactly what it was yet.

Chapter Eleven

A Very Yorkshire Christmas

Her phone was screeching. Was it an alarm? Had she overslept? Missed a flight?

No. Worse. It was her mother.

Eva's phone vibrated across the nightstand like an angry hornet, the screen blazing with notifications. Twenty-three texts. Each one escalating in panic and capitalisation. The final message simply read: "ANSWER YOUR PHONE NOW OR I'M CALLING THE EMBASSY."

Sandy Coleman did not make idle threats.

Eva grabbed the phone just as it began its next attempt, her mother's contact photo—taken at last year's country club gala—filling the screen with its perfectly coiffed disapproval.

"Finally!" Her mother's voice burst through the speaker before Eva could even say hello. "Do you have any idea what I've been going through? I've not slept a wink since you left, Eva Coleman. All. Week."

"Mom, it's five in the morning here—"

"I'm well aware of the time difference," Sandy interrupted, her Tennessee drawl sharpening into something that could cut glass. "Your father had to give me a Xanax. A Xanax, Eva! You know how I feel about unnecessary medication."

Eva sat up, pulling the duvet around her shoulders. The brass key tumbled off her nightstand, hitting the floor with a thud.

"I'm fine, Mom. I told you I was extending my trip—"

"Extending your trip?" Sandy's voice climbed an octave. "That's what you call this? Not 'having a breakdown in a foreign country'? Not 'abandoning all responsibility to play Nancy Drew'?"

In the background, Eva could hear her father's measured voice suggesting her mother take a breath. Robert Coleman had spent thirty-five years perfecting the art of gentle intervention, though it rarely worked.

"I'm working on something," Eva said carefully, already knowing how this would land.

The silence that followed was so complete Eva took her phone from her ear and looked at the screen to make sure the call hadn't dropped.

"Working. On. Something." Each word was a precision strike. "You mean this 'mystery' Courtney mentioned when I cornered her at the Kroger?"

Damn it, Courtney.

"It's research into local history—"

"It's a waste of time!" Sandy exploded. "You should be here, fixing your life. Do you know what people are saying? Linda Patterson announced to the entire book club that you'd had a nervous breakdown. I had to lie and say you were on a work trip."

"Maybe I did have a breakdown," Eva said quietly. "Maybe that's okay."

"Okay? OKAY?" Her mother's voice reached frequencies only dogs could hear. "Nothing about this is okay! You're almost thirty years old, Eva. No husband, no clear career path, and now you're gallivanting around England like some . . . some . . . bohemian!"

Despite everything, Eva almost laughed. In Sandy Coleman's world, 'bohemian' was the worst possible insult, conjuring images of unwashed artists and people who shopped at thrift stores by choice.

"I'm trying to figure things out—"

"By playing detective? This isn't you, Eva. This impulsive, irresponsible behaviour. What am I supposed to tell people?"

And there it was. The heart of it.

"Is that what matters?" Eva asked. "What you tell people?"

"Of course it matters! Our reputation, our standing in the community—"

"Mom," Eva interrupted, surprising herself with her steadiness. "Who are you without me?"

"What kind of question is that?"

"You just said it. You don't know what to tell people. But this isn't about you or your book club or what Linda Patterson thinks. This is my life."

"Your life?" Sandy's voice cracked, and suddenly she sounded less angry and more afraid. "Your life is here, Eva. With your family. Who am I if I'm not . . . if you don't need . . ."

The words hung between them, an ocean of expectation and fear and love so tangled it was hard to separate the threads.

"I have to go," Eva said softly.

"Eva Ann Coleman, don't you dare—"

She ended the call.

The phone immediately began buzzing again, but Eva turned it face down. Her hands were shaking—she wasn't entirely sure if it was from the cold, or the emotion or both. Unable to face her mother's barrage again, she grabbed the phone and opened Instagram, seeking the mindless comfort of other people's curated lives.

This was a mistake.

The first post was from Jennifer at Monarch Music: a close-up of her left hand sporting a diamond that could be seen from space. He proposed at the Ryman! Where we first met! #NashvilleLove #CountryMusicDreams

Scroll.

Her college roommate Rachel: Baby #3 on the way! The twins can't wait to be big sisters!

Scroll.

Even Blake—Blake who couldn't buy his own Secret Santa gift—had posted from Santorini. Best vacation ever with this amazing woman. #CoupleGoals #LivingMyBestLife

Scroll.

Her sister Lily: Just closed on our dream home! Five bedrooms for all those future grandbabies Mom keeps asking about ☺

Eva tossed her phone aside, pulling her knees to her chest. The room felt smaller suddenly, like the walls were closing in. Everyone else was collecting life milestones like her Dad collected baseball cards, while she was literally going backwards, trying to solve the mystery of a dead woman's lost love in a city where the radiators clanged like ghost chains.

By the time she made it downstairs, showered but nowhere near refreshed, Eva felt like she'd already been awake for three long days. The smell of beans, bacon and proper English tea drew her to the dining room, where Florence was arranging the morning spread with her usual military precision.

"Morning, love," Florence said, then stopped, taking in Eva's face. "Oh dear. Sit. Tea first, then talk." Eva knew by now that tea in Britain could cure almost everything. But not this.

Eva sank into her usual chair. The dining room was empty, pale morning light filtered through lace curtains.

Florence returned with a pot of tea in a cosy shaped like a Christmas pudding, complete with felt holly leaves that had seen better days. She poured a cup, added milk without asking, and then, instead of bustling away, sat down across from Eva with a definitive plop.

"Right then," Florence said. "What's wrong? And don't say nothing. I've run this inn for forty years. I know that look. Was it your mum?"

Eva almost choked on her tea. "How did you—"

"That particular combination of exhaustion, guilt and fury? That's mothers." Florence's eyes twinkled with understanding. "Mine once drove four hours to tell me I was disappointing the family by not marrying the butcher's son. Turned up at two in the morning with a three-page letter she'd typed up on her old Remington and made me read it aloud."

"She made you read it aloud?"

"Said she wanted to make sure I absorbed every word. Even brought carbon copies for my sisters." Florence

168

poured herself tea. "The butcher's son is in prison now, so I feel I made the right choice. But you didn't come down looking like death warmed over to hear about my mother. What did yours say?"

Eva wrapped her hands around the warm cup. "She thinks I'm wasting my time here. That I should be home, fixing my life, finding another suitable boyfriend, being who she needs me to be."

"And what do you think?"

"I don't know. That's the problem. I've spent so long being what everyone else wanted that I don't even know what I want anymore."

Florence studied her. "Let me ask you something. What does your heart want?"

"I don't know," Eva admitted.

"Your mind?"

"To be practical. Go home, get another boyfriend, job, make everyone happy."

"And your gut?"

Eva was quiet, considering. "My gut says there's something here I need to understand. About Margaret, about myself, about . . . something."

Florence nodded. "It's clear a lot happened before you got here, love. Failed relationships, family expectations, a life that looked right but felt wrong. This trip—it's not really about Margaret Wells, is it?"

"No," Eva admitted. "I don't think it is."

"Sometimes we need to get properly lost before we can find ourselves. And sometimes," Florence added, rising to refill the teapot, "we need to stop running long enough to let the right things catch up." She paused at the sideboard, her hands stilling on the china crockery. "Everyone makes decisions they think are right at the time. Keeping secrets, protecting people, holding on to things that maybe should have been shared." Her voice had gone soft, distant. "What matters is what we do when we realise the weight of those choices."

She turned back, her usual brisk manner returning, but Eva caught something in her expression—a flicker of old guilt, perhaps, or recognition.

"More tea, love?"

She bustled away, leaving Eva to contemplate her cryptic wisdom and wonder what exactly was trying to catch up with her.

It didn't take very long, as twenty minutes later Charlie appeared in the doorway, looking uncharacteristically uncertain. He wore his usual uniform of jeans and a sweater—forest green today that brought out the flecks of gold in his eyes. In contrast to his usual cool demeanour, today he carried himself like a man approaching a spooked animal.

"Morning," he said, hovering at the threshold. "Florence said you were down here."

"Did she also tell you to check on the pathetic American?"

"No." He stepped into the room. "Actually, I came to ask if you'd like to see Castle Howard. The Christmas decorations are worth the trip. And it's meant to be clear today. Mostly clear. Partially clear. Look, it probably won't rain the entire time. Dry like."

Eva studied him suspiciously. "Did Florence put you up to this?"

Charlie's brow furrowed. "No? Why would—" Understanding dawned. "You think I'm here out of pity."

"Aren't you?"

"Eva." He moved closer. "I'm here because I want to show you something beautiful. Because despite our . . .

discussion yesterday, I don't actually think you're a complete disaster of a tourist anymore. And because Tilly's been moping since she realised you weren't on this morning's walk."

"Tilly's been moping?"

"Devastated. Tragic, really. She's written sad poetry. It's all very dramatic."

Despite everything, Eva smiled. "Well, we can't have Tilly writing sad poetry."

"How about I let you settle into the morning, get a cuppa down you and some decent food and I'll be back this afternoon to pick you up?"

"Deal," Eva smiled to herself.

* * *

The drive to Castle Howard took them through countryside that looked like it had been painted every possible shade of green. Charlie's Land Rover handled the narrow roads with its usual rattling determination, while Tilly sat between them, occasionally sighing with deep contentment. Eva leaned her head against the window, looking out to the hills rolling ahead of her. Closing her eyes for a moment, she thought of the last time she sat in Charlie's car like this. The truck all cosy, Tilly's tail tapping against her leg, the way Charlie reached out and caressed her face . . .

"So," Charlie said, pulling her from the daydream as they turned onto a tree-lined drive, "rough morning?"

"Phone call with my mother," Eva admitted. "She thinks I'm having a breakdown."

"Well, are you?"

Eva considered this. "Maybe? But it feels more like a . . . breakthrough? If that makes sense. Jeez I sound like those therapists you see in movies. But honestly, it's like I've been sleepwalking through my life and suddenly I'm awake and have no idea where I am."

"That sounds terrifying."

"It is," Eva agreed. "But also . . . freeing? For the first time, I'm not following anyone else's plan."

Charlie glanced at her. "Even if that plan involves following mysterious notes through Yorkshire?"

"That's my choice, though. Mine. Not my mother's, not Richard's, not anyone else's."

They crested a hill, and Castle Howard spread before them like something from a dream. The baroque palace rose from manicured grounds, its dome and wings creating a symphony in stone. But it was the Christmas decorations that stole Eva's breath—thousands of lights outlining every architectural detail, making the building shimmer like it had been dusted with stars.

"Oh," she breathed.

"Wait until you see inside," Charlie said, and there was something in his voice—pride, maybe, in belonging. The kind that came from sharing something beloved. "I know how much you love a fairy tale, this year's theme is Sleeping Beauty."

Leaving the car windows down, Charlie promised Tilly they'd be back as soon as the interior wander of the house was done. Like the good girl she was, Tilly curled up on the passenger seat to take a nap while waiting. The inside was even more spectacular. Each room had been transformed into scenes from the fairy tale—enchanted forests of silver birch and evergreen, spinning wheels draped with golden thread, and in the great hall, an enormous canopy bed surrounded by thorny roses that climbed towards the painted ceiling.

"It's beautiful," Eva said, then caught herself. "Though I suppose you think those fairy tales I dote on are just pretty lies we tell ourselves."

Charlie was quiet for a moment, studying a display of a hundred spinning wheels, each one holding a single red rose. "Maybe," he said finally. "Or maybe they're warnings. Sleeping Beauty pricks her finger because she's curious, because she's been sheltered from the truth. Then she sleeps for a hundred years while the world moves on without her."

"That's a dark interpretation. Disney definitely don't depict it that way, Blackwood."

"You think?" Charlie moved to the next room, where mirrors reflected infinite versions of them both. "Or is it honest? She wakes up to find everyone she knew is gone. Everything's changed. The world moved on while she was frozen in time."

Eva thought of her life in Nashville—the job she'd kept out of obligation, the relationship that had been slowly suffocating her, the careful construction of a life that looked perfect but felt like sleepwalking.

"Maybe she needed that sleep," Eva said softly. "Maybe sometimes we need to stop, even if it means the world changes while we're gone. Because the alternative is staying awake in a life that's slowly killing you."

Charlie turned to look at her then, something shifting in his expression. "Like my grandmother," he said quietly. "She stayed 'awake' through her whole life, doing whatever she thought was the right thing for others. Never let herself stop long enough to chase what she really wanted."

They moved into the chapel, where instead of the paper angels, a massive rose bower had been created, with thousands of silk roses in every shade from white to deep crimson. The afternoon light through the stained glass turned them into jewels.

"She brought me here every Christmas," Charlie said. "Said fairy tales weren't about the happy endings—they

173

were about the choices that made the story. The princess who chose to touch the spindle. The prince who chose to fight through the thorns. The castle that chose to sleep alongside her." He paused. "She said the real tragedy wasn't the sleeping—it was all the people who stayed awake but never really lived, they just sort of existed."

*　*　*

After a further walk around the inside of the house in contemplative silence, the two retrieved Tilly and ended up outside, wandering through the grounds as the afternoon sun cast long shadows across the frost-touched grass. They found a bench overlooking the atlas fountain, now still for winter, and sat watching the light change on the palace façade.

"I thought Florence put you up to this," Eva admitted. "I'm sorry."

Charlie looked genuinely confused. "Why would you think that?"

"Because yesterday I found out about your grandmother, we were basically arguing and I could tell you didn't want to see me after that. Now today you're being nice to me. You must be able to see how I thought your sudden change in temperament may have been . . . connected."

"Eva." Charlie turned to face her fully. "I'm here because I want to be. Because despite everything—or maybe because of it—I like spending time with you. You're . . . unexpected."

"I thought you didn't like anyone but Tilly."

"I don't, usually." He ran a hand through his hair, messing it endearingly. "People are complicated. They want things, they leave, they disappoint you. Dogs are simple. They love you or they don't, and they're honest about it either way. No matter how far I throw that ball for Tilly to fetch, she always finds her way back to me."

"That's a lonely way to live."

"It's a safe way to live," Charlie corrected. "Or it was. Until this American tourist spilled wine on my maps and started asking questions about things I'd spent years not thinking about."

Eva pulled her coat tighter as the wind picked up. "Can I tell you something?"

"Of course."

"My mother asked me who she was without me. And the horrible thing is, I've been asking myself the same damn question. Who am I without her expectations, without Richard's plans, without the life everyone else mapped out for me? The one I've been blindly going along with because I was scared to rock the applecart."

Charlie was quiet for a moment. "Maybe that's the wrong question."

"What do you mean?"

"Maybe it's not about who you are without those things. Maybe it's about who you are despite them. Or alongside them. Or . . . I don't know. I'm rubbish at metaphors."

"I think you're better at them than you give yourself credit for," Eva said softly.

They sat watching the palace glow in the late afternoon light. Tilly had found a stick and was carrying it around proudly, occasionally bringing it to them for approval. Just like Charlie said she would.

"My parents barely remember I exist," Charlie said suddenly. "They call on my birthday—usually a day late actually—and send Christmas cards with those awful family newsletters where they detail their humanitarian work and forget to mention they have a son."

"Charlie . . ."

"They left me with Gran when I was seven. Said it would just be for a few months while they got settled in their new posting. That was twenty-five years ago, Eva." His voice was matter-of-fact, but Eva could hear the old hurt underneath. "Gran raised me. Told me stories, taught me to love this place, gave me roots when my parents were too busy saving the world's history to save a place at the dinner table for their son."

"That must have been so hard."

"It was. But it was also . . . not. Gran was brilliant. Difficult and complicated and carrying her own grief, but brilliant. She loved me. That was more than a lot of people get." He looked at Eva. "The thing is, I spent so long being angry at my parents for leaving that I almost missed what I had. A grandmother who chose me every day, even when choosing me reminded her of everything she'd lost."

"Is that why you reacted so strongly when I was researching her?"

Charlie sighed. "Part of it. I've spent years trying to reconcile the grandmother I knew with the woman I discovered in her letters. She was so heartbroken, Eva. So full of regret. But she was also the person who taught me to ride a bike and make proper Yorkshire puddings and find beauty in old maps. How do you hold all of that at once?"

"Maybe that's what makes us human," Eva suggested. "The ability to be broken and whole at the same time. Have you ever seen the Japanese art kintsugi? It's this process where they take broken vases or ceramics and fill the cracks with gold. It's supposed to stand as a reminder that the broken or damaged is still beautiful."

She let the words float between them as they sighed and sunk into one another in the gardens.

*　*　*

As they walked back to the car, Castle Howard glowing behind, Eva felt a shift inside herself. Not a solution to all her problems, not a clear path forward, but something smaller and more important: the beginning of believing she might be worth her own story.

They climbed into the Land Rover, Tilly immediately claiming her spot between them with a satisfied huff. *She could get used to this.* Charlie started the engine, then paused, reaching behind his seat.

"I got you something," he said, almost shyly, pulling out a package wrapped in brown paper. "Saw you looking at it at the market the other night."

Eva unwrapped it carefully, her breath catching when the paper revealed the green leather journal from the craftsman's stall. It was even more beautiful than she remembered, the leather soft under her fingers, the brass clasp gleaming in the afternoon light filtering through the windscreen.

"Charlie," she whispered. "I can't accept this from you—this is too much—"

"It's not," he interrupted. "You're a writer, even if you've forgotten. And let's face it, you're living a story worth documenting. Gran would have said the same." He paused, then added quietly, "Maybe you can't judge a book by its cover, but you can tell when one deserves to be written in."

Eva clutched the journal, tears threatening again but for entirely different reasons than this morning. She thought back to the tattered notebook she'd boarded the plane with, filled with shopping lists and to do tasks. To the chaotic pages of Inn stationery she'd scribbled across. Looking down at Charlie's gift, she saw this as something more than just a journal. "Thank you. This is . . . it's perfect."

"Well," Charlie said, clearly uncomfortable with the emotion of the moment, "Tilly picked it out really. I was just the one with opposable thumbs and a credit card."

Eva laughed, the sound bright in the confines of the car. She opened the journal to the first page, running her fingers over the blank paper that seemed full of possibility.

"What will you write?" Charlie asked, pulling out of the car park.

"I don't know yet," Eva admitted. "But for the first time in a long time, that thought feels like the beginning of something rather than the end."

Chapter Twelve

The Trail of Kindness

Eva woke with a sense of purpose she hadn't felt in years. The green leather journal Charlie had given her lay open on the bedside table, its first pages already filled with fragments of Margaret's story. Outside, York was dressed in frost, the December morning crisp and bright—the kind of day that made everything look like a Christmas card.

She dressed quickly, not even bothering to style her hair, something she had done every day since her mother told her she looked unkempt unless the length of her ponytail was smooth. But today Eva left her long, loose waves to cascade free over her shoulders down her cream sweater and coat. Today, she would follow Margaret's trail properly, armed with Charlie's tentative blessing and her own growing certainty that this story needed to be told.

Her first stop was Fossgate, where Mr Trinkett had mentioned an elderly shopkeeper who'd known Margaret personally. The shop—Whitby's Antiquarian Books—was squeezed between a modern café and a vintage clothing store, its window display thick with dust and appearing unchanged since approximately 1862.

A bell tinkled as Eva pushed open the door, releasing the scent of old paper and leather bindings. Behind the counter sat a man who seemed to be composed entirely of wrinkles and wisdom, his thin hands sorting through a stack of Victorian postcards.

"Mr Whitby?" Eva ventured.

He looked up, eyes sharp behind wire-rimmed spectacles. "Haven't been called that in years. Most people just call me Arthur. You're the American asking about Margaret Wells."

News travelled fast in York. "Yes, my name is Eva. I—"

"Saved my life, she did." Arthur set down the postcards with careful precision. "Not dramatically, mind you. Margaret wasn't one for dramatics. But she saved it all the same."

Eva pulled out her journal, and Arthur nodded approvingly. "Good. Someone should write it down proper."

"My father died at Dunkirk," Arthur began, his voice steady despite the weight of memory. "Left Mum with four boys and a shop full of books nobody could afford to buy. I was the youngest, just a baby thankfully — my eldest brother was fourteen at the time and convinced he'd have to leave school, get work and provide for my mother."

He stood, moving to a shelf behind the counter with surprising agility. "Then one day, he came home to find his schoolbooks for the next year already waiting. A little rough around the edges, they were second hand, but they were his. Mum swore she hadn't bought them."

"Margaret?"

"Took him three years to work it out. She'd come in the shop, chatting with Mum about this and that. Must have seen the worry, understood what wasn't being said." Arthur pulled down a leather-bound ledger, its pages yellow with age. "Found this after Mum died. Margaret had been contributing to our account, making it look like general sales, but it was for us. Clever woman."

He opened the ledger, pointing to entries in faded ink. "See? 'Mrs M. Wells—Various titles.' Every month like clockwork, right through my teenage studies."

"Did you ever thank her?"

"Tried to. Went to her house when I was eighteen, full of grand speeches." Arthur smiled. "She served me tea, listened politely, then said she hadn't the faintest idea what I was talking about. Said I must have her confused with someone else. Had that way about her—made you feel foolish for trying to unmask her kindness. Always wanted to redirect the praise of thanks to someone else. Selfless."

Eva made notes, thinking of Charlie's words about his grandmother helping everyone but herself. "Did she seem happy?"

Arthur considered this. "Content, maybe. But there was always something . . ." He trailed off, searching for words. "A person's eyes tell you a lot, Miss Eva. It was almost like she was watching life through a window. You know? Present but not quite participating. She was a beautiful woman, though. Inside and out, had that dark hair and those eyes that seemed to see right within you."

* * *

Eva's next stop was The Olde Stables pub, where Florence had said the hospital administrator took his lunch every day. She found Dr Malcolm Hartley exactly where promised, nursing a pint and working his way through a crossword.

"Margaret Wells?" He set down his pen when Eva introduced herself and her mission. "Now there's a name that deserves remembering."

Dr Hartley had the kind of voice made for storytelling—rich and measured, with the hint of a Yorkshire accent beneath his educated tones. "I've been at York Hospital for forty years. Started as a junior doctor, worked my way up. But the stories about Margaret—they were legend long before I arrived."

He pulled out a tablet, surprising Eva with his tech-savviness. "Digitised all the old records last year. Dull work, but fascinating too." His fingers moved across the screen with practiced ease. "Here we are. Margaret Wells, Voluntary Aid Detachment, 1943 to 1947."

"Four years?"

"Stayed on after the war ended. That was unusual—most VADs couldn't wait to get back to normal life. But Margaret . . ." He showed Eva a black and white photograph on the screen. A group of nurses standing outside the hospital, and there in the middle, a young woman with dark hair and a measured smile.

"She worked primarily with the traumatised soldiers. What we'd now call PTSD, though back then it was 'shell shock' or 'lack of moral fibre'." His voice carried old anger at the term. "Margaret understood that sometimes the wounds you couldn't see left just as much damage as those that needed stitches. She started things, initiatives, clubs I guess you could call them. She had a weekly reading group, art therapy sessions before anyone even called it that. Small things that made big differences in those men's lives."

"I heard she left notes?"

"Ah, yes. The famous notes." Dr Hartley smiled. "Started with the soldiers who couldn't sleep. She'd leave little poems, quotes, sometimes just a few words of encouragement on their bedside tables for them to find in the small hours. Word got around. Soon patients were specifically asking for 'the note nurse'."

He swiped to another document. "See this? Discharge report from 1945. 'Patient shows marked improvement in mood and outlook. Attributes recovery to therapeutic interventions by VAD Wells.' That's medical speak for 'Margaret's magic worked again'."

"Magic?"

"That's what the patients called it. Margaret's little magics. Never anything grand—a book that arrived just when someone needed it, a conversation that changed a perspective, a note that made someone feel recognised and heard in their struggles." He looked at Eva over his glasses. "You know she paid for a young soldier's train ticket home when he was discharged? Told him the hospital had a 'transportation fund'. There was no fund, Eva."

Eva thought of the brass key in her pocket, of Florence's worried face over the inn's finances. Patterns repeating through generations. "She gave a lot."

"Everything, some would say. I honestly don't know how she managed it all." Dr Hartley's expression grew thoughtful. "I treated her once, years later when I was still junior. Came in with pneumonia, wouldn't admit how sick she was. Kept trying to check on other patients from her bed. I asked why she didn't have many family visiting. She said her family was the whole of York."

"That's beautiful."

"You think so?" He took a long pull of his pint. "Or is it sad? Woman gives everything to strangers, keeps nothing for herself. Makes you wonder why, doesn't it? She was devoted to anyone but herself, what makes a person do such a thing? She was lucky to have her grandson in the end, I think."

* * *

Eva's final stop was the York Library, where the head librarian, Mrs Patricia Chen, had agreed to meet her in the local history section. The room smelled of old paper and furniture polish, dust motes dancing in the afternoon light streaming through tall windows.

"Margaret Wells established our children's reading program in 1946," Mrs Chen said, pulling out a cloth-covered album. "Called it 'Stories for Tomorrow' because she said these children would be the storytellers of our future."

The album was filled with photographs—children clustered around Margaret as she read, their faces rapt with attention. Some wore patched clothes, some had the hollow look of wartime poverty, but in every photo, they were smiling.

"Many of these children had lost fathers in the war," Mrs Chen explained. "Margaret understood that stories could fill some of those hollow spaces. She came every Saturday without fail, even when she was ill."

"Did she ever read her own stories?"

Mrs Chen's expression grew careful. "She wrote the most beautiful tales. I've heard of some of the fragments—stories about brave girls and lost princes, about bridges between worlds and love that transcended time. But she never thought they were good enough to share properly, she only ever read a short excerpt when really pushed by keen listeners. Always said she was still practicing."

"Practicing for what?"

"The right moment and the right tale she said. The story that truly mattered." Mrs Chen closed the album gently. "I don't think she ever completed it. Or maybe she did and just couldn't bear to tell it after all that waiting."

She led Eva to a display case near the back of the room. "This is one of our Christmas traditions, started by Margaret in 1946."

Inside the case was a collection of small, wrapped packages—books, mittens, toys. A sign read: 'Take what you need, leave what you can. Christmas magic is meant for sharing.—M.W.'

"Every December, people still contribute," Mrs Chen said. "Anonymous gifts for anyone who needs them. Last year, a single mother found a winter coat in her size with a note that said 'For the late-night walks when the baby won't sleep.' That's pure Margaret magic—knowing exactly what someone needs before they even ask."

As they walked back through the stacks, Eva noticed small sprigs of dried mistletoe tucked above certain sections — Poetry, Letters, Romance.

"Margaret?" she asked, pointing.

"Every year until she passed," Mrs Chen confirmed. "But never in the obvious places. She'd put them where people lingered alone—above the grief counseling books, the war memoirs, the section on starting over. Said mistletoe shouldn't just be for those already in love, but for those who'd forgotten it was possible."

Eva thought of Charlie's gentle forehead kiss at The Shepherd's Rest, how he'd called it 'technical compliance' when really it had been something far more careful, more considerate. Like Margaret's mistletoe—placed where it might remind someone that tenderness could exist even in unexpected moments.

"Did it work?" Eva asked. "Did anyone ever . . .?"

"Once," Mrs Chen smiled. "A widower and a young mother, both reaching for the same book on helping children through loss. They've been married twelve years now. Margaret sent them a note on their wedding day that just said: 'Some bridges are worth crossing, even when you can't see the other side'."

* * *

Eva made her way back to the inn as the winter sun began its early descent, her notebook full of stories, her heart full of questions. She found Charlie in the pub area, Tilly at his feet, both staring morosely at the unlit fireplace.

"Successful hunting?" he asked without looking up.

"Very." Eva sat beside him, pulling out her journal. "Your grandmother was extraordinary, Charlie. The lives she touched, the kindness she spread—"

"I know." His voice was quiet. "But knowing and understanding are different things."

They sat in silence for a moment, Charlie drumming his finger against his leg in deliberation with his own thoughts. Then, he stood abruptly as he decided. "Come on. If you're going to write about her, you should see the rest."

He led her upstairs to a room she hadn't noticed before—small, tucked under the eaves. Charlie produced a key and unlocked it, revealing what appeared to be a storage room. Boxes lined the walls, all carefully labelled in Charlie's neat handwriting.

"After she died, I couldn't bear to throw anything away," he admitted, pulling down a box marked 'Notebooks—1943-1950'. "Florence helped me organise it all. Said someday someone would want to understand."

186

Inside were Margaret's journals—not diaries exactly, but notebooks filled with observations, story fragments, sketches. Eva handled them reverently, aware she was holding pieces of a life.

"Look," she breathed, opening one at random. The page was covered in Margaret's careful handwriting, a story about a girl who collected stars in jam jars. But the next page was torn out, leaving only jagged edges.

"There are gaps," Charlie said, anticipating her question. "Pages torn out, entire notebooks missing from certain periods. I think . . . I think there were things she couldn't bear to leave behind, even in death."

"What things?"

Charlie was quiet so long Eva thought he wouldn't answer. Then: "Something deeper, more private? Maybe writing she couldn't bare to read over herself. Like love letters, maybe. She was careful about what story she left behind."

Eva traced the torn edges with her finger. "Did you look for the missing pages?"

"No." Charlie's voice was firm. "She chose what to keep and what to destroy. That's her right."

They spent the next hour going through notebooks, Eva reading passages aloud while Charlie provided context. Margaret's voice emerged from the pages—witty, observant, heartbreakingly lonely at times.

"'The soldiers think I'm healing them,'" Eva read, "'but they're wrong. They're healing me, showing me that broken things can still be beautiful, that incomplete stories can still have meaning.'"

"That's from 1945," Charlie said softly. "The American must have already left by then."

Eva looked up sharply. "You know about the American?"

Charlie's laugh was bitter. "Hard not to. She never said his name, but he haunted everything. The way she flinched at the accent, the way she always happened to be busy on the fourth of July, the way she kept every Stars and Stripes newspaper even though she never read them."

Eva pulled out the brass key. "Charlie, I think this might—"

"Oh, aren't you two cosy!"

They turned to find Florence in the doorway smiling, but her usual cheerfulness was forced, her eyes red-rimmed. She moved into the room with the careful steps of someone holding themselves together by will alone.

"Florence?" Charlie stood immediately. "What's wrong?"

She sat heavily in an old armchair, looking suddenly fragile in a way Eva had never noticed before. "I suppose there's no point putting it off any longer."

"Putting what off?" Charlie knelt beside her chair, his earlier stiffness replaced by genuine concern.

Florence pulled a letter from her cardigan pocket, official-looking with a bank's letterhead. "Final notice. We have until 24th of December to pay the mortgage arrears, or they'll begin foreclosure proceedings."

"What?" Charlie snatched the letter, scanning it with growing fury. "How long has this been going on? Why didn't you tell me?"

"Six months," Florence admitted. "Business has been slow, and the roof repairs last spring . . . I kept thinking I could turn it around."

Eva remembered the night she'd seen Florence with her papers and calculator, the worry etched on her face. "I should have said something," she murmured. "I saw you that night, working on the accounts . . ."

"Not your fault, love," Florence said tiredly. "This has been coming for a while. Maybe it's time to admit defeat. Aidan Finchley's been making offers—"

"Aidan?" Charlie's voice could have etched glass. "You've been talking to Aidan?"

"He's been very persistent. Says he could convert the inn to luxury flats, give me enough to retire comfortably . . ."

"Over my dead body." Charlie stood, pacing the small room like a caged animal. "This inn has been in our family for sixty years. Gran saved it once—"

"And look where that got her," Florence interrupted sharply. "A lifetime of pouring everything into this place, and for what? So I could lose it anyway?"

The silence that followed was heavy with history and hurt. Eva felt like an intruder by being privy to the conversation, but couldn't seem to move.

Finally, Florence stood, smoothing her cardigan with hands that trembled slightly. "I'm not discussing this anymore tonight. We all need sleep and clear heads. We'll talk in the morning."

She left, her footsteps heavy on the stairs. Charlie stared after her, still holding the foreclosure notice.

"I can't lose this place too," he said quietly. "It's all I have left of her."

Eva moved closer, not quite touching but offering presence. "We'll figure something out."

"We?" Charlie looked at her, something vulnerable in his expression.

"We," Eva confirmed. "Your grandmother spent her life saving things that mattered. Maybe it's time someone returned the favour."

Charlie studied her for a long moment, then nodded slowly. "Tomorrow, then. We plan tomorrow."

They locked Margaret's room carefully, but Eva noticed Charlie pocket one of the notebooks—one from 1946, its cover worn soft with handling. Whatever was in those pages, he wasn't ready to share it yet.

Back in her room, Eva sat at the desk with her green journal, trying to process everything she'd learned. Margaret Wells: nurse, storyteller, guardian of broken soldiers and lost children. A woman who gave everything and kept nothing, who wrote beautiful stories but never her own happy ending.

And now Florence faced losing the inn Margaret had once saved, while Charlie guarded his grandmother's memories like wounds that wouldn't heal.

Eva picked up the brass key, turning it over again in the lamplight, a practice that had become habitual but brought her comfort. Whatever door this opened, she had a feeling it held answers they all needed. But first, they had to come up with a plan to save the inn. Margaret had left a legacy of small magics and quiet kindnesses—surely there was enough left to save the place she'd loved.

Outside her window, York slept under its blanket of frost and history. Tomorrow would bring hard truths and even harder choices. But tonight, Eva fell asleep thinking of a woman who believed in the power of stories to heal, and wondered if maybe—just maybe—the right story could still save them all.

Chapter Thirteen

A Place Worth Saving

Eva woke before dawn, her mind already racing with half-formed plans. The inn's mortgage deadline loomed like a storm cloud, and she couldn't shake the image of Florence's trembling hands holding that foreclosure notice. She grabbed her phone and typed a message to Charlie quickly:

Eva: Are you okay? We need to talk to Florence about the inn.

His response came faster than expected for 5.47 a.m.

Charlie: Already awake. Be there by 7. We'll figure this out.

*   *   *

After showering, Eva dressed quickly in leggings and her warmest sweater, then made her way downstairs. The inn was quiet in that particular early morning way, all creaking floorboards and the distant hum of the ancient boiler. She found Florence in the kitchen, already up and mechanically preparing breakfast, her movements lacking their usual brisk efficiency. Despite the inn being far from full, Florence continued to prepare for a morning service. Eva admired her sense of 'the show must go on' attitude, but still felt saddened by the reality of the situation.

"Couldn't sleep either?" Florence asked without turning around.

"Not really." Eva poured herself tea from the ever-present pot. "Florence, we need to talk about the inn. Properly talk."

Florence's shoulders sagged. "Yes, I suppose we do." She abandoned the eggs she'd been whisking and sat heavily at the kitchen table. "I've been fooling myself, haven't I? I really thought I could turn it around if I just worked harder, stayed open longer, made greater offerings, like serving better breakfasts."

"How long has it been bad?" Eva asked gently.

"Really bad? Two years, if I'm honest. Started when the new Premier Inn opened near the station. Then that boutique hotel in the city centre with its Instagram-ready rooms and cocktail bar." Florence's hands twisted in her lap. "I don't know how to spread the word like those clever sorts do. What do you kids call it? Going viral? Oh I don't know. There's all kinds here, we've got this shop—it sells ceramics or something—people queue down the street just to buy the little figurines for fifteen pounds. Fifteen pounds!"

Eva remembered passing The Shambles, the lines of tourists eagerly waiting to purchase their little pieces of York. Eva narrowed her eyes, thinking.

"Started six months ago," Florence continued. "Some influencer posted about it, said it was the only place to go when you're in York or some such nonsense. Went viral on TokTok. Or TokTik? No matter. Now they can't keep their stock on the shelves, it's gone by lunchtime! Meanwhile, I've got the actual history of York in every beam and brick, and I can't fill three rooms." Her laugh was bitter. "Can't compete with that, can I? Not with creaky floors and radiators that sing opera at three in the morning."

"But that's what makes this place special—"

"Special doesn't pay the bills, love." Florence rubbed her eyes. "Bookings are down forty percent. At the moment, I've got you and maybe one other room filled. The Christmas market helps, but January through March?" She shook her head. "Ghost town."

"Ghost . . . town . . ." Eva repeated slowly, her mind suddenly racing. "Florence, that's it!"

"What's it?" Florence looked at her with concern. "Are you feeling all right?"

"The ghosts! The trinkets! Don't you see?" Eva's words tumbled out in excitement. "That shop is selling a story, like a manufactured mystery. But you have the real thing—Margaret's tale, the inn's history, all of it!"

"Eva, love, I don't think—"

"No, wait, hear me out." Eva's marketing brain was fully engaged now, the pieces clicking together and wheels turning. If only she felt this passionate in her actual job. "People waited in line for those . . . trinkets because someone told them a story that made those trinkets special. But this inn, Margaret's legacy—that's authentic. That's real. We don't need to manufacture mystery when we have actual history that's even more compelling than fiction. A story. It's about a story!"

Florence opened her mouth to respond, but the door opened and Charlie arrived as promised, looking haggard but determined. He kissed Florence's cheek and accepted the mug of tea Eva pushed towards him. Eva looked upon him as he sat at the table with them. His forehead was etched with worry and there was nothing more she wanted than to ease his stress. Despite the way he was clearly feeling, Charlie remained calm in his speech and looked between the women before speaking. It was a silent attempt at telling them they were okay, they could do this together.

"Right," he said. "Let's hear it all. No more secrets."

*　*　*

During the hour's discussion, Florence laid everything out plainly: six months of mortgage arrears, depleted savings, credit cards maxed from the roof repairs. The numbers were stark, undeniable.

"How much to catch up?" Charlie asked.

"Thousands of pounds I don't have Charlie. By 24th of December."

Charlie winced. "And Aidan's offer?"

"Enough to pay off everything and set me up in a nice little flat somewhere." Florence's voice was carefully neutral. "He's been very . . . persistent. Discreet, which I've been grateful for, but persistent nonetheless."

Eva had been quiet during the financial discussion, but her mind was attempting to work through the problem like she would have done at Monarch Music. Not with spreadsheets and profit margins, but with something more fundamental: a story. Marketing was just storytelling, after all, and the inn had stories to spare.

"What if we could show people what this place really is?" she said suddenly. "Not compete with the boutique hotels or the Premier Inn, but offer something they can't—real history, real connection to York's past."

"A marketing campaign?" Charlie's tone was sceptical. "Eva, this isn't Nashville. We don't do the whole flashy—"

"Not flashy. Authentic." Eva pulled out her journal, flipping through the notes she'd made about Margaret. "Think about it—people are literally queuing for junk and photo opportunities on The Shambles. Imagine what they'd do for real history, real stories. Your grandmother's work during the war, the lives she touched, the inn's role in York's history—people would come for that. The kind of travellers who want more than just a place to sleep." Eva's heart quickened. She felt alive and excited like never before. "We could create a trail, like a treasure hunt through York following Margaret's notes, ending here at the inn where—"

"No." Charlie's response was immediate and sharp as a knife. "Margaret's story isn't a marketing tool."

"I'm not suggesting we sell out with it, I—"

"Aren't you?" Charlie stood abruptly, his chair scraping against the floor. "You want to turn my grandmother's private memories and her pain into a tourist attraction? Make her another ghost to sell to gullible tourists? 'Come stay where the tragic nurse lived'?"

"That's not what I meant—"

"You don't know what she wanted, Eva." His voice was rising. "Some of this is private. Some of it should stay buried."

Eva stood too, matching his intensity. "Maybe I don't know what she wanted. But I know what the inn *needs* right now. And it's this."

"You've been here for five minutes," Charlie said coldly. "You think that gives you the right to dig up our family's history and sell it to the highest bidder? To turn my grandmother into another York attraction, like those bloody ceramic figures?"

"I'm trying to help!"

"I don't need your help." He grabbed his coat. "And neither does Margaret's memory."

The door slammed behind him, leaving Eva and Florence in ringing silence.

"Well," Florence said after a moment. "That went about as well as expected."

"I don't understand," Eva said, sinking back into her chair. "All those people yesterday—they loved her, remembered her kindness. Why wouldn't he want to share that?"

Florence was quiet for a long moment, then rose and went to an old Welsh dresser in the corner. From behind a stack of dishes, she pulled out a wooden box, its surface worn smooth with age.

"Charlie isn't the only one holding on to pieces of Margaret," she said, setting the box on the table. "She left this with me many years ago. Said to keep it safe until the right moment."

Eva stared at the box. It was locked, with no visible key. "What's in it?"

"I don't know. Never opened it. Couldn't if I tried, it's locked. Margaret said—" Florence's voice grew soft, "—'Some things are meant to be discovered by the right person at the right time.'"

"And you think I'm the right person?"

"I think you're here for a reason." Florence pushed the box towards Eva. "But be careful what you dig up, love. Some stories are buried for a reason. The past has teeth, and Margaret . . . she knew how to keep secrets."

Eva picked up the box, surprised by its weight. The wood was dark with age, and she could feel something shift inside when she tilted it.

"The key," she breathed, pulling the brass key from her pocket. It had become a habit to carry it with her while wandering round York. Something like a lucky charm, it brought her a sense of comfort and served as a reminder that she was here for a reason. "The one from behind the plaque, it must be."

It fit perfectly.

Florence stood. "I'll leave you to it. But Eva—remember that Margaret was a real person, not just a character in a story. She was wonderful, but she also made choices that hurt people, including herself. Whatever's in that box, it could change how you see her. Please keep that in mind."

After Florence left, Eva sat alone with the box. She could wait for Charlie, try to convince him to open it with her. But time was running out for the inn, and Charlie clearly needed space to process.

She thought of all the fairy tales she'd read, all the boxes that shouldn't be opened, all the warnings about curiosity. But this wasn't a fairy tale. This was real life, with real consequences. The inn needed saving, and maybe—just maybe—Margaret had left them the key to doing just that.

Eva turned the key.

Inside, the first thing she saw was a photograph: Margaret, young and radiant, standing beside a tall man in an American uniform. They were in front of the inn, snow on the ground, and Margaret's smile was different from any Eva had seen in other photos—unreserved, completely alive.

Beneath the photo was a bundle of letters tied with a faded ribbon, a leather diary, what looked like architectural drawings, and at the very bottom, an envelope addressed in shaky handwriting: *For whoever discovers this—please understand.*

Eva's hands trembled as she picked up the diary. Whatever secrets Margaret had kept, whatever story she'd been too afraid or ashamed to tell, it was all here. The real story, not the sanitised legend York had built around her.

For the first time since arriving in York, Eva felt the full weight of what she'd stumbled into. This wasn't just about saving an inn or solving a mystery. This was about understanding why some love stories don't get happy endings, why some sacrifices aren't noble but necessary, why a woman might spend her whole life atoning for a choice made in wartime.

She opened the diary to the first page, Margaret's handwriting clear despite the years:

January 1, 1945. I met a wonderful man today. Walter. He says it like it's music—Wall-ter, with that American drawl that makes the nurses giggle. He's dying, though he doesn't know it yet. The doctors give him two months. I give him forever, because that's what you give to love when you find it in the middle of hell . . .

Eva felt tears prick her eyes. Whatever came next in these pages, she understood with sudden clarity why Charlie was afraid. Some stories, once told, changed everything.

But the inn was worth saving. Florence was worth fighting for. And this time, despite Charlie's hesitancy, Margaret's truth—however painful—could be the key to preserving what she'd loved most. During her trip, Eva had come to realise that in life, we don't always get what we want but sometimes we do get what we need. Right now, she needed to do this.

And so, Eva began to read, stepping out of the fairy tale and into the messy, complicated, achingly human reality of a woman who'd loved and lost and spent the rest of her life trying to make amends.

Chapter Fourteen

Betrayals

Eva sat at the small desk in her room, Margaret's wooden box open before her like Pandora's box itself, its contents spread across the worn wood. The diary's leather cover was cracked with age, but the pages inside were surprisingly intact, as if grief itself had acted as a preservative.

Beside the diary lay a photograph of a handsome American soldier in uniform, a bundle of letters that had been tied up with ribbon, and what appeared to be some kind of diagram or map, carefully folded.

She'd been reading for hours, lost in Margaret's world of 1945 York—a city of wounded soldiers and exhausted nurses, of hope wearing thin and love blooming in the most unlikely circumstances. Margaret's handwriting grew more passionate as the entries progressed, documenting her growing feelings for an American soldier named Walter.

January 8, 1945—Found the most curious thing today. A note tucked inside 'Pride and Prejudice' in the hospital library. 'Even Mr Darcy needed time to heal,' it said. No signature, but I have my suspicions about the American in Ward 3.

The Mansion House has made for such a strange hospital—its ballroom now filled with iron beds where dancing couples once waltzed, crystal chandeliers casting light on bandages instead of ball gowns. Sometimes I forget this was ever anything but a place of healing, though Sister Matthews says we'll all be displaced once the war ends and York's grand buildings are returned to their proper purposes. Where will all these broken men go then, I wonder?

January 15, 1945—He left another! This time in 'Wuthering Heights'—Heathcliff had nothing on Yorkshire weather.' Made me laugh despite everything. I may have left a reply in 'Jane Eyre' . . .

February 14, 1945—Valentine's Day, though we're not supposed to take note of such things in wartime. But Walter noticed. Left a paper heart on my desk at the nurses' station, made from a letter from home. 'My heart's already across the ocean,' he said when I found him watching. 'Might as well make it official.' Our library book courtship is becoming something more and I don't know what to do. Or maybe the problem is that I do, but I just can't bring myself to pull away. I should walk away. Should remember that I am engaged to Thomas, a good Yorkshire man who is waiting ever so patiently for the war to end. But Walter's smile lights a fire within me and is rapidly undoing all of my careful plans.

Eva's phone rang, jarring her from 1945 back to the present. She almost ignored it—probably her mother again—but something made her check the screen.

Richard.

Her blocked Richard. Calling from what must be his office line.

She stared at the phone, letting it ring. Then, on the fourth ring, she answered.

"Eva, thank God." Richard's voice was different—less polished, more human. "I know you blocked me, and I deserve that, but I had to talk to you."

"How did you even—"

"Listen, I know I have no right to call, but I've been thinking—"

"Richard—"

"I made a mistake, Eva. A huge mistake. I've been miserable since that night at Kayne Prime. I miss you. I miss us."

Eva sank onto the bed, Margaret's diary still in her hand. "There was no 'us', Richard. There was you and who you wanted me to be."

"That's not true. We were good together."

"We were convenient together. There's a difference."

"Eva, please. I realise now what I threw away. I want another chance. I'll do better, be better—"

"Richard." She surprised herself with how steady her voice was. "You're not a bad person. You're just not my person."

"What does that even mean?"

Eva thought of Charlie in the rain, singing country music in a Yorkshire pub. Charlie handing her a green journal because he believed she had stories worth telling. Charlie's walls and wounds and the way he looked at her like she might be worth letting them down for.

"It means I've found something here. Something real."

"In England? Eva, you barely know anyone there—"

"I'm not talking about someone else. I know myself here. For the first time in years, I feel as though I'm not acting like someone the world has told me to be, I'm just living. I know what *I* want here."

"And what's that?"

"I'm sorry Richard, but it's not you and not us." The words came out gentle but final. "Not the life we were building. I want messy and complicated and real. I want someone who sees me, not just the version that fits someone's ideals, or what they've imagined for themselves"

Richard was quiet for a long moment. "This is about someone else, isn't it? You've met someone."

"This is about me, Richard. But in the spirit of being completely honest and authentic with myself, yes, there's someone. Someone who drives me crazy because he's so stubborn, but makes me laugh because he isn't afraid to be silly and he looks at me like I'm worth knowing. The real me, not the sanitised version."

"I could be that person—"

"No, you couldn't. And that's okay. You'll find someone who fits your vision perfectly. Someone who wants the same things you want. But that's not me. It never was."

"Eva—"

"Goodbye, Richard. I mean it this time. Please don't call me again."

She ended the call and put her phone face down, a finality to the motion that felt good. Then she sat in the silence of her room, waiting to feel . . . something. Regret, maybe. Or doubt.

Instead, she felt free. And suddenly, crystal clear about her feelings for Charlie. This was in fact crazy. She hadn't known Charlie for long. But sometimes the length of time didn't matter. Sometimes you met someone and every conversation felt like continuing one you started years ago. Sometimes a few weeks of real connection meant more than years of going through the motions. She thought of Margaret and Walter—three months that changed a lifetime. Time wasn't the measure of love; truth was.

She picked up her phone again and typed a message to the man she could feel herself unravelling for:

Eva: We need to talk about the key and about your grandmother. I've found another notebook and there are things in here that I think you should know.

The message showed as delivered but not read. After some anxious tapping, she tried again:

Eva: Charlie, please. This is important. The inn needs us to work together.

Nothing.

Eva: I'm sorry about this morning. You were right—some stories are private. But Florence gave me this for a reason.

Still nothing. He was clearly still upset about their argument this morning, about her suggesting they share Margaret's story in an attempt to save the inn. Time was running out, she'd had to open the box no matter what could be inside—its secrets might be the only thing that could help them now.

Eva turned back to Margaret's diary, her heart heavy. The entries from March 1945 were increasingly desperate:

March 20, 1945—*Walter grows stronger every day. He's nineteen, barely older than I am. Yesterday he managed to walk the length of the ward without assistance. The doctor says he'll be discharged soon, sent back to his unit or perhaps home. The thought terrifies me. How did this happen? How did I let myself fall so completely for someone I cannot have? Thomas writes faithfully every week, planning our future. A cottage near the cathedral, children,*

Sunday roasts with his parents. A good life. The right life. But when Walter looks at me, I see a different future—one across an ocean, full of uncertainty and adventure and a love that makes my chest ache. I'm a terrible person. I know this. But I cannot seem to stop.

The next entry made Eva's throat tight:

March 28, 1945—Walter has asked me the unthinkable. I'm not sure if it's due to his injuries or the fear of what may come next with the war, but he has asked me to come with him. After the war, he said. To Pennsylvania, where his family own a farm. 'Marry me, Maggie,' he said in a stolen moment when the ward was at its quietest. (No one else has ever called me Maggie, only him.) I know it's crazy and too fast and all wrong, but I love you. I'll make you happy, I swear it.' I couldn't speak. Couldn't breathe. Couldn't do anything but cry. Because I want to say yes with every fibre of my being. But Thomas. My parents. My duty. My life here. How can I throw it all away for a man I've known three months? How can I not?

Eva turned the page, but the next entry was dated two weeks later:

April 12, 1945—He's gone. I arrived at the hospital this morning to find his bed empty, stripped bare. Like a ghost, my Walter has left me. Discharged in the night, Sister Matthews said. Immediate deployment. No warning, no goodbye, no chance to give him an answer. Perhaps it's better this way. Perhaps this is God's way of keeping me from making a terrible mistake. There's a bitterness within me at my choice being taken. I know Thomas's mother has begun planning our wedding for after the war. Last week she told me the story of finding her own dress. Still, I sit and smile and nod. Polite, well-mannered Margaret always doing the right thing. If only they could read the notes Walter and I *had passed to each other in the secrecy of the dark. Today, I feel as though I'm drowning in broad daylight. I'll never see Walter again, my heart bleeds.*

But this is for the best. This is for the best. This is for the best. (If I write it enough times, perhaps I'll believe it.)

Eva had to stop reading, tears blurring her vision. She understood now why Charlie was so protective of his grandmother's memory. This wasn't the story of a noble woman who chose duty—this was the story of a woman who'd had love ripped away before she could choose at all. The diary made it seem like Walter had abandoned her, but what if there was more to the story? What if Charlie had grown up believing his grandmother had been callously left behind when that wasn't quite the case? Eva was a hopeless romantic at heart and she needed to know the truth behind this secret love affair.

She picked up the bundle of letters, all from Walter during his time in the hospital. They progressed from polite ("Dear Nurse Wells, thank you for the extra blanket last night") to playful ("Maggie, that smile of yours could power all of London") to desperate ("I know I have no right to love you, but I do. God help me, I do").

At the bottom of the pile was one letter different from the rest—still sealed, addressed to Margaret in Walter's handwriting. He'd written 1946 at the envelope's seal but a US postmark dated the letter to the 1980s. *Strange.*

Eva stared at it, her heart racing. An unopened letter. Whatever was inside had been too painful for Margaret to read, even decades later. Or maybe her sense of duty and respect to her husband told her that this letter was best left buried in the past. Something in her gut told her this was meant for Charlie—the truth his grandmother had never been able to face and one he didn't know.

She carefully placed the unopened letter in her bag. She wouldn't open it without Charlie. It wasn't her secret to discover alone. But she needed air, needed to think, needed to process everything she'd learned.

She gathered Margaret's diary and her own journal ready to head to a small café she'd discovered, tucked away on a side street that tourists never found. Writing would help her work through the events of the day.

* * *

The café was warm and quiet, smelling of coffee and cinnamon. Eva settled into a corner table and opened her journal, trying to organise her thoughts. She'd been writing for perhaps twenty minutes when the bell above the door chimed. She glanced up automatically—and froze.

Eva had been avoiding Aidan since their drinks at The Vaults, which was easily done since he never seemed to frequent the real York—the cosy pubs, the ancient streets, the places where locals gathered. He preferred the polished venues that blew up on Instagram and lacked any real character, carbon copies that could have been in any city.

But here he was standing with his chest puffed out and eyes scanning the café, his designer coat now dusted with rain. Their eyes met, and the corners of his mouth pulled into a smirk that made her stomach sink.

"Eva, Eva, Eva," he said, approaching her table with purpose. "Causing quite the stir of emotions for that little old inn, aren't you?"

"What are you talking about?"

"I thought I had the agreement in the bag weeks ago and then little miss USA had to show up and be a little flea in Florence's ear."

"Aidan I—"

"Well tough luck Eva, because that inn is mine." He produced a folded document from his coat, laying it on the table between them. "Preliminary sale agreement for the Riddle & Quill. Signed by Florence just yesterday."

Eva's blood ran cold. She grabbed the document, scanning it with growing horror. Florence's signature was there, shaky but there was no denying it. She'd signed the document.

"She wouldn't—"

"She would, and she did." Aidan leaned back, satisfied. "The inn will make beautiful luxury flats, don't you think?"

"This can't be legal. Charlie doesn't even know—"

"Charlie isn't the owner. Florence is. And she's made her choice." He studied her with those calculating eyes. "It's a pity really, you're as bad as Charlie, trying to save that place. But you're wasting your time, Eva. It's happening whether you like it or not."

"There must be a way to stop this—"

"There isn't." Aidan stood, buttoning his coat. "Construction assessments begin tomorrow. The bank's deadline is 24th of December, but with this agreement in place, they'll extend if needed. It's over."

He paused at her table, looking down at her with something like pity. "You should go home, Eva. Back to Nashville. There's nothing left for you here except false hope and old ghosts."

He left, the bell chiming mockingly in his wake.

Eva sat alone in the café, her hands shaking as she stared at the copy of the agreement Aidan had left behind. And somewhere in York, Charlie still wasn't answering her messages, unaware that everything was falling apart.

She pulled out her journal and wrote with trembling hands:

Richard called today. Wanted me back. Six months ago, I would have cried with relief, would have been on the next plane home. But I'm not that Eva anymore. That Eva believed in perfect plans and safe choices. This Eva knows that love isn't about convenience, timing or fitting into someone's vision. It's about finding someone who sees you— really sees you—and chooses you anyway. Messy, imperfect, complicated you.

Charlie isn't answering. He's hurt and angry and has every right to be. I pushed too hard this morning, suggested using his grandmother's story without understanding how much pain it still causes him.

And Florence . . . I can't believe she'd sell to Aidan without telling us. There must be more to this story. She loves that inn. It's her whole life.

Tomorrow is December 22nd. Two days until the deadline. Two days to save the inn, to convince Charlie to stay, to figure out what really happened between Margaret and Walter.

Two days to decide if I'm brave enough to fight for what matters, or if I'll end up like Margaret—spending the rest of my life regretting the chances I didn't take.

She closed the journal and carefully tucked the unopened letter deeper into her bag. Through the café window, York continued its ancient business of existing, indifferent to the small dramas playing out in its streets. But Eva was learning that small dramas could change everything—a nurse falling for a soldier, a lost woman following breadcrumbs through a strange city, a grandson trying to outrun his heritage.

She thought of Margaret's diary entry: *This is for the best. This is for the best. This is for the best.*

"No," Eva said aloud to the empty café. "It wasn't for the best. And I'm not making the same mistake."

She had two days to save everything that mattered. Time to stop reading other people's stories and start writing her own ending.

Chapter Fifteen

The Letter That Changes Everything

Eva found Florence in the inn's small office, surrounded by towers of paperwork that seemed to have multiplied overnight. The room smelled of old paper and Florence's lavender hand cream, mixed with the bitter scent of reheated coffee that had gone cold hours ago. The older woman looked up as Eva knocked on the doorframe, her reading glasses sliding down her nose, a red pen still poised over columns of numbers that refused to add up to anything good.

For the first time since arriving at the Riddle & Quill, Eva saw Florence as she truly was—not the bustling innkeeper with endless energy, but an old woman carrying the weight of too many years and too many worries.

The desk lamp cast harsh shadows across Florence's face, highlighting the deep grooves around her mouth and the purple smudges beneath her eyes.

"We need to talk about Aidan's offer," Eva said softly, closing the door behind her. The latch clicked with a finality that made her stomach clench.

Florence's hands stilled on the papers, the rustling silence suddenly oppressive. Outside, a dog barked—sharp and insistent in the cold night air. "How do you know about the agreement?"

"He showed me. At the café." Eva moved closer, her boots creaking on the old floorboards that dipped in the middle from decades of footsteps. She noticed the slight tremor in Florence's hands as she set down her pen. "He seemed to get a kick out of sharing it with me. How could you sign it, Florence?"

"I signed a preliminary agreement." Florence's voice was steady, but her eyes were wet, catching the lamplight like winter puddles. "Nothing's final yet. I wanted . . . I just needed to have options."

"Florence—"

"I'm too old for this, Eva." The words came out sharp, defensive. She stood abruptly, her chair scraping against the floor with a sound like fingernails on wood. "I've been fighting to keep this place afloat for God knows how long. I can't fight forever."

Eva sat down across from her, the leather chair releasing a soft wheeze of protest, its springs long past their prime. Through the window behind Florence, she could see frost creeping across the glass, transforming the lights of York into impressionist smears of gold and white. "What if you didn't have to fight alone?"

Florence laughed, but there was no humour in it. "With what army? Charlie's maps don't pay the mortgage. My regular guests are aging faster than the building. And you . . ." She paused, studying Eva with those sharp blue

211

eyes that seemed to catalogue every detail, every tell. "You'll go home eventually. Back to your real life."

"This feels like my real life," Eva said quietly, her fingers finding the worn edge of Margaret's diary in her bag, the leather soft as skin beneath her touch. "More real than anything I had in Nashville."

"Feelings change. People leave." Florence's voice carried the weight of experience, each word dropping like stones into still water. "That's what Margaret learned too late."

Eva pulled out the diary, its pages whispering secrets as she set it on the desk between them. The leather cover bore the marks of countless handlings, oil from fingers that had traced its surface in joy and sorrow. "I've been reading Margaret's diary. The one from the box you gave me."

Florence's hand moved involuntarily towards the diary, then stopped, fingers hovering inches away as if the leather might burn on touch. "You've read it all then?"

"Most of it. About Walter, about how he left—deployed without warning, without goodbye. She writes about it like he abandoned her, but . . ." Eva hesitated, watching dust motes dance in the lamplight like tiny ghosts. "There's an unopened letter. From 1946. From him."

Florence was silent for a long moment, her fingers worrying the edge of an invoice until the paper began to fray, leaving tiny white fragments on the dark wood. "She could never bring herself to open it. I remember her showing it to me once, years ago. Said some questions were better left unanswered."

"But she kept it."

"She kept everything that mattered. Hidden away, locked up tight, but kept all the same." Florence's eyes went distant, focusing on something beyond the frost-etched

212

window—perhaps seeing Margaret as she'd been, young and broken and determinedly cheerful. "I suspected there was more to the story. The way she'd flinch at American accents, the way she'd go quiet every fourth of July. But in those days, you didn't talk about such things. Maybe if we were sisters, cousins don't exactly have the same clout and of course there was always the age difference so I missed out on some of those types of conversations."

"Your family never spoke about it?"

"Never, think about it Eva, it would have been a scandal at that time. Falling in love for a stranger when your hand is promised to another? No, she did the 'right' thing. She swallowed the pain and married Charlie's grandfather—Thomas—in 1946 just as she said she would. Had Charlie's mother, Sarah. Built a life. A good life, by all accounts. But of course, there was always something . . ." Florence shook her head. "Like she was living someone else's story."

Eva thought of her own life in Nashville, the careful construction of an existence that looked perfect from the outside. Her hands found each other in her lap, fingers twisting together—a nervous habit her mother had always hated. "I know that feeling."

"I expect you do." Florence's gaze sharpened. "Is that why you're really here, do you think? Running from your own Walter?"

"No," Eva said, thinking of Charlie, of the way he'd looked at her in the Castle Howard grounds. "I think part of me has only just found my version of Walter and I'm trying my best to run towards him."

Florence was quiet, studying her. "Charlie doesn't know you have all this, does he? Margaret's diary, the letters?"

"Not yet. He's been avoiding my messages since yesterday."

"He's protecting her the only way he knows how," Florence said gently. She moved to the window, her reflection ghostlike in the dark glass as she looked down to the frosty scene below her. "He grew up thinking his grandmother was abandoned by a careless American soldier. It shaped him, that story. Made him careful with his heart. I know you've met Sophie. I'm sure you can imagine how that break up went from the little you've seen of her. That factors in too, of course."

"God I know, but what if that's not the whole truth? What if Walter had reasons—"

"What if he did?" Florence interrupted, turning back with a swish of wool cardigan. "What if that letter contains explanations, apologies, declarations of undying love? It doesn't change what happened. Margaret lived her whole life without him. Made her choices, for better or worse."

"It just seems so unfair," Eva said. "All that love, wasted."

"Was it wasted?" Florence asked. "She helped hundreds of people find their own happiness. She saved this inn, built a community, raised a family. Maybe it wasn't the life she'd dreamed of, but it was a life. A good one, in its way."

They sat in silence, the weight of Margaret's choices heavy between them. Finally, Florence stood, moving to the window that overlooked the inn's small garden.

"I don't want to sell to Aidan," she said quietly. Her breath fogged the glass, obscuring the view of bare rose bushes and frost-silvered grass. "This place is all I have left of her, of the family we built here. But wanting something and the reality of it are very different things. Unless a miracle happens by 24th of December . . ."

Eva stood too, determination crystallising in her chest. "Then we make a miracle happen. We have two days—"

"Eva." Florence's voice was gentle but firm. "This isn't a fairy tale. This is real life, with real consequences. Sometimes the dragon wins. Sometimes the castle falls."

"And sometimes," Eva said, thinking of Margaret's courage in the face of impossible circumstances, "sometimes ordinary people do extraordinary things. Not because it's easy, but because it matters."

Florence studied her for a long moment, then smiled—a real smile this time, one she hadn't seen from the innkeeper since she first arrived. "You're very like her, you know. Margaret. That same stubborn hope."

"Is that a good thing?"

"Ask me in two days," Florence said. "Now go find Charlie. He needs to know about all this. About the diary, the letter, everything. And Eva?" She paused. "Be gentle with him. Some wounds we inherit from the people who loved us."

Eva climbed the stairs to her room, each step creaking a different note—the inn's wooden symphony that she'd grown to love. Her head was spinning with everything she'd learned. She needed to think, to figure out what came next. The room felt different now—not a temporary refuge but something more. She moved to the wardrobe, intending to organise her thoughts along with her clothes, a coping mechanism that was tried and tested whenever she could feel some sort of meltdown happening. Pulling hangers out at random, she was interrupted by heavy footsteps on the stairs.

The footsteps were uneven, angry—taking the stairs two at a time, then a surprise pause, like a deep breath before continuing. She knew it was Charlie before he arrived, could feel his approach like electricity before a storm.

Charlie appeared in her doorway, his face a tempest of emotions. His hair was wild, as if he'd been running his hands through it, and his coat still bore traces of the December cold—tiny crystals of frost melting into dark patches on the wool. "Florence told me you have Margaret's diary. That you've been reading it."

"She gave me a box," Eva said carefully, aware of how the air in the room seemed to thicken with his presence. "And with the key I found I was able to open it. Florence must have known they'd be a match. She said Margaret wanted—"

"Margaret's dead," Charlie cut her off, his voice sharp as winter wind. "She doesn't want anything anymore."

"Charlie—"

He interrupted her—"ahh I see, you're running away already?" His voice was bitter, as he cast his eyes over the clothes haphazardly laid out on the bed. The sight seemed to confirm something for him—his shoulders sagged slightly, as if he'd been expecting this. "God, I should have seen this coming. Things get complicated and before you know it, it's time to hop on a flight back to the bloody US of A. Or did you get bored and decide this little trip was over?"

Eva felt anger flare, hot and sudden. Her hands clenched at her sides, nails digging into palms. "You don't know anything about me. Or why I'm here."

"Don't I?" Charlie stepped into the room, his presence filling the small space like smoke. "You're here because you're running from something. Bad breakup, wasn't it? So you decided you needed an adventure, a distraction for now and then a story to tell your friends back home. 'The Christmas I solved a mystery in York.' How charming."

216

"That's not—"

"And now you've got your story, haven't you? My grandmother's tragic love affair, the lost American, the family secrets. Perfect material for whatever blog post or Instagram story you'll no doubt share."

"Stop it," Eva said, her voice low and dangerous. She could feel her pulse in her throat, taste copper in her mouth. She'd never been so angry in her life. Or had she, but never been honest enough with herself to truly feel it?

"Why? Because the truth hurts?" Charlie's eyes were wild, the careful control she'd seen him maintain cracking like ice under pressure. "You're treating Margaret's story like a fairy tale. Like something with a happy ending just waiting to be discovered. It's not a fairy tale—it did not end happily ever after." He laughed bitterly. "You know what happens when you devote yourself to stories and books instead of life? You end up like one. On the shelf. Collecting dust. That's what happened to her—surrounded by other people's stories because she couldn't write her own ending, the one she got instead was sad and lonely."

"I know that!" Eva shouted, surprising them both. The words echoed in the small room, seeming to bounce off the sloped ceiling. "I've read her diary, Charlie. Every painful entry. I felt her heartbreak, her regret. I understand—"

"You understand nothing!" Charlie roared back. His face was flushed, a vein pulsing at his temple. "You didn't catch her crying every year on the fourth of July like clockwork. You didn't see her flinch when American tourists asked us for directions. You didn't hold her hand when she was dying and hear her whisper a name that wasn't my grandfather's."

The silence that followed was deafening. Charlie stood there, chest heaving, his breath visible in the cold room—

when had it gotten so cold? He looked as surprised by his outburst as Eva felt.

"Walter," Eva said softly. "She said Walter's name?"

Charlie's face crumpled. It was like watching a wall collapse—sudden and complete. "She just asked him over and over 'why did you do it?' It was awful. My mum tried to tell her it was okay, that Grandad—Thomas—understood. But she just kept apologising to a ghost."

Eva moved without thinking, reaching for the wooden box on her desk. The wood was warm under her fingers, as if it had been waiting. "Charlie, there's something you need to see."

"I don't want—"

"There's a letter." She thrust the box at him. Her hands were shaking slightly still, the adrenaline in her veins from the fighting made the contents rattle—a sound like bones. "From Walter in 1946. She didn't get it until later, she never opened it."

Charlie stared at the box like it might bite him. His Adam's apple bobbed as he swallowed hard. "No."

"You need to read it. You need to understand—"

"I said no!" He snatched the box from her hands, clutching it against his chest. She could see his knuckles white with pressure, could hear his breathing—ragged and uneven. "Whatever's in here, whatever excuses or explanations he had, it doesn't matter. He left her. She waited, and he left."

"But what if—"

"There is no 'what if'," Charlie said, already backing towards the door. "There's only what happened. And what happened is that Margaret Wells spent her whole life paying for loving the wrong man."

He was gone before Eva could respond, his footsteps on the stairs heavy and uneven, punctuated by the slam of the front door that rattled the windows in their frames. She stood alone in her room, surrounded by half-organised clothes and unfinished stories.

This was it—her dark night of the soul, as her English teacher, Ms Jensen would have called it. The moment when the heroine must choose: give up and go home, or stay and fight for something that might be impossible.

Eva sank onto the bed, the mattress springs creaking a familiar protest. She outstretched her arms creating a clothing snow angel and sighed amongst the mess. Rolling onto her side she reached out and pulled her green leather journal towards herself. The pages already held so many observations about York, about Margaret, about her own journey. She turned to a fresh page, the paper crisp beneath her fingers.

She thought of Richard's call, of the easy path back to Nashville and a life that would never quite fit. She thought of Florence, signing papers she didn't want to sign because she saw no other choice. She thought of Charlie, so wounded by his grandmother's pain that he couldn't see past it to the love that had caused it. To Sophie and the way she had broken Charlie's heart all the same.

And she thought of Margaret, eighteen years old, looking to Walter's empty hospital bed and choosing duty over desire.

Eva picked up her pen and wrote:

Sometimes the bravest thing is to stay.

Not because it's easy—it's not. Every instinct screams to run, to return to the safe and known and manageable. But there's a different kind of courage in planting your feet and saying: this matters. These people matter. This story matters.

Charlie thinks I don't understand, but I do. I understand what it's like to live someone else's version of your life. I understand the weight of other people's expectations, the way they can shape you into someone you don't recognize. I understand the fear of wanting something so much it might destroy you.

But I also understand this: Margaret's story isn't finished. It echoes through generations, shaping lives, breaking hearts, building walls. Charlie carries her regret like armour. Florence holds her secrets like penance. And somewhere in an unopened letter is a truth that might change everything.

I could leave. Pack my bags, catch a flight, return to Nashville and pretend these weeks were just a strange detour. But I know now what Margaret knew then—some choices you can't unmake. Some people you can't unlove. Some stories demand to be finished, even if the ending isn't happy ever after.

So, I'm staying. To fight for the inn. To fight for Charlie, even if he doesn't want me to. Or, doesn't want me. As hard as that is to write. But I'm here to fight for the truth of Margaret's story, whatever it might be.

Because sometimes the bravest thing isn't letting go. Sometimes it's holding on.

Eva closed the journal and stood, moving to the window. York sprawled below her, ancient and eternal, its cobblestone streets slick with frost that caught the streetlights like scattered diamonds. Somewhere out there, Charlie was walking those streets with Margaret's box clutched to his chest, carrying the weight of generations of heartbreak.

She had two days to save the inn. Two days to convince Charlie that some stories deserved better endings. Two days to prove that *this* American tourist might just be exactly what this particular fairy tale needed.

Eva began reorganising her clothes, hanging them back in the wardrobe with careful deliberation. Each garment was a small act of defiance—the cable-knit cardigan she'd worn on her country walk with Charlie when he'd kissed her under the mistletoe, the green sweater she'd worn to the Christmas dinner, the jeans still stained with Yorkshire mud. With each hanger that clinked against the rail, she was making a declaration: I belong here.

Through her window, the Minster bells began to toll—ten o'clock, their bronze voices carrying across the frozen city. Eva pressed her palm against the cold glass, feeling the vibration of the bells through the window, through her bones.

Margaret Wells had spent over fifty years with her hand pressed against the window of what might have been, watching life pass by on the other side of the glass. Eva Coleman wasn't going to make the same mistake.

Not when the glass could still be broken.

Not when the story was still being written in ink that hadn't yet dried.

Chapter Sixteen

Everything Unravels

Here's the thing about construction crews: *they don't knock*. They just appear outside your window at dawn with measuring tapes and clipboards, treating your home like a corpse they're about to dissect. Which, Eva supposed as she watched two men in hard hats photograph the inn's Tudor beams, wasn't far from the truth.

'Thornfield Construction: Building Tomorrow's Heritage' read the van parked outside, though Eva saw it more like a hearse at a wake. Eva had always thought corporate slogans were the poetry of capitalism—pretty words to disguise ugly intentions. "They're early," Florence said when Eva found her in the kitchen, stirring porridge with the mechanical precision of someone whose mind was elsewhere. "Aidan said they wouldn't start until after Christmas."

"Aidan says a lot of things." Eva poured tea from the ever-present pot, noting how even Florence's secret weapon—

the sheep-shaped tea cosy—looked dejected this morning. "Most of them are lies dressed up in expensive disguises."

Florence almost smiled. Almost. "You're starting to sound like Charlie."

"God help me."

They watched through the window as one of the men held up his phone, documenting the inn's distinctive timber framing with the clinical efficiency of a medical examiner. Click. Click. Click. Each photo another nail in the coffin.

Eva's phone buzzed. Aidan. She could smell the cologne through the screen.

Aidan: Good morning, Eva. I hope you slept well. Could we meet for coffee? I have a proposition that might interest you.

"Speak of the devil," Eva muttered.

"What does he want now?" Florence asked.

"To offer me something I don't want while pretending it's exactly what I need. It's his signature move, apparently."

Another text appeared.

Aidan: The café on Goodramgate in 20 minutes? My treat.

Eva grimaced, locked her phone and placed it in her back pocket. She would just ignore him, then he'd go away, right? But something made her pause. *Know your enemy*, her father always said. And she needed to understand Aidan's plans if she had any hope of stopping them.

Eva: Fine. 20 minutes.

*　*　*

Eva was surprised by the chosen location. The independent coffee shop didn't seem to be Aidan's scene at all. With its mismatched chairs and woven blankets over bean bags, he must have picked this spot to impress her, or at least try to lull her into a false sense of security. Eva was on high alert, she knew exactly what kind of guy Aidan was. He'd already arrived by the time she got there, sitting at a corner table with two cups waiting.

"Eva," he said warmly, standing as she approached. "Thank you for coming. I took the liberty of ordering you a latte—is that all right?"

"It's fine," Eva said curtly, sitting down but not removing her coat. "What do you want, Aidan?"

"Straight to business. I like that." He leaned back, studying her with those calculating eyes. "I have a proposition for you."

He pulled out a sleek folder, sliding it across the table. "My company—Thornfield Development—we don't just renovate buildings. We create narratives around them, document their histories, connect the past with the future. You know, really sell it to the people. Anyway, we need someone with your skills."

Eva opened the folder to find glossy brochures of his previous projects. The photography was beautiful, the marketing copy was polished. But something felt hollow about it all.

"You want me to write marketing copy?"

"I want you to be our Chief Narrative Officer." The title rolled off his tongue with emphasis on each word. *How many times has he practiced this speech*? "You'd travel to our sites across Britain, maybe Europe eventually. Research the buildings' histories, spin the stories that make people fall in love with them."

He went on to name a figure that made Eva's eyes widen. But it wasn't just the money—it was the travel. The idea of exploring more places like York, diving into their histories, uncovering their stories. She could stay in Britain legally, with a real visa. She could take trains to Scotland, ferries to Ireland, maybe even the Channel to Paris.

"Tell me more," she heard herself say.

Aidan's smile widened. "We have projects everywhere. Bath, Edinburgh, Canterbury. You'd spend time in each location, really get to know the buildings, the communities. Full creative freedom to write whatever the hell you want. The goal is to sell someone a story and get them to sign on the dotted line."

Eva's mind was spinning. For a moment she'd seen herself wandering through Bath's elegant streets, researching the lives of the people who'd walked those Georgian squares. Scottish castles. Welsh mining villages. All of it waiting to be explored. But what Aidan now described seemed more like selling out.

"You could document our heritage preservation efforts," Aidan continued. "Chronicle how we breathe new life into dying buildings. They're all the better for it, Eva."

"Sure, because you have so many 'heritage preservation efforts'," Eva said dryly. "And anyway, why me? You barely know me."

"Because you're not rooted here. You're not weighed down by generations of Yorkshire stubbornness. You understand progress." He leaned forward. "And frankly, you're wasted here. Following ghost stories through a dying city, mooning after Charlie Blackwood—"

"I'm not mooning after anyone," Eva protested.

"Aren't you?" Aidan's smile was knowing. "He's never going to choose you over this place, Eva. Charlie's married to the past. You could do so much better."

"Like working for you?"

"Like building an actual future." He pulled out his phone, showing her photos. "This is our Bath project.

Twelve units, each one preserving the period features while offering modern luxury—"

"How much of the original building is left?" Eva interrupted.

"Well, the façade, obviously. Some of the nicer interior elements. The things that matter."

"And who decides what matters?"

Aidan's eyes hardened slightly. "The market decides."

Eva stared at the photos, thinking of Nashville—how quickly the honky-tonks had given way to rooftop bars, how the old recording studios became boutique hotels. She'd watched her city transform, historic music venues demolished for condos marketed to people who complained about the noise from the clubs that had been there first. Progress, they called it. But Eva had seen what progress looked like when it had no respect for the past—it was erasure dressed up in glass and steel.

"You know what I've learned, living in Nashville?" Eva said slowly. "Change isn't inherently good or bad. It's necessary. But there's a difference between evolution and extinction. Between adapting a story and deleting it entirely."

Aidan tilted his head. "That's an interesting perspective."

"It's an American perspective," Eva corrected. "We're so young as a country that we tear things down without thinking. A hundred-year-old building? Ancient by our standards. But here? That's practically new construction. Maybe that's why I can see what you're doing more clearly —I've watched my own city forget itself in real time."

Eva stared at the photos. "So, what's your plan for The Riddle & Quill?"

"Ah." Aidan sat back. "I thought this may be a sticking point in our conversation."

"Luxury apartments?"

226

"Twelve units, possibly fourteen if we convert the attic space. It's really the kindest thing—"

The coffee shop door chimed. Eva glanced up automatically and her heart stopped. Charlie stood in the doorway, his eyes moving from her to Aidan to the glossy brochures spread between them. His expression shifted from surprise to realisation, then to something that looked horribly like betrayal.

"Charlie—" Eva started, but he was already backing away.

"Don't let me interrupt," he said coldly, and then he was gone.

"Charlie!" Eva jumped up, but the door had already closed behind him.

"Let him go," Aidan said calmly. "He was bound to find out eventually."

"You knew he'd come here."

"I suspected. This is his usual coffee run time. Old habits die hard." Aidan began to gather his papers, but Eva could hardly hear him as the blood rushed up her neck into a flush through her ears. "The offer stands, Eva. 23rd of December. Think about what kind of future you really want," he called after her, but she was already running out of the door.

Eva barrelled outside, but Charlie had vanished into York's maze of streets. Her heart was pounding—not from the run, but from the look on his face. She'd seen him angry before, defensive, hurt. But never like that. Never like she'd personally driven a knife into his back.

Eva wandered the streets for an hour, lost in thought. What did she do? What did Charlie think? The twinkle of the Christmas lights seemed to diminish around her into angry eyes.

* * *

When she returned to the inn, the construction crews had multiplied as afternoon approached. There were surveyors, architects, workers with clipboards making notes about load-bearing walls. The timeline wasn't just accelerating; it was in freefall.

She found Florence in the kitchen, the older woman's face flushed from having to compete with the cacophony of tools and vehicles screaming from every direction. But before she could explain about Charlie, Florence grabbed her arm.

"THANK GOD YOU'RE BACK!" Florence bellowed over the pounding of a hammer somewhere above them. "CHARLIE'S BESIDE HIMSELF—TILLY'S MISSING!"

"What?" Eva shouted back, leaning in close.

"SHE WAS IN THE GARDEN THIS MORNING WHILE HE WAS WORKING!" Florence's voice cracked from the strain. A sudden bang from the dining room made them both flinch. "HE LET HER OUT FOR FIVE MINUTES AND NOW SHE'S GONE! IT'S BEEN OVER AN HOUR!"

Eva's stomach dropped. Tilly never ran off. Never. She was Charlie's constant, his one uncomplicated relationship. If something had happened to her . . .

"Which way did he go?"

"Towards the Minster, then the market. He's checking all her usual spots."

Eva ran out again, calling Tilly's name as she went. She found Charlie near the Christmas market, frantically questioning vendors.

"Have you seen a spaniel? Black and white, very friendly. She never does this, never runs off—"

"Charlie," Eva called.

He whirled around, and the wild desperation in his eyes made her forget everything else. His hair was

228

sticking up where he'd been running his hands through it, and he was only wearing one sock with his hastily-pulled-on shoes.

"She's gone," he said, his voice cracking. "I was reading the letters, I only let her out for five minutes, and she's just gone. What if she's hurt? What if someone took her? What if—"

"We'll find her," Eva said firmly. "Where have you looked?"

"Everywhere. The Minster grounds, all around the market, Knavesmire, the museum gardens. She's not anywhere."

They spent the next hour searching together, calling until their voices were raw. Charlie grew more frantic with each empty street, each "Sorry, haven't seen her" from concerned locals.

"Tilly! Tilly, come!" His voice was breaking now, desperation bleeding through. "She's all I have."

"Charlie—"

"Everything else is complicated," Charlie kept talking as if Eva hadn't spoken. "The Inn, Gran, you. But Tilly, Tilly just loves me. No questions, no conditions, just love."

"You have—" Eva began.

"Did he offer you a job?" The question came out of nowhere as they checked behind the bins near The Horse and Hound. "Aidan. Did he offer you a position with his company?"

Eva's heart sank. Even in his panic about Tilly, he couldn't let go of what he'd seen. "Yes, but—"

"Of course he did." Charlie laughed bitterly, still scanning the street for any sign of Tilly. "That's how he works. Find the weakness, make the offer. Sophie, the city council, now you."

"I didn't accept it!"

229

"Yet." He turned to face her fully, tears gathering in his eyes—whether from fear for Tilly or anger at her, she couldn't tell. "But you were tempted, weren't you? All that travel, all those stories to uncover. Better than being stuck in York with a failing inn and a bitter mapmaker who can't even keep track of his own dog."

"That's not—Tilly! Here, girl!" Eva called, then turned back to Charlie. "We can talk about this later. Right now, we need to find her."

"What if we don't?" Charlie's voice broke completely. "What if she's gone like everything else? My parents, Sophie, Gran, soon the inn, probably you—"

"Stop it." Eva grabbed his shoulders. "We're going to find her. She's probably just found something interesting and lost track of time. You know what she's like."

But as another hour passed with no sign of the spaniel, even Eva began to fear the worst. They'd covered every street in central York, checked every park, every hidden corner Charlie knew.

"The river," Charlie said suddenly, his face going pale. "What if she went to the river?"

They ran towards the Ouse River, Charlie calling Tilly's name with increasing desperation. The December sky was darkening, making it harder to see. Soon it would be fully dark, and a black and white dog would be invisible in the shadows.

The Ouse appeared before them like a dark wound through the city, its surface black and oily in the fading light. The water moved deceptively fast, carrying bits of debris—branches, plastic bottles, things Eva didn't want to identify. The current was stronger than it looked from the bridges, churning and pulling at the banks with quiet violence.

"She's never gone to the river alone," Eva said, trying to reassure him, but her voice came out thin. The water scared her—it was nothing like the lazy rivers back home. This was ancient and hungry, swollen with December rain.

"She's never run off at all!" Charlie snapped, then immediately looked stricken. "I'm sorry. I'm just—"

"Scared. I know."

They searched along the riverbank, Charlie getting closer and closer to the water's edge, calling and calling. The path was slippery with moss and mud, and Eva's heart lurched every time he leaned out over the water, scanning the surface for any sign of black and white fur. The river seemed to mock them with every splash and gurgle—was that debris hitting a bridge support, or something else? A branch bobbing in the current looked horrifyingly like a tail for one heart-stopping moment.

"There!" Charlie pointed, scrambling down the bank. But it was just a plastic bag, caught on a submerged shopping trolley. He stood knee-deep in the freezing water, staring at it like it had personally betrayed him.

"Charlie, come back," Eva pleaded. "You can't go in there. The current—"

"What if she tried to swim across? What if she fell?" His voice was raw. "Dogs can swim, but if she hit her head, if the current got her—" He was wading deeper, the water now at his thighs, the cold making him gasp.

Eva grabbed his arm, pulling hard. "Charlie, stop! You can't help her if you drown!"

They stumbled back onto the path, Charlie shaking from cold and fear. The river continued its relentless flow, indifferent to their panic. In the growing darkness, every shadow on the water could be Tilly, every sound could be her struggling. His voice was almost gone now, reduced to a hoarse whisper.

"Tilly, please. Please come back." He sank onto a bench, his wet trousers clinging to his legs, water pooling around his feet. The Christmas lights reflected on the river's surface, creating a mockery of stars on water that could have swallowed his best friend. "She's all I have that I can always rely on, Eva. The one thing in my life that isn't weighed down by history or regret or other people's choices. If I've lost her too . . ."

Eva sat beside him, her own eyes burning with tears. Seeing Charlie like this—broken, desperate, stripped of all his careful defences—was devastating. She wanted to comfort him, but what comfort could she offer when Tilly was still missing?

"We'll keep looking," she said softly. "We won't stop until we find her."

Charlie looked at her then, his eyes red-rimmed and lost. "Why did you meet with him? Really?"

"To understand his plans. To know what we're fighting against."

"And the job?"

"I was curious," Eva admitted. "The travel, the writing—it was tempting. But Charlie, I didn't accept. I wouldn't. Aidan would have me out there writing fabricated fantasies, anything for a sale. I would never do that."

"Wouldn't you?" His voice was hollow. "When the inn's gone and there's nothing keeping you here?"

Before Eva could answer, Charlie was on his feet again. "We can't sit here. I have to keep looking."

They searched until their feet ached and their voices were gone. The Christmas lights came on across the city, festive and bright, mocking their desperation. Somewhere in York, Tilly was lost or hurt or worse, and Charlie was unravelling with every passing minute.

"She's all I have," he kept saying, like a mantra. "She's all I have left."

And Eva, watching him fall apart, and absorbing the pain he felt realised with terrible clarity that she was falling in love with this difficult, complicated man. And he might never believe her on what he'd seen in that coffee shop, even if they found Tilly safe.

The cathedral bells chimed eight o'clock at night. They'd been searching for hours. Charlie stood in the middle of Stonegate, turning in circles, calling Tilly's name into the darkness with a voice that had no sound left.

He looked utterly lost.

"We'll find her," Eva whispered, not sure if she was trying to convince him or herself. "We have to find her."

But York stretched out around them, ancient and vast and full of places a small spaniel could disappear. And tomorrow was 23rd of December—the deadline for Aidan's 'safety net'.

If they even made it to tomorrow.

Chapter Seventeen

What We Find When We're Lost

They'd been searching for so long. Eva's voice was completely gone, reduced to a whispered rasp. Charlie wasn't even calling anymore—just walking with grim determination, checking every shadow, every doorway, every possible place a spaniel might hide.

The Christmas market was closing down, vendors packing up their wares, and several had joined the search after hearing about the missing dog. "We'll keep an eye out," they promised, but Eva could see that even they thought it was hopeless. Eight hours was too long. Something had happened.

"Maybe we should go back to the inn," Eva suggested gently. "Check if she's returned home—"

"She hasn't." Charlie's voice was flat, defeated. "Florence would have called."

They were standing in The Shambles, where they'd first met over spilled wine that now seemed like a lifetime ago. The narrow street was empty except for a few late tourists taking photos of the crooked buildings.

"Charlie," Eva said softly. "We need to think differently. Tilly's smart. If she's not in any of her usual places, maybe she found somewhere new. Somewhere . . ." She paused, remembering Tilly's talent for finding hidden things. "Somewhere only she would think to look."

Charlie turned to her, a flicker of hope in his exhausted eyes. "Like where?"

"Hidden gardens. Forgotten spaces. The kind of places tourists never find." Eva pulled out her phone, ignoring the fourteen missed calls from her mother. "When I was exploring yesterday, I noticed some gates that looked like they led nowhere. Behind shops, between buildings. The kind of places that look abandoned but—"

"But might be perfect for a curious spaniel." Charlie was already moving. "There's one off Fossgate. Another behind the old bakery on Gillygate."

They split up briefly, checking the hidden spaces Eva had noticed during her wanderings. It was Charlie who called out—not Tilly's name, but Eva's, his voice cracking with emotion.

Eva ran towards the sound, finding him standing at a gate so overgrown with ivy it was nearly invisible. Through the tangle of dead vines, she could hear it—a familiar bark.

"She's in there," Charlie said, his hands shaking as he fought with the rusted latch. "I can't get it open—"

"Together," Eva said, adding her hands to his. The gate groaned, protested, then finally swung inward with a shriek of old hinges.

The garden beyond was like something from a storybook Eva had read as a child—tiny and forgotten, surrounded by the backs of buildings that had turned their faces away. In the centre, next to a stone bench that was more moss than stone, sat Tilly. Her tail started helicoptering the moment she saw them.

"Tilly!" Charlie crashed to his knees, and the spaniel bounded into his arms, covering his face with kisses.

She was covered in dirt and dead leaves from whatever adventure she'd been on. Twigs stuck out from her fur at odd angles, and her paws were caked with mud that she immediately, generously, shared with Charlie's coat.

As Tilly covered his face with kisses, Eva noticed something that made her breath catch—tangled in the spaniel's collar was a small sprig of mistletoe, fresh and green despite the season, as if she'd found the one living piece in the entire forgotten garden and decided to wear it home like a prize.

"You stupid, wonderful, infuriating dog. Don't you ever—ever—do that again."

He buried his face in her fur, his shoulders shaking. Eva realised he was crying—really crying, all the fear and relief and exhaustion of the hours searching poured out. She knelt beside them, her own eyes burning, one hand on Charlie's shoulder and the other stroking Tilly's silky ears, carefully extracting the mistletoe sprig and tucking it into her pocket. It felt warm against her fingers, like a blessing or a sign—Margaret's garden offering up one last bit of magic, delivered by a muddy spaniel who knew exactly where they needed to be.

"She's okay," Eva whispered. "She's okay, Charlie."

"I thought I'd lost her." His voice was muffled against Tilly's fur. "I thought she was gone like everything else."

They stayed like that for several minutes, a small huddle of relief in the forgotten garden. Finally, Charlie lifted his head, wiping his face into his own shoulder to absorb the tears that had involuntarily fallen. His eyes were red, his defences completely shattered.

"Let me get her lead on," he said, his voice still shaky. He pulled the leash from his pocket, clipping it to Tilly's collar with hands that trembled slightly. "I'm not taking any chances."

Tilly, for her part, seemed perfectly content to be leashed, sitting proudly as if she'd accomplished something important by leading them here.

"Eva," Charlie said, one hand firm on Tilly's lead. "What I said earlier, about the job, about you leaving—"

"You were scared," Eva said gently. "And you had just seen me with Aidan, looking at brochures—"

"Looking tempted." Charlie's voice was quiet but steady. "And you were, weren't you? The travel, the writing, the chance to stay in Britain properly."

Eva took a breath, choosing honesty. "Yes. For about five minutes, I was tempted. On the surface, it sounded like everything a practical version of Eva would have wanted. Security, with a hint of adventure and a 'real career'." She met his eyes. "But I'm not practical Eva anymore. I haven't been since I followed a mysterious book to York and spilled wine on a grumpy mapmaker. Plus, I know I can't trust the lines Aidan spins. You taught me that remember."

"You didn't accept?"

"Charlie." She waited until he was looking at her, really looking. "I couldn't accept. How could I help him package history for profit when I've seen what real history means? When I've walked these streets with you, heard Margaret's

237

story, felt the weight of what we'd lose?" She paused. "When I've fallen in love with this place and everyone in it?"

Charlie studied her face in the dim light filtering through the overgrown garden. "Everyone?"

"Well, Tilly mostly," Eva said, her heart hammering. "But I suppose her difficult owner has grown on me too."

Something shifted in Charlie's expression—a wall coming down, maybe, or a door opening. But before he could respond, Tilly stood and trotted to the bench, her lead pulling taut as she pawed at something beneath it.

"What have you found now?" Charlie asked, keeping a firm grip on the leash as he followed her.

It was Eva who knelt down to investigate what Tilly had been pawing at. Beneath the bench, she pulled out a small metal box, rusted with age. Inside, wrapped in oilcloth, was another of Margaret's notes—this one dated 1994, the writing shakier but still recognisable.

"Read it," Charlie said quietly, wrapping Tilly's lead around his hand an extra time.

Eva read aloud, her voice soft in the quiet garden:
"December 1994

I come here when the memories are too heavy. This was where we met in secret, after he could walk again. Where we planned a future that never came to pass.

He asked me to wait for him. Said he'd come back after the war, that we'd have that farm in Pennsylvania, that life we'd dreamed of between hospital walls.

I wish I'd known if he'd have waited for me. If I'd been brave enough to follow him, would he have kept his promise? Or would I have been just another war bride forgotten when real life resumed?

I'll never know. That's my penance for choosing safety over love. But sometimes I sit here and pretend he did come back. That I was brave. That love was enough.

MW"

When she finished, Charlie was sitting on the bench where his grandmother had sat for over fifty years, Tilly pressed against his legs, her lead wrapped securely around his hand. The weight of all those visits, all that regret, seemed to settle over the garden like fog.

"She never knew," Charlie said quietly. "She spent her whole life wondering, and she never knew the truth."

"What truth?" Eva sat beside him, the cold stone seeping through her jeans.

Charlie reached into his coat with his free hand and pulled out a letter—yellowed with age, the envelope bearing Walter's time stamp of 1946. "I read Walter's letter. While Tilly was missing, before I realised she was gone, I finally read it."

His hand shook slightly as he unfolded it, still keeping Tilly's lead secure with the other. "They put him back on the ground, to serve. But he was sent home after being wounded again. Badly this time—lost partial use of his left arm. By the time he could write, months had passed. He didn't know if she'd waited, if she'd moved on. He was afraid."

"Afraid of what?"

"That he'd ruin her life. That she'd feel obligated to a damaged soldier who couldn't even work his family's farm properly anymore. So, he wrote to release her." Charlie's voice caught. "He said he loved her too much to make her choose between duty and happiness. That he wanted her to find someone whole, someone who could give her the life she deserved."

"Oh, Charlie." Eva felt tears sliding down her cheeks.

"They both chose what they thought was noble," Charlie said bitterly. "And they both spent the rest of their lives regretting it. He never married—there's a postscript from his sister, after he died in 1987. She thought Margaret should know that he'd kept her picture by his bed for forty years."

The silence in the garden was complete, even the distant sounds of York muffled by the surrounding buildings. Eva thought of Margaret coming here for decades, sitting on this bench, wondering. Never knowing that across an ocean, Walter was wondering too.

"All that love," Eva whispered. "All that time. Wasted because they were too afraid to fight for it."

"Or too noble," Charlie said. "Too concerned with doing the right thing to see that the right thing was each other."

He turned to her then, his eyes intense in the dim light. "Eva, when I saw you with Aidan today, looking at those brochures, I thought—I was so sure you'd choose the practical path. The safe or set path Aidan was paving for you."

"Like Margaret did?"

"Like everyone does, eventually." His voice was raw. "My parents chose their careers over me. Sophie chose New York. Even Gran chose duty over love."

Eva reached for his free hand, lacing their fingers together. His skin was cold from the December night. "I'm not basing my decisions on obligation anymore, Charlie. I'm choosing York. I'm choosing the inn, Florence, mystery tours with Trinkett, and hidden gardens full of history." She squeezed his hand. "I'm choosing the cranky mapmaker who shows me hidden angels before singing

240

country music in pubs and loves his dog more than most people love anything."

Charlie stared at their joined hands. "Even if the inn closes tomorrow? Even if there's no magical happy ending?"

"Especially then." Eva thought of Margaret's note, of all those decades of wondering. "I'd rather fail at something real than succeed at something that doesn't matter. I'd rather be here, fighting a losing battle with you, than anywhere else with a fancy title and a corporate credit card."

Charlie lifted their joined hands, pressing his lips to her knuckles in an old-fashioned gesture that made her heart skip. "You terrify me, Eva Coleman."

"Good," she said. "You terrify me too. But maybe that's okay. Maybe being terrified means it matters."

Tilly, apparently deciding the emotional moment had gone on long enough, stood and shook herself, then headed purposefully towards the gate, pulling Charlie along.

"I think she's telling us it's time to go home," Charlie said, but he didn't let go of Eva's hand, managing to hold on to both her and Tilly's lead as they walked.

They made their way back through York's ancient streets, Tilly trotting ahead but frequently checking to make sure they were following, Charlie keeping the lead short. The Christmas lights reflected in puddles from the afternoon rain, turning the city into something magical despite everything hanging over them.

"Tomorrow's the deadline," Eva said as they approached the inn.

"I know."

"The construction crews were multiplying when I left. Aidan's confident he's won."

241

"He probably has." Charlie's voice was steady, accepting. "But maybe winning isn't the point. Maybe the point is that we tried. That we didn't just let it happen without a fight."

They paused outside the inn, looking up at its crooked Tudor frame, its windows glowing warmly against the night. Tomorrow it might belong to Aidan's company, destined for conversion into soulless luxury flats. But, tonight, it was still theirs—still home.

"Whatever happens tomorrow," Eva said, "I want you to know that I'm not going anywhere. Not unless you want me to."

Charlie turned to her, something vulnerable and hopeful in his expression. "What if I never want you to?"

"Then I guess I'm staying," Eva said simply. "At least for the time being. Not for forever. But for now."

He smiled then—a real smile that transformed his face. "Just like that?"

"Just like that."

Something about the way he looked at her confirmed her fear was just that: a silly little fear, not reality. Charlie felt something for her, she knew it and damn it she was going to be brave enough to find out exactly what that was.

* * *

Florence appeared in the doorway, relief flooding her face when she saw Tilly. "Thank God! I was about to organise a search party." She looked between them, noting their joined hands, and something in her expression softened. "Come in, all of you. There's soup on the stove and decisions to make. Tomorrow's coming whether we're ready or not."

As they followed Florence inside, Charlie finally relaxed his death grip on Tilly's lead, though he didn't unclip it until they were safely inside with the door closed. Eva felt the weight of Margaret's final note in her pocket. Tomorrow was 23rd of December—the deadline that would change everything. But tonight, she'd found something in a forgotten garden that Margaret had spent over half a century looking for: the courage to choose love over safety, hope over certainty.

Whatever tomorrow brought, Eva wouldn't spend the rest of her life wondering what if. She'd learned that much from a nurse who loved an American soldier, and a spaniel who knew exactly where to lead them when they were lost.

Sometimes the best discoveries weren't the ones you went looking for, but the ones that found you when you were brave enough to stop running.

Chapter Eighteen

The Story Worth Telling

Sitting on the inn's lounge sofa, Eva found herself entangled with Charlie, Tilly at their feet. Cosy and comfortable, she snuggled into his chest, before reality rudely awoke her. The two must have dozed off on the sofa last night after their epic search for Charlie's four-legged friend. Florence had covered them in a blanket. Eva thought, *how sweet of her to*—"Crap, Florence! Charlie, wake up!"

* * *

Eva burst into Florence's office without knocking, her hair still wild from the spooning session she'd just awoken from. Still, she clutched her journal like a weapon.

"Don't you dare sign anything," she announced.

Florence jumped, sending a cascade of bills sliding across her desk. Her reading glasses slipped down her nose as she blinked up at Eva. "Good Lord, you nearly gave me a coronary. It is half five in the morning, what are you doing up? I—"

"The papers. From Aidan. Whatever legal nonsense he's wrapped in a bow and delivered with his snake-oil smile." Eva collapsed into the chair across from Florence, her breath coming in puffs. "Promise me."

Florence carefully realigned the scattered papers, a gesture Eva recognised as buying time. "The deadline on Aidan's safety net offer is midnight tonight, love. The bank won't accept righteous indignation as collateral on the twenty-fourth,."

"No, but they might accept this." Eva slapped her journal on the desk between them, pages fluttering like moth wings. "Margaret's real story. Not the tragedy Aidan will peddle to his journalist friends when he tries to give this place a sellout story."

"Ah. Morning love," sighed Florence as Charlie's frame entered through the doorway. He still appeared to be shifting the sleep from his eyes after Eva's rude awakening. Florence's fingers found the manila folder from Thornfield Development, its corporate logo gleaming like a threat. "You heard about how he does that, then. Believe me, he's already briefed me on how he's going to share: 'The Tragic Romance of York's Lost Nurse.' I wanted to throw my teapot at him."

"Did you?" Eva questioned, insulted even hearing it.

"I considered it. But it's good china." Florence's mouth twitched up. "Besides, assault charges would complicate the bankruptcy proceedings."

Charlie leaned forward, accidentally crushing an invoice for plumbing repairs that looked older than he was. "What exactly is Aidan planning? The truth, Florence."

Florence sighed, casting her eyes between the two of them and suddenly looking ancient. "He's got that journalist friend of his ready to run a feature. Tomorrow's edition. 'The Heartbreak Behind The Riddle and Quill Inn.' Complete with artistic photos of empty rooms and dramatic quotes about love lost." She pushed her glasses up her nose. She tried to say it casually, but Eva could hear the pain and embarrassment behind the words. "He's betting the threat of the sensational story will either force us to sell immediately to avoid the attention, or drive up interest so he can flip the property for twice what he paid."

"That manipulative little—" spat Charlie.

"Quite." Florence's smile was sharp. "His exact words were 'Everyone loves a tragic romance. We'll have tour buses by New Year's.'"

Eva felt something fierce and protective rise in her chest. "Not if I write the real story first."

"You? Write? Eva, love, you said you hadn't written anything since you were a teen, do you really think you ca—"

"Yes, and I will." Eva stood taller, energy crackling through her like lightning before a storm. "I'm going to write Margaret's real story right now. All of it. Not the tragedy, but the triumph. I'm calling it 'Margaret's Trail of Magic'."

Florence raised an eyebrow. "The whole thing?"

"Every damn word. Time is of the essence Florence, we have to perform magic!" Eva's hands were already itching for her keyboard. "The Christmas funds, the reading programs, the lives she saved. The veterans she housed, the children she fed, the love she multiplied across this entire city. And yes, I'll include Walter—but as one chapter in a full life, not the defining heartbreak." She turned to Charlie, searching for his approval.

"That's a lovely thought, but how does one day of writing combat Aidan's media machine?"

"Because truth is more interesting than tragedy," Eva said. "Always has been. People think they want the dramatic story, but what they really want is to believe that broken hearts can still do beautiful things."

Florence opened her desk drawer—the one that stuck and required jiggling—and pulled out Margaret's wooden box. She must have retrieved it when Charlie called her over to tell her Tilly was missing. "She wasn't perfect, you know. Had a tongue like a whip when crossed. Once poured a pint over a man's head for suggesting nurses were just failed doctors' wives."

"Even better," Eva grinned. "Perfect people make terrible stories."

"Then you'll need this." Florence pushed the box across the desk. "Charlie here has the rest, but . . . be gentle with her memory, love. She wasn't a saint. She was just a woman who made a choice."

"That's what makes her extraordinary," Eva said softly, taking the box. "Saints don't have to choose."

Box in hand, she turned to Charlie. Talking to him with her eyes only, she begged him to let her do this.

*　*　*

Back in her room, Eva transformed her desk into command central. Photos fanned across the wood like tarot cards telling a life. She'd stolen Florence's Scotch tape and now Margaret's timeline decorated her wall—1944 on the left, early 2000s on the right, five decades of quiet kindness mapped in yellow sticky notes. Both she and Charlie stood back and looked at their creation in awe. While he was hesitant at first, he'd tried his best to hear Eva's plea to tell his grandmother's story as it should be told. He'd tasted the bitter fear of losing Tilly just yesterday and there was

247

no way he could risk that feeling with the inn, Florence or especially Eva. He had to at least let her try.

* * *

With Charlie vacating the room to give her some space to get in the writing mindset, Eva made herself a cup of tea using the room's miniature kettle, cracked her knuckles like a pianist before a concert, and began to type:

"We love our tragic heroines best when they're beautiful corpses. Catherine Earnshaw wasting away on the moors. Juliet in her marble tomb. We want our broken-hearted women aesthetic and finite, their pain wrapped up neatly with a bow.

Margaret Wells refused to give in to a tragedy. She lived.

Eva thought about it all as she typed. Margaret lived through rationing and rebuilding. She lived through marriage to a good man she respected but didn't burn for. She lived through raising children and burying a husband and watching the world change around her. She lived, and in living, she loved—not with the desperate passion of youth, but with the steady, transformative love of someone who understood that hearts, like bones, grow stronger at the broken places.

* * *

Eva wrote all through the day, fuelled by Florence's tactical tea deliveries (the room kettle just couldn't fill the epic sized mug she needed) and her own desperate desire to get this right. She wrote about the library where Margaret had worked, slipping notes into books to tell people 'You matter', 'Tomorrow can be different' and 'Someone believes in you.' Simple phrases that became lifelines for damaged soldiers learning to live again with shaking hands.

She wrote about Christmas 1952, when Margaret had noticed children pressing their noses against toy shop windows. By Christmas Eve, mysterious baskets had appeared on doorsteps throughout York—oranges and walnuts, hand-knitted mittens, and small toys. The Christmas Angel, they'd called her, never knowing it was the head nurse who'd organised it all, encouraging shopkeepers into donations with surgical precision.

When she got to Walter, she paused. This was the tricky part—how to tell a love story without making it the only story. She thought of her own failed relationships, how she'd tried to build her entire identity around loving men who couldn't love her back the same way. The difference was, Margaret had chosen to love anyway—just differently. She flexed her fingers and typed:

In 1945, Margaret Wells fell in love with an American soldier named Walter Lorne. They wrote notes in library books, planned a future on a Pennsylvania farm, dreamed the dreams of eighteen-year-olds who think love conquers everything.

He left without saying goodbye—deployed in the night, no warning, no explanation, just gone. She waited. He never came back.

Although this is where other stories would end, Margaret had over sixty more years to live.

Eva continued to inform the reader of how she spent them at bedsides and Christmas markets, in council meetings and charity drives. She spent them teaching children to read and veterans to hope. She spent them proving that love isn't just what happens between two people in the dark—it's what happens when you decide the world deserves better than your broken heart.

She kept writing, her eyes burning, her back aching. The radiator clanged its evening song. Her tea went cold, then colder. At 7 p.m., she opened Margaret's box and found a photograph—Margaret in her forties, surrounded by children at the library, every face turned towards her like flowers to the sun. On the back, in spidery handwriting: 'Tuesday story time, 1973. My favourite hour of the week'.

Eva taped it to her wall and kept typing.

She wrote about the inn being saved in 1947, the Christmas Angel Project of 1952, the reading room established in 1963. She wrote about a woman who transformed heartbreak into an engine of grace. Not a saint—saints didn't have Margaret's sharp tongue, her weakness for sherry or her habit of 'accidentally' tripping rude customers at the tea shop. Saints didn't write letters to the council calling them 'complete nincompoops' for trying to close the veterans' shelter. Saints didn't keep a flask in their handbag for 'medicinal purposes'.

Just a person who chose, every day, to be useful rather than bitter.

By the time she typed the last word, her laptop clock read 7.06p.m. Florence had moved the office printer into her room earlier in the day and so Eva began to print her first draft. She'd go through a hard copy she decided, spell-check, edit, make sure she'd captured not just the facts but the feeling of a life lived in service to joy. She saved the document with shaking fingers, then nearly jumped out of her skin when Florence knocked on the door.

"Come in," Eva called, her voice hoarse from disuse.

Florence entered carrying yet another pot of tea and something more precious—hope in her eyes. "Is it finished?"

"Just." Eva gestured at the pages resting in the printer. "But Florence, even if it's good, how do we—"

"Get it to the right people?" Florence's smile was sly. "Already sorted. James Hartwell at the Yorkshire Herald owes me more favours than I can count. His mother was one of Margaret's Christmas Angel recipients back in '58. I rang him an hour ago."

"The Yorkshire Herald would publish this?"

"James is waiting for it right now. Has held space in tomorrow's edition—Christmas Eve morning. It'll be online by midnight, in print by dawn." Florence moved to look at the printout. "May I?"

Eva nodded, watching nervously as Florence skimmed through sections of the article.

"This is it," Florence said softly. "This is Margaret's real story. Send it to James now—here's his direct email." She handed Eva a business card that looked like it had lived in her apron pocket for years. "He said if we get it to him by ten, he can have his best editor review it tonight."

"But what about Aidan's journalist friend?"

"Different paper," Florence said with satisfaction. "Smaller circulation. And James has already heard whispers about Aidan's sensationalist piece. He's no fan of developers who treat history like a commodity. Your story will run as the lead feature, with a note about the heritage trail and tomorrow's gathering at the inn."

Eva's hands trembled as she attached the document to an email. "What if it's not enough?"

"Then at least the truth will be out there," Florence said. "Margaret's real legacy, not Aidan's twisted version. That matters, love. Truth always matters."

"Okay, let me do one more read through and then we can share it."

"Right then," Florence said briskly, though Eva caught her wiping her eyes. "You rest for a bit. Charlie's been busy with the trail all day, but he'll want to know it's done."

Eva took the pages from Florence to look at the document one last time. She'd proofread it properly, she just needed to close her eyes for a moment . . .

*　*　*

Charlie found her shortly after she'd nodded off, face smooshed against her keyboard, one hand still reaching for her cold tea. Scrawled pages covered every surface—the desk, the floor, her bed. The unlocked laptop screen's light caught the photos on the wall, making Margaret's face glow like a benediction. Tilly padded in behind him, lead wrapped twice around his wrist, and gave Eva's dangling hand an investigative sniff.

"Eva?" Charlie whispered, then louder: "Eva."

Nothing. She'd even managed to fall asleep with perfect typing posture, because of course she had. There was a crease on her cheek from her keyboard, and her glasses sat askew. She looked like a disaster. She looked perfect.

Charlie looked to the document placed on top of the printer and laid his eyes on Eva's first draft. Picking up the story, his eyes began to scan. As he read, his hands stilled. His breath caught.

She'd done it. She'd captured Margaret—not the martyr he'd feared she'd write or the victim the papers wanted, but the complicated, stubborn, gloriously human woman who'd raised him. But more than that, Eva had found the thread that connected them all: a woman turning private grief into public good, one small kindness at a time.

252

He kept reading, sinking into the corner of Eva's mattress as Tilly settled at his feet. When he reached the section about Walter, his eyes burned:

```
Margaret Wells and Walter Lorne loved
each other for three months in 1945. It
wasn't enough time. It was a lifetime.
Both things can be true.
```

The simplicity of it—the truth of it—hit him like a physical blow. Charlie pulled out Walter's letter—the one he'd finally read during those terrible hours when him and Eva were fighting. He'd memorised parts already, the words seared into his brain:

```
"My dearest Maggie,
By the time you receive this, I hope
you've found happiness. I was shipped back
to battle without warning, then home rather
quickly. My arm, as you know, was worse
than we thought. I've started this letter
a hundred times over during the past few
months, but couldn't find the words.
The truth is, I'm broken, Maggie. Not
just my arm. The things I've seen, the
things I've done—they've left marks that
won't heal. I wake up screaming. I can't
hold a coffee cup without shaking. What
kind of life is that for a woman like you?
You deserve someone whole. Someone who
can give you dancing nights, Sunday dinners
and babies who'll run in your garden
without their father flinching when they
move too fast.
I love you too much to make you settle for
half a man. I know that there is someone
```

already waiting who deserves you far more than me. Be happy.

All my love, Walter

P.S. (Added by Mabel Lorne, 1987)—My brother died last Tuesday. It's only this following week that I found this unsent letter. He never married. I thought you should know he kept your picture at his bedside all these years. His last word was your name.

Charlie wiped his eyes with his sleeve. All that waste. All that noble stupidity. Two people so busy trying to save each other from pain that they'd caused infinitely more. He looked at Eva, drooling slightly on her keyboard, and felt his heart crack open.

On the screen there was a draft email ready to be sent, article included. Eva was second guessing herself. But after reading the article, Charlie knew that what she had written was perfect. She'd channelled some part of herself in order to tell Margaret's truth, and for that he'd be eternally grateful. Maybe he could be brave for both of them. Holding his breath, he clicked send.

"Eva," he said softly, touching her shoulder. "Eva, wake up."

She stirred, making an indignant noise that might have been "five more minutes" or possibly "death to morning." Her eyes fluttered open, focused on him, then went wide.

"Charlie? What time—oh no, the pages!" She tried to stand, got tangled in her chair, and would have fallen if Charlie hadn't caught her elbow. For a moment they were close enough that he could see the exact shade of brown in her eyes, like tea with honey.

"The pages are fine. I've read them." He steadied her, their faces suddenly very close. "Eva, they're perfect. It's ready, I've sent it."

"You read them? All of them?" She was adorably rumpled, her hair flat on one side, keyboard marks on her cheek. "Even the part where I called her 'beautifully belligerent'? And you've sent it!?"

"Especially that part, yes." Charlie's voice was rough. "It's exactly what she was. Beautiful and belligerent and absolutely refusing to let the world be less than it could be.

"Every word." He held up Walter's letter. "And this. I want you to finally read this too."

Eva's face softened as she took the fragile paper from him. "Oh, Charlie. What does it say?"

He told her, watching her eyes fill as he recited Walter's words about being broken, about wanting Margaret to have better. When he got to the part about waking up screaming, Eva's hand found his. When he reached the sister's postscript, she made a small, wounded sound that he felt in his chest.

"They were both idiots," she whispered.

"Noble idiots," Charlie agreed. "Tragic, self-sacrificing idiots who robbed themselves of decades of happiness because they each thought they knew what was best for the other."

"My therapist has a word for that," Eva said with a watery laugh. "She calls it 'catastrophising your way out of joy.'"

"Your therapist sounds smart."

"She'd have had a field day with these two." Eva gestured at the letter. "Can you imagine? 'I love you too much to let you love me'. The ego of it. The absolute arrogance of deciding someone else's happiness for them."

They stood there in the dawn light, surrounded by the scattered pages of Margaret's life, the weight of all that wasted love heavy between them. Without thinking, Charlie reached up and fixed Eva's crooked glasses. His fingers lingered against her temple.

"Charlie," Eva said quietly. "We can't let the inn go. We can't let Aidan turn it into some soulless—"

"We won't." The certainty in his voice surprised them both.

"The deadline is in a few hours."

"I know."

"We have no money, no legal standing, no—"

Charlie stopped her with a finger to her lips, a gesture that made them both freeze. The air between them went electric. "What we have," he said slowly, "is Margaret's story. The real one. The one you just spent all day writing."

"A story won't pay the mortgage."

"No, but it might do something better." His eyes were bright now, that manic gleam she'd seen when he talked about his maps. "What if we made Margaret's trail real? Physical? Something people could walk, touch, experience?"

Eva's exhausted brain tried to keep up. "Like a heritage trail?"

"Exactly. Every place she touched, every life she changed. Mapped, marked, unmissable."

Eva looked at him in awe. This was a brilliant idea, people would love it! "But Charlie, we have next to no time, how can we plot that all out?"

"We don't need to. Margaret did it for us."

"What?" Eva was tired and now even more confused.

"The diagram. Eva, do you remember the diagram in the box? I thought it was just decorative, but when I took a

256

closer look it was as clear as day. Margaret created a map. It was a literal guide to where she had hidden all her notes.

"The veterans' corner, the library, the orphans' Christmas spot, the hidden garden where she went to grieve, all of them." His speech seems to speed up with each location added.

Eva's exhaustion vanished. "Charlie, you genius. That's it. That's our trail."

They looked at each other, breathless with possibility. Then reality crashed back like cold water.

"Charlie, the deadline is midnight. We have just hours."

"Good job I've already made a start on it then, isn't it? With a little help, of course . . ."

"Charlie Blackwood, what have you been up to while I've been writing miste—"

Instead of answering, Charlie did something that stopped Eva's heart. He stepped forward, cupped her face in his hands, and kissed her forehead—gentle, reverent, a blessing and a promise. She could smell his soap, feel the calluses on his palms from years of drawing maps.

"I think," he said softly, "that Margaret Wells spent her life proving that impossible things happen when people choose kindness over fear."

Eva felt herself sway towards him, exhaustion and emotion making her brave. Her hands found his chest, feeling his heartbeat race to match hers. "What do we do now?"

For a moment, they just looked at each other. Eva thought he might kiss her properly. Thought she might die if he didn't. The evening room was chilly now that she'd left the blanketed seat at her desk.

Then Charlie pulled her into a fierce embrace, his arms wrapping around her like he was trying to hold all the pieces of her together. She felt him shake slightly—exhaustion or emotion, she couldn't tell. Maybe both.

"We save it," he whispered into her hair. "We save all of it."

Eva buried her face in his shoulder, breathing him in. "Together?"

"Together." He pulled back just enough to look at her, his eyes bright with unshed tears and something that looked dangerously like hope. "I know how to save the inn. Let me show you the real people of York too."

"Show me the way." Eva's voice was steady now, sure. "What's the plan?"

* * *

"Then the last stop leads us back to the Inn," Charlie's smile was radiant as he finished walking Eva through the crash course of the trail he'd marked out for Margaret's Map. While she'd been hard at work writing, Charlie had rallied every man, woman and child in the vicinity to get Margaret's points adequately marked. A good thing no one had retired to bed yet. His friends from the Christmas dinner get together and fellow stall owners had divided and conquered each of the zones. Together, they'd created beautiful handmade markers that labelled each spot. Even Sophie had managed to shake off her ego and offered to help.

"So, what's next?"

"Now? We set Trinkett loose on the town's people while they're jolly and weaponise his theatrical tendencies. We're going to rally everyone who's ever been touched by Margaret's kindness. We'll make this city remember why some things are worth saving."

"And if it doesn't work?"

"Then we'll have tried." He squeezed her hand. "Margaret would expect nothing less."

Eva squeezed back, feeling the weight of the past and the possibility of the future all tangled up in this moment. "For Margaret, then."

"For Margaret. For Florence. For the inn." His eyes held hers. "For us."

Before Eva could unpack everything in that 'us', Charlie was already heading for the door, battle plans forming. "Trinkett will be our voice on the ground. The stall I bought your notebook from, that's owned by a really cool local artist, he created fliers this afternoon that we've had people posting door to door, we're going to hand out the last of them now. I want to see a queue winding through the streets of York tomorrow morning to understand Maragaret's story.

"Charlie," Eva called after him. "We need to sleep. Both of us."

He turned back, grinning like a man about to charge into glorious battle. "Sleep is for people who aren't trying to save Christmas. Come on, Coleman. Let's go make some magic."

And despite her exhaustion, despite the impossible odds, despite the keyboard marks on her face, Eva tightened the scarf around her neck and followed him into the night. Because sometimes the best stories weren't about the endings you got, but the battles you chose to fight.

And sometimes, if you were very lucky, the battle was worth it because of who stood beside you.

Margaret Wells had taught them that.

Chapter Nineteen

The Christmas Miracle

"Where the bloody hell is Trinkett?" Charlie questioned. He was practically bouncing on his heels as they stood outside the inn at 6.47 a.m. It was already past dawn, which meant that The *Yorkshire Herald* had published Eva's article, and townsfolk would be reading her words over the coming hours. She hadn't yet allowed it to sink in. They had other matters to attend to first. The December air bit at their cheeks, and somewhere nearby, church bells were already practicing for Christmas day. Tilly, sensing adventure, was doing her best impression of a sled dog, straining against her lead. "He knows everyone. He IS everyone."

"It's not even seven," Eva protested weakly, though she was already buttoning her coat. The adrenaline from their all-nighter hadn't worn off—if anything, it had transformed into something electric and urgent. Her breath formed clouds in the frosty air, and the scent of someone's wood fire made the morning feel impossibly festive. "Won't he be—"

"Preparing his morning dramatics? Absolutely." Charlie grinned. "Which means he'll be awake, caffeinated, and ready to weaponise his entire contact list. Or at least, those he couldn't get a hold of last night."

The two were running on less than an hour's sleep and a scary amount of caffeine. Both Charlie and Eva were a bundle of nervous energy. In the final hours of last night, they'd sat together with Florence and sighed with relief as she agreed to not sign Aidan's final piece of paper. The safety net was being pulled from beneath them but if they were going down, they were 'going down swinging' as Florence had said with a gritty attitude.

Before they left, Charlie grabbed something from the parlour—a large rolled paper he'd been working on through the night. "Wait until you see the final piece of the puzzle," he said, his eyes bright with discovery.

*　*　*

They found Trinkett in The Shambles, adjusting his Victorian top hat in a shop window's reflection. Fairy lights still twinkled in the medieval overhangs, and the faint sound of *God Rest Ye Merry Gentlemen* drifted from a nearby shop already preparing for the day. His magnificent moustache twitched when he spotted them approaching like people on a mission.

"Ms Coleman! Mr Blackwood!" He swept off his hat in an elaborate bow. "You both look positively unhinged. How delightful."

"We still need your help," Eva said without preamble. "The inn—"

261

"Say no more." Trinkett held up a gloved hand. "We've all heard the whispers about Thornfield Development, that appalling Aidan creature, over the last few months. It's a bloody tragedy what they're planning to do to Florence's inn and I can't imagine the story they'll spin about our Margaret." His eyes glinted dangerously. "Is the counter-offense continuing as planned?"

Charlie carefully unrolled his creation against the wall, and Eva gasped. He'd walked her through Margaret's original diagram, but this—this was art.

"I told you I was busy while you were writing," Charlie explained, holding the corners flat. "I went back to Margaret's diagram. Like I said, at first I thought it was just decorative—you know, stars and swirls. But then I noticed the stars had numbers. Tiny ones. And the swirls weren't random—they were paths."

The original diagram had been simple pencil on yellowed paper, but Charlie had transformed it into a watercolour masterpiece. Delicate blue lines traced through a painted map of York, connecting location to location like veins of kindness. Each stop was marked with a golden star, and in Charlie's precise architectural hand, he'd added labels: 'Library—first notes, 1946.' 'Mrs Morrison's shop—wedding dress, 1962.' 'Milk route, Gillygate—coins for the Trinkett family.'

"Wait," Trinkett said, his finger hovering over that last entry. "The Trinkett family?"

"Every hidden note, every secret kindness," Charlie confirmed. "All those years of leaving York better than she found it."

Trinkett traced the path to his grandmother's house, his pale cheeks turning a soft red. "She used to find coins in her milk bottles when times were tight. Said it was the milk fairy." His voice cracked slightly. "It was Margaret, wasn't it?"

"According to this," Charlie tapped the date notation, "every Tuesday from 1953 to 1961."

Trinkett pulled off his gloves and wiped his eyes quickly. "Right. Well. That settles it." He pulled out his phone with the determination of a general preparing for battle. "I have calls to make!"

"We're saving the inn," Charlie and Eva said in unison.

"Excellent. Focused. I like it." His fingers flew across his phone screen. "I'm cancelling today's tours and calling in every favour I've accumulated in twenty years of showing people around this city. Mrs Henderson owes me for not mentioning her great-aunt's smuggling operation on tours. Dr Hartley's been trying to get me to include the hospital in my route. Oliver at The Horse and Hound—his grandfather knew Margaret personally."

"You think they'll help?" Eva asked.

Trinkett looked genuinely offended. "My dear girl, this is Yorkshire. We queue politely, we complain about the weather, and we rally like Vikings when one of our own is threatened. Margaret Wells IS York. They'll help."

*　*　*

By 8.00a.m., Trinkett's network had activated like some sort of benevolent sleeper cell. Eva and Charlie arrived at Whitby's Antiquarian Books to find Arthur already pulling boxes from his back room. The shop smelled of cinnamon and old paper, and he'd put on a recording of King's College choir that made everything feel sacred.

"Trinkett called," he said by way of explanation. "Told me you were creating Margaret's Trail." He opened a box with reverent hands. "These are from her reading

263

program. 1946 to 1967. Every book she donated, every child she taught. I kept records because . . ." His voice wavered. "Because someone should remember."

He pulled out a leather journal, its pages filled with careful entries. "Look here—Christmas 1947. She brought thirty books wrapped in brown paper. Each one had a child's name on it and a note inside." He showed them a preserved slip of paper: 'For Tommy—adventures await those brave enough to read them.'

"Mr Whitby," Charlie said softly. "We can't ask you to—"

"*You're* not asking. *I'm* telling." Arthur pulled out a photograph—Margaret surrounded by children, books piled high around them. Their faces glowed in what was clearly candlelight, and someone had drawn paper snowflakes for the windows behind them. "See that boy, third from left? That's me. She taught me to read when everyone else had given up. Said I wasn't slow, just saw words differently." He looked up fiercely. "I inherited this bookshop proudly because Margaret Wells believed in a dyslexic child with no father to guide him. You think I wouldn't fight for her memory?"

* * *

The Horse and Hound was already in full Christmas mode when they arrived. Garlands hung from the beams, and the fire crackled with unusual warmth. They pushed through the heavy door to find Oliver on the phone, gesturing wildly.

"—don't care if it's short notice, Dennis. Margaret's grandson needs us." He paused. "The architect one. Yes, the one with the lovely girlfriend—" He spotted them and winked. "They're here now. Bring your tools and anyone else from the Tuesday lot."

Eva swallowed hard and pretended that she wasn't just called Charlie's 'girlfriend.'

He hung up and beamed at them. "Right, that's six carpenters, two electricians, and a plumber who owes Margaret's fund his sobriety. What do you need built?"

Eva felt her throat tighten. "You don't even know what we're planning."

"Don't need to. It's for Margaret." Oliver reached behind the bar and pulled out not just a ledger, but a wooden box marked with Margaret's star symbol. "This has been behind our bar since 1946. We open it every Christmas Eve and read the names." He opened it carefully, revealing hundreds of small cards. "Every person able to raise a glass in here on Christmas day due to Margaret's kindness. We remember them all."

He pulled out one at random. "23 December, 1958. The Morrison family. Father out of work, four children, no money for Christmas." He flipped it over. "Margaret's fund provided the Christmas dinner that year. The eldest Morrison boy grew up to be a teacher. Comes in every December to add to the fund."

"The Margaret Wells my father told me about," Oliver continued, carefully replacing the card, "wouldn't want some superficial development named after her. She'd want this—people helping people, the way she taught us."

*　*　*

By 10a.m., York had transformed into something from a Christmas fairy tale. What started as a desperate plan had become something extraordinary. The path to the inn bloomed with pop-up stalls decorated with white lights and evergreen boughs. The December cold had brought out the vendors' creativity—braziers burned between the

265

stalls, roasting chestnuts and warming mulled wine that scented the entire street.

Mrs Henderson's pottery stall displayed bowls glazed in Margaret's favourite colours. She'd arranged them on white cloth with sprigs of holly between them. "She commissioned these during the war," she explained to growing crowds. "Said beautiful things helped people heal. Always ordered extra before Christmas—'for those who need something lovely,' she'd say."

Dr Hartley had created a medical history display, but he'd softened it with Margaret's own Christmas decorations from the hospital—paper angels made by patients, a knitted nativity scene, photographs of ward Christmas parties where Margaret, in her starched uniform, could be seen leading carols.

"Margaret Wells pioneered trauma treatment before we even had a name for it," he explained to a group of visitors. "But at Christmas, she was pure magic. Used to dress as Father Christmas for the children's ward. Only nurse I ever met who could make a beard look dignified."

The library had sent their entire children's department. They'd created a reading corner with books bearing Margaret's bookplates, arranged around a small Christmas tree decorated entirely with paper ornaments—each one containing a quote from Margaret's hidden notes.

"We've been preserving these for decades," the head librarian explained, adjusting an angel made from pages of *Peter Pan*. "Waiting for the right moment to share them."

Eva stood in the inn's doorway, breathing in the mingled scents of pine, cinnamon and snow, watching it all unfold with a kind of breathless wonder. Inside, each room had become a chapter in Margaret's story. Florence had found boxes of Margaret's Christmas decorations and the volunteers had used them throughout—paper chains made by long-ago children, glass baubles that caught the light like tears, a wooden star that Charlie recognised from his childhood.

The parlour held Charlie's map as a centrepiece, now framed and surrounded by battery-powered candles that made the golden stars seem to pulse with life. The dining room displayed the love letters between Margaret and Walter—not as tragedy, but as prologue to a life fully lived.

"Your young man knows what he's doing," Florence said, appearing beside her cradling a cup of tea in Margaret's best Christmas china—red roses and gold rims. They watched Charlie directing volunteers, his usual awkwardness replaced by focused purpose. She'd found an old Santa hat somewhere and placed it on his head thinking he'd take it off straight away. Instead, he wore it unselfconsciously, with a bit of extra tinsel caught in his hair.

"He's not my—" Eva started, then stopped. "He might be. I don't know. It's complicated."

"Love always is." Florence smiled. "Especially at Christmas. All those songs about mistletoe and miracles put pressure on people. But Margaret taught me that the best love stories aren't the ones that happen because of the season. They're the ones that happen despite it—messy and real and choosing each other when everything's chaotic." Florence sighed to herself. "The inn looks bloody brilliant, what you've both done here, it's something special," she caught herself as her voice began to shake. "Thank you for bringing us together like this, all of us."

* * *

By mid afternoon, the inn looked like a scene from *A Christmas Carol* had come to life. Local media had arrived to find a story that wrote itself. Carollers had appeared spontaneously, their voices weaving between the stalls. Someone had brought a snow machine, causing artificial flakes mixed with the real ones to begin falling at the entrance of the inn. Local news arrived alongside the journalists, it seemed a snowball effect had occurred on multiple levels. The word truly had spread quickly . . .

Eva's phone buzzed. Her mother. Again. She'd sent seventeen texts since Eva had gone dark last night, but Eva had been too caught up in the magic to check them properly.

The afternoon brought unexpected revelations, each one wrapped in its own Christmas story. A woman in her eighties arrived with a suitcase, snow dusting her silver hair like a crown.

"I'm Helen Morrison," she announced. "Margaret Wells helped create my wedding dress in 1962. It was two weeks before Christmas, and I was crying outside the shop because I couldn't afford anything nice for my Boxing Day wedding." Her eyes sparkled. "The shopkeeper and Margaret helped me pick one of their cheaper dresses, then Margaret took it away to alter. She made it so beautiful."

She opened the suitcase. Inside, preserved in layers of tissue paper, lay a beautiful 1960s wedding dress. "I've kept it all these years. My granddaughter wore it last Christmas. Generations of Morrison brides have been blessed with it, all because Margaret Wells believed everyone deserved magic." The stories continued to multiply like lights on a tree.

Charlie found Eva in the kitchen, where Florence was pulling tray after tray of mince pies from the oven— "Margaret's recipe," she said simply. They were both taking a moment to breathe. His hair was sticking out wildly beneath the Santa hat, his shirt was now untucked and there was paint on his cheek from helping with signs.

"Look what we did," he said wonderingly.

"Look what she did," Eva corrected. "We just reminded people."

The sound of *Silent Night* drifted in from outside, and for a moment they just stood there, surrounded by the warmth and scent of Christmas, feeling the weight of what they'd created. Refusing to think about the looming fate of the inn.

Bang on time, the front door slammed open with characteristic drama.

"What the bloody hell—"

Aidan stood frozen in the doorway, snowflakes still melting on his expensive coat, his usually perfectly styled hair looking slightly windswept, *had he ran here?* Aidan stared at the controlled chaos around him. The sound of children laughing at the puppet show outside mixed with the brass band that had just started "Hark! The Herald Angels Sing."

"Charlie," he managed. "I figured I'd give Florence a bit of breathing room this morning before I came to collect the signed papers and instead found—what is this?"

"This," Eva said, stepping forward, "is what you were about to destroy."

Aidan's gaze landed on Charlie's map, the candlelight illuminating it in all its glory. He moved towards it slowly, his expression unreadable.

"Margaret drew this?" His voice had lost its usual corporate smoothness.

"She mapped every kindness," Charlie confirmed. "Every life she touched. A lifetime of leaving love notes in the margins of York's story."

For a long moment, Aidan studied the map. Behind him, through the window, they could see an elderly couple requesting roasted chestnuts to share on their wander. His finger traced the path from the hospital to the orphanage to the inn itself.

"The local publicity you've garnered just today," Aidan said slowly. "This is generating actual attention. It'll lead to tourism."

"It's generating more than that," Eva said. "It's generating community. Memory. The kind of thing your development would erase forever."

A child's laughter drew their attention to the reading corner. Here, Arthur was showing children how Margaret had hidden notes in books. One little girl pulled out a slip of paper that read 'You are braver than you know' and clutched it like treasure. Her mother shed a tear, whispering "I found the same note when I was seven."

Something shifted in Aidan's expression. "We used to come here as kids at Christmas. Your Gran would make us all hot chocolate with candy canes and tell stories by the fire." He touched the map again. "I guess I'd forgotten."

"Aidan—" Charlie started.

"Wait, just let me think a second." Aidan pulled out his phone, scrolling through messages with increasing agitation. "The numbers could work. Heritage site, living museum, Margaret's Trail as an actual attraction . . ." He looked up. "Christmas tours alone would pay for maintenance. Add in the wedding venue potential, the literary connections . . ." His business mind was visibly working, but there was something else there too—a softness around his eyes as he watched a family discover Margaret's advent calendar, each door revealing a small act of kindness to perform.

"Actually," Aidan said, "this is better than demolition. Heritage tourism, authentic York history, multi-generational appeal . . ." He smiled suddenly, a genuine childlike glow that Eva had not seen from him before. Perhaps there was a purer side of Aidan after all. "Fair play to you, Charlie boy. You've really got something here."

"You mean—"

"I mean the sale's off. We're going to need to find another way to help Florence aren't we?" Aidan pocketed his phone. "Besides, can you imagine the press if I demolished a Christmas miracle? I'd be the Grinch of Yorkshire."

Relief flooded through Eva so fast she felt dizzy. Charlie made a sound somewhere between a laugh and a sob. Outside, as if on cue, the brass band struck up *Joy to the World*.

"I need to call the lawyers," Aidan said, already moving towards the door. "And possibly grovel to the heritage committee. We'll definitely need to hire Trinkett for the marketing." He paused. "Your Gran always said Christmas was when magic was strongest during storytime. Suppose she was right about that too."

Aidan nodded once, sharply. "I'm going to talk to Florence about a potential loan to approach the bank with today, combine that with the donations that you've already received today and we'll be getting somewhere. We'll sort it Charlie, the proper way." He smiled again and was gone.

Eva and Charlie now stood alone in the parlour, surrounded by the gentle chaos of their miracle. The smell of warm mince pies wrapped around them like a blanket. Through the windows, snow had begun to fall in earnest, dusting the market stalls in white and making everything look like a snow globe come to life.

"We did it," Eva breathed.

"You did it," Charlie corrected. "I was ready to let it go. You fought."

"We did it together," Eva insisted, and something in her tone made Charlie step closer.

They were standing in the doorway between the parlour and the hall, where Florence had hung not just one sprig of mistletoe but an entire bower, tied with red ribbon and little silver bells that chimed softly in the cool air currents. The sounds of celebration floated around them—carols, laughter and the clink of glasses as people toasted Margaret's memory.

Charlie reached up to tuck a strand of hair behind Eva's ear, his fingers lingering against her cheek. "You have glitter in your hair by the way," he said softly.

"You're wearing a Santa hat," she countered.

"It's Christmas," he said, as if that explained everything. And maybe it did.

"There's mistletoe," she whispered, glancing up at Florence's elaborate creation. "Margaret's magic strikes again."

"I don't need mistletoe to want to kiss you," Charlie said, "but I'll take all the magic I can get."

His hands framed her face, and Eva's eyes fluttered closed. The kiss was everything she'd longed for over the past few days as she'd grown ever closer to Charlie. Their connection had become deeper, more certain. Eva's arms wound around his neck, and she could taste cinnamon from the mulled wine, feel the soft wool of his jumper under her fingers. The Santa hat fell off somewhere amidst the embrace, and Eva was just thinking she could stay here forever when—

The front door burst open with enough force to rattle the windows.

"Eva Coleman!"

Eva's eyes flew open. She and Charlie sprang apart like guilty teenagers, but not quickly enough. Her mother stood in the doorway, snow swirling dramatically behind her, looking like an avenging angel in Burberry.

Her father peered around her shoulder, arms full of what appeared to be every craft item from the market. "Oh, hello darlin'! Are we interrupting?"

"Yes," her mother said crisply, her eyes fixed on Eva. "Yes, Robert, I believe we are."

Eva smoothed down her hair, very aware that she probably looked thoroughly flustered at this point. Charlie, for his part, was trying to look cool, calm and collected while his Santa hat lay incriminatingly at his feet.

"Hello, Mom," Eva said, with as much dignity as she could muster while her lips still tingled from kissing.

Chapter Twenty

The Ending She Chooses

"Perhaps we should talk somewhere private," Sandy Coleman suggested, her voice carrying the same tone she'd used when Eva was seven and had decided to give herself bangs with craft scissors.

Eva glanced at Charlie, who gave her an encouraging nod before tactfully steering her father towards the market stalls. "Mr Coleman, have you seen the medieval stonework? It's actually quite fascinating . . ."

Her father went willingly, already pulling out his phone to photograph everything. "Sandy!" he called back. "They have actual medieval masonry techniques on display!"

"Go on, Robert," her mother said with fond exasperation. "Just don't buy any more pottery. We barely fit what you bought earlier in the hand luggage case!"

Sandy sighed and turned back to Eva. "Your father and his enthusiasms. Shall we?"

Eva led her mother to the snug, the quietest room in the inn. The fire crackled warmly, and Margaret's wooden box sat open on the side table, her treasures catching the light. Sandy paused in the doorway, taking in the photographs, the displayed letters, the careful recreation of a life lived in kindness.

"So," she said, settling into an armchair with the precision of someone preparing for a negotiation. "You were going to miss family Christmas, for this?"

"I know." Eva sat across from her, hands folded in her lap like she was nineteen again, calling home to explain why she'd changed her major from pre-law to English. "Mom, I—"

"Twenty eight years, Eva. You've never missed Christmas. Not when you had the flu. Not when you were in college. Not even the year you were dating that terrible musician." Sandy's voice wavered slightly. "Everyone is at home in the family, except you. And now us too apparently!"

Eva felt tears prick her eyes. "I'm sorry. I didn't mean to hurt you."

"Then explain this to me." Sandy gestured around the room, encompassing the inn, the celebration outside, Charlie's Santa hat still visible on the parlour floor. "What is all this? What are you doing here instead of coming home for the holidays?"

Eva took a deep breath. Outside, she could hear the carollers starting *Good King Wenceslas*, and the sound gave her courage. "I'm writing again. Really writing. Not press releases or marketing copy. Mom, I wrote a real story about a real person who changed lives."

"You could write in Nashville."

"No, I couldn't." Eva met her mother's eyes. "In Nashville, I was drowning. Going through the motions. Following the plan you'd laid out for me since I was five."

"That plan was to help you succeed—"

"That plan was to keep me safe. To keep me close." The words came out gentler than Eva intended. "Mom, look at Lily—she's running a tech startup in Seattle. Maddie is a partner at her firm. They found their own paths. Why couldn't you let me find mine?"

Sandy's perfectly composed façade cracked slightly. "Because you're different from them. You've always been more . . . sensitive. More likely to get hurt."

"Or maybe you just decided that's who I was," Eva said. "And I believed you. Just like I believed all the fairy tales about princesses waiting to be rescued. Turns out, some of us have to rescue ourselves."

They sat in silence for a moment, the fire popping softly. Through the window, snow continued to fall on the Christmas market, making everything look like one of the Hallmark movies Eva loved so much.

"The story you wrote," Sandy said finally, "the one you handed over to the press here? Ms Jensen saw it online, do you remember her? She sent me an email about it, God knows how she saw it, or how she still has my email. That woman loved you in school, though. I didn't have a moment to read it on the way here. But maybe if I do, I'll understand more?"

Eva was not used to the sight of her mother backing down. But she recognised this olive branch for what it was and took it gratefully. In the end, that's all she'd ever wanted. For her mother to truly see and understand her and to appreciate her passion for writing the way Ms

Jensen always had. Maybe York could gift them that too this Christmas.

* * *

Eva poured the fresh pot of tea that Florence had left sat between her and Sandy. In her pocket her phone buzzed.

Courtney: EVANGELINE COLEMAN! Your article is going viral! My mother-in-law just texted me about it. Call me the SECOND you get home. I need every single detail about York and especially about this guy.

"The Yorkshire Herald published it this morning." Eva showed her mother the screen. 'Margaret's Trail of Magic: How One Woman's Kindness Transformed York.'

Sandy read in silence, her expression unreadable. Eva watched her mother's eyes move across the screen, taking in the story of Margaret Wells, the Christmas traditions she'd started, the lives she'd changed, the love she'd spread despite her own broken heart.

"The comments," Sandy noted, scrolling down. "People are sharing their own stories. This one—'My gran used to talk about the Christmas Angel who left homemade confectionery in 1953. Now I know who she was.'" She looked up. "You did this in one day?"

"The story was already there. I just . . . told it."

Sandy closed the laptop carefully. "The writing is good, Eva. More than that. It's better than anything you've done before."

"Thank you."

"When are you coming home?"

Eva took a deep breath. This wasn't exactly how she'd wanted the conversation to go. "I haven't decided yet. I

277

need to help them get the trail established, finish some interviews and do some write ups."

"And then?"

"I don't know." Eva stood, moving to the window where she could see her father enthusiastically photographing a medieval doorway while Charlie patiently explained the architecture. "This trip has changed me, Mom. Made me realise I've been living the life everyone expected me to live, not the one I want."

"Which is?"

"That's what I need to figure out. Maybe it's not Nashville. Maybe it's not even America. I just know I can't go back to being the person I was before."

Sandy joined her at the window. "That boy—Charlie. Is he part of this change?"

Eva smiled warmly. "Maybe. But this isn't about him. It's about me finally deciding who I want to be. No more waiting for someone else to write my happy ending."

Her mother was quiet for a long moment. Then: "Your father and I always wondered where you got your love of stories. Now I think maybe you were just waiting to find the right one to tell."

"Mom . . ."

"I'm still not happy that you're missing our family Christmas," Sandy said, but her voice was softer now. "But I suppose, well, I suppose sometimes you have to let go of some older traditions in order to grow and move forwards. That's how new traditions are created, right? It's decided, we're staying. Merry Christmas Eve, Eva."

* * *

By evening, the inn was glowing with Christmas Eve warmth. The article had done exactly what Eva hoped—

reminded York why the inn mattered. All day, locals had been stopping by with their own Margaret stories, and Trinkett had already fielded three calls about organising proper tours of the trail. Florence and Aidan appeared to have reached an agreement that meant the inn stayed in Florence's family, but Aidan would have a hand in supporting the trail.

The pub was packed for the celebration. Eva squeezed through the crowd, recognising every face—these people had rallied to save something that mattered. Oliver was behind the bar, telling anyone who'd listen about Margaret's fund. Arthur Whitby had brought some of the preserved books from Margaret's reading programme to display. Dr Hartley was explaining Margaret's innovations in trauma care to Eva's fascinated father.

"Eva!" Jean from the tea shop appeared with a tray. "I've been telling everyone about your article. My mother called—she remembers finding one of Margaret's notes in 1967. Said it changed her whole perspective on life."

George from the fudge shop joined them, beaming. "Three people came in today because of your story. Said they wanted to support the businesses on Margaret's Trail. You've done something wonderful here."

Eva stepped away from the crowd and found herself gazing out the window, thinking of how much had changed because she decided to take a trip. She let a mysterious book lead her on a journey she never thought possible.

She couldn't help but smile.

Tilly meandered into the room, huffing and grinning from ear to ear, tailed by Charlie.

"Hiding from your admirers?" Charlie said holding two glasses of mulled wine in chipped yet ornate mugs.

"Just catching my breath." She accepted the wine gratefully. "I can't believe how many people came."

"You gave them something to fight for. A story that mattered." He paused, looking uncharacteristically nervous. "Speaking of which, we should probably talk."

Eva's stomach fluttered. "About?"

"About what happens next. You're supposed to be leaving soon."

"Yes."

"And I'm obviously staying here."

"For now," Eva said carefully.

Charlie's eyebrows rose. "For now?"

"I've been thinking." Eva set down her wine, turning to face him fully. "You've lived in York your whole life. You've never been anywhere else. And that's beautiful—this place, these roots. But Charlie . . . when was the last time you did something just for you? Not for Margaret's memory, not for family obligation, but for Charlie Blackwood?"

He opened his mouth, then closed it, looking stunned.

"What if," Eva took a deep breath and continued. It was time to be bold. "What if you came to visit me? Saw America? Gave yourself permission to explore?"

"Eva, I can't just—"

"Why not? The inn is safe. Your project is done. Tilly has Florence wrapped around her paw." She took his hands. "You've been living in other people's stories your whole life. Maybe it's time to write your own. Think of the places you'll get to see, the maps you could be designing wherever you go!"

Charlie stared at her for a moment and, at first, she panicked. *This was a bad idea. He doesn't want to leave York for an adventure. Of course he doesn't, and he sure as hell doesn't want to abandon it for some girl.* But the initial confusion in his eyes seemed to settle as fear gave way to possibility.

"You want me to come to Nashville," he said slowly.

"For a visit. *Just* a visit. See how it feels to be somewhere new." Eva squeezed his hands. "I'm not asking you to give up York. I'm just asking you to give yourself the chance to see what else might be out there. For both of us."

"Like a fairy tale in reverse," Charlie murmured. "Instead of the princess leaving everything behind for the prince, we both get to choose."

"Exactly. No rescuing required. Just . . . choosing."

Before Charlie could respond, Florence appeared in the hallway. "There you are! Come, both of you. I have something for Eva."

They followed her back to the main room, where Florence clinked her own glass for attention. The crowd quieted.

"Friends," Florence began, her voice carrying. "Margaret Wells saved this inn in 1947. She saved it over and over again through the years with fierce advocacy. And this week, her memory saved it once more, through the story Eva told, the trail Charlie created, and the community that rallied to preserve it."

She pulled out a wrapped package. "Eva, dear, would you come here?"

Eva made her way through the crowd, aware of all the eyes on her, including her mother's. Florence handed her the package with ceremony.

Inside was Margaret's green leather journal—the one Eva had found that first day, now professionally restored. The gilt edges gleamed, and the lock had been repaired.

"Florence, I can't—"

"Margaret would want you to have it," Florence said firmly. "Some stories need new endings. And you're rather good at providing them."

Eva clutched the journal, feeling the weight of history in her hands. "Thank you. For everything."

"No, love. Thank you. You've given us all the greatest Christmas gift—hope."

As the evening wore on, Eva found herself pulled into conversation after conversation. Her parents had integrated seamlessly into the gathering—her father deep in discussion about Roman Britain with Dr Hartley, her mother actually laughing at one of Trinkett's theatrical stories.

"You've done something special here," Mrs Morrison said quietly, approaching Eva by the fire. "Margaret would be so pleased to know her story is being told properly. Not as tragedy, but as triumph."

"That was always the real story," Eva said. "People just needed reminding that not all fairy tales end with 'happily ever after'. Some end with 'happily ever choosing'."

Near midnight, as the celebration began to wind down, Eva said goodnight to her parents who'd been given a room at The Riddle and Quill Inn by Florence. Heading outside to the small terrace behind the inn, Eva took a moment for herself. Snow was still falling softly, muffling the sounds of York settling into Christmas night. It was here that Charlie found her.

"I've been thinking about what you said," he began without preamble. "About living in other people's stories."

Eva waited, watching the snow catch in his dark hair.

"You're right. I've been so focused on preserving the past that I forgot to imagine a future." He turned to her, eyes bright with something new—excitement mixed with terror. "I'll come to Nashville. In February, after I finish the renovations needed on the property."

"Really?"

"Really. I want to see your world. Meet the infamous Courtney. Eat whatever grits are." He smiled ruefully. "Terrifying as it is, I want to see who Charlie Blackwood might be outside of York."

"And I'll come back," Eva said. "To help launch the trail properly. To see who Eva Coleman might be when she's choosing her own adventure. And not following mysterious books that fall."

"Is that really how this all started?" Charlie asked.

"I got dumped, and booked the first flight to London. And yes, Margaret thumped me quite literally on the head."

"You really do have a way with stories."

A familiar clicking of claws made them look down. Tilly sat at their feet, tail wagging, a sprig of mistletoe tied to her collar with a red ribbon.

"Did she have that earlier?" Eva asked, laughing.

"Florence might have helped," Charlie admitted. "She did say Margaret believed in giving fate a push sometimes."

"How are you going to manage to kiss me once Christmas is over?" Eva teased. "When there's no convenient mistletoe?"

Charlie pulled her closer, his voice low and warm. "I'm sure we'll be able to create our own piece of magic. In York. In Nashville. Wherever our story takes us."

The kiss was different this time—still passionate, but also full of promise. Of planes to catch and cities to explore and stories yet to be written.

Later, alone in her room, Eva sat with her notebook— the one Charlie had kindly gifted her. Its pages were once crisp and blank, now it overflowed with scrawls of Margaret's story, waiting to be shaped into something more.

She opened Margaret's restored journal and found a blank page. After a moment's thought, she wrote:

December 25th The Riddle & Quill Inn, York

Once upon a time, a lost girl came to York looking for Christmas magic and found something better—the courage to write her own story.

Margaret Wells taught her that love isn't just what happens between two people—it's what happens when you decide the world deserves better than your broken heart. It's choosing kindness when bitterness would be easier. It's believing in magic even when the signs aren't clear.

Soon, I'll go home. But home doesn't mean what it used to. And in February, Charlie will follow—not because it's a fairy tale, but because we're both brave enough to see what happens when you stop living the story everyone else wrote for you.

I don't know how our story ends. But I know it will be one we choose to write together, one page at a time.

She closed the journal, putting the sprig of mistletoe from her apartment, still carefully wrapped in tissue, in the notebook. Eva looked out of the window at York sleeping under its blanket of snow. The Christmas lights twinkled like stars, each one a small miracle, a tiny act of faith in the darkness.

She didn't need signs anymore.

But she saw them anyway.

Acknowledgements

Thank you to HarperNorth for taking a chance on this story and giving it a home. Your enthusiasm from day one made me believe this book could really happen. To my brilliant editor, Megan Jones, whose patience seems infinite and whose insight is invaluable—thank you for understanding what I was trying to say even when I didn't, for knowing exactly which dark night of the soul was important, and for somehow making the editing process feel less like surgery and more like sculpture. This book is immeasurably better because of you.

To my dad, who taught me that the best stories are worth telling twice, and then editing three times more. Your wisdom echoes through every chapter. Your feedback has been a masterclass in storytelling, and your belief in me has been unwavering.

England changed me in so many ways throughout my life. As a teenager, walking down London streets with my sisters while my parents taught journalism classes, you first whispered your possibilities to me. But it was Oxford—where you truly claimed me. Living in your city of dreaming spires, I discovered my love of walking, a way of following in the footsteps of my literary heroes.

Morning walks with our dogs—our Doberman Hugo and English Springer Spaniel, Millie (yes, that is actually Tilly) in places that I'd exclaimed "looked like Pride & Prejudice!", afternoons wandering through college quads, evenings when the golden light hit those honey-coloured stones just right—you were teaching me how to see stories everywhere. Oxford, you showed me that history isn't the past; it's a living thing that breathes through ancient walls and speaks through worn cobblestones.

And then there was York. Visiting with Hugo and Millie, we fell completely in love with your medieval streets that twist and turn like they're keeping secrets, your pubs that welcome muddy dogs and muddy boots with equal warmth, your Yorkshire Dales stretching endlessly with paths that beg to be explored. York, you showed us that adventure doesn't require leaving the country—sometimes it's just a train ride away, with two dogs and a sense of wonder. You gave us The Shambles on misty mornings, riverside walks along the Ouse, and the kind of proper Yorkshire welcome that makes you feel like you've always belonged.

To the most incredible online community, thank you for buying this book and forever being part of the story. Thank you for your encouragement and love. The milk vending machine is just for you!

And Michael. Where do I even begin? You've been my first reader, my toughest critic, and my fiercest champion. Thank you for the sacrifices and dedication you made to make this book a reality.

Thank you for those first Christmas markets we discovered together, when we were just wide-eyed tourists drinking glühwein and marvelling at the lights. Who would have thought that our obsession would grow into leading river cruise trips, sharing that magic with others? You saw my joy and said, "Let's make this our life." You always do that—take my dreams and find a way to make them bigger.

Together we discovered the magic that is European Christmas markets and you know how much writing this book meant to me. You've made it possible. For the countless cups of tea that appeared at my desk without being asked for, for taking over everything else in our life when I disappeared into this book, for reading the same chapters multiple times and still finding something encouraging to say. Thank you for walking the dogs in the rain so I could keep writing, for talking through plot problems at midnight, for celebrating every small victory and minimising every crisis.

You moved across an ocean with me—twice—and never once made me feel like my dreams were too big or too impractical. When I said I wanted to write about England, you said "of course you should." When I doubted myself, you never doubted me. This book exists because you made space for it to exist, because you protected my writing time like it was sacred, because you believed it mattered. You don't just support my dreams; you expand them. You make me braver than I would ever be alone. Every adventure is better because you're in it, and this book is no exception.

My best decision, always and forever.

Harper
North

Book Credits

Fionnuala Barrett
Peter Borcsok
Sarah Burke
Alan Cracknell
Jonathan de Peyer
Anna Derkacz
Morgan Dun-Campbell
Tom Dunstan
Kate Elton
Sarah Emsley
Andrew Furlow
Simon Gerratt
Imogen Gordon Clark
Lydia Grainge
Monica Green
Natassa Hadjinicolaou
Emma Hatlen
Jess Haycox
Jo Ireson

Megan Jones
Jean-Marie Kelly
Taslima Khatun
Holly Kyte
Rachel McCarron
Millie Morton
Alice Murphy-Pyle
Adam Murray
Genevieve Pegg
Amanda Percival
Dean Russell
Florence Shepherd
Colleen Simpson
Eleanor Slater
Hilary Stein
Emma Sullivan
Katrina Troy
Claire Ward
Ben Wright

For more unmissable reads,
sign up to the HarperNorth newsletter at
www.harpernorth.co.uk

or find us on socials at
@HarperNorthUK

Harper
North